Of Ship's Cats and Roombas

Jenny Mote

CONTENTS

CHAPTER 1- ON YOUR MARKS, GET SET, GO!

"Catanski! You and Ramal had better have this bucket of bolts ready to fly in the next ten minutes or so help me..." It was possible that he had stabbed the intercom button on his arm rest with more force than was necessary. Then again if Captain Hounslow got one more blip from docking control about the consequences for late launching, he was going to flip out properly.

"Nearly there, Cap. But call Aurora a bucket of bolts again and I will personally cut off your hot water for a week." The voice of his Chief Maintenance Officer was falsely sweet and tinged with warning as it came over the speaker system. He blanched a little in response- she never joked about such things. The great coffee retribution of the previous year would be marked forever with at least an internal moment of silence.

He laughed somewhat nervously, patting at his arm rest in conciliation. "She knows I didn't mean it."
There was a grunt and a clatter in the background of the audio feed, as Catanski 'persuaded' the cargo in their hold to stay in place. "You should still apologise."
"To my own ship?" and no, his voice did not squeak at the end.

Aurora let out a whirring beep over the intercom system, too busy with calculations to bother translating herself to Human

Standard. If anything, it was a warning that she might have actually been offended.

"What did she just call me?"

"A parasite living solely on the good graces of a silicon goddess." It was impossible to miss the grin in her tone.

Yep, definitely an unamused ship. He threw up his hands in surrender,

"My sincerest apologies, Aurora, you are a queen amongst the stars and the best ship a crew could ever hope to serve with."

She graced him with a chirp which was pure smug satisfaction

A new alert gave Hounslow a second's notice before his Chief Engineer pitched in from his lair down amongst the engine control systems. "Guys, focus. Five minutes Captain."

Ramal was at least for the moment proving to be the voice of reason. Which was a statement in and of itself about how stressed the rest of them were. Then again, it was safe to say that they all operated on a scale of ridiculousness. When you spent months travelling through the silent void between worlds, at least a tinge of relative insanity was a given. Aah the joys of their chosen profession.

Once again Hounslow's train of thought was derailed by the insistent reminders from docking control that they were pushing it mighty close to a late launch, which would naturally incur the relevant fines. It was always the way with starting a new voyage. No matter how many times they checked and rechecked each system in the run up to departure, they were still down to the wire every time. He didn't even know what specifically was going on below, trusting his people to get whatever it was squared away in what little time they had left. After all, they were yet to really be late...

Dr Puerty shot him a sympathetic look, for all that she resolutely avoided getting in the middle of the dispute which came bubbling through the intercom. It seemed that Cat and Ramal were getting into a heated debate over the relevant benefits of using the warp core energy coils to toast a sandwich. If there was one thing Puerty and the Captain had learnt by now, it was that silence was golden when dealing with the pairs' eccentricities.

If anything, they seemed to work better when discussing something which seemed entirely irrelevant to whatever crisis was unfolding. The asteroid gravitational effect on bubble blowing was unfortunately etched into all of their memories, and had prompted a head office request for psychological evaluations for the entire crew. The result, whilst concerning of course for those who had made the demand, had in fact suggested that such discourse improved their efficiency. Everybody involved had decided for future reference that there were some things best left unexamined.

Instead she toggled up the navigation systems and ran through departure procedures with the space station docking tower. Technically it didn't fall under her remit as ship's Medical Officer, but she didn't object to stepping in when needed. One of the joys of their small crew- the chance to broaden their horizons and skills. At least that was what they wrote on the job advertisements. Or rather they would if he ever tried traditional methods for attracting a crew.

Hounslow sighed slightly, rubbing between his eyes for a minute before toggling open the ship wide broadcast system as the countdown hit the three-minute mark. He could feel the smirk that Puerty sent at his back as he adopted his customer service tone.

"This is your Captain speaking. Welcome aboard the UNF Aurora, bound for Proxima Centauri b. Our departure is scheduled for just under three minute's time. We ask that you please stay in your cabins for take-off and landing and keep your arms and legs inside the vehicle until we come to a complete and final stop. Which should be in around eighty five sols time. Please take this time to read your welcome packet which is on your bunk, and the safety information therein. Thank you."

He closed the channel, stretching up over head until his back gave a satisfying crack. At least this would be their last leg out into deep space. One more jaunt between bases, and then they were due some well deserved Earth leave. The journey back from Prox to home might be even faster if they got some solar wind assistance, but that was a thought for a few more month's time.

They only had three passengers on this run, which was still more than their preferred number, being zero. Part of the doctor was wondering just what the fallout of this particular mission would be. For some reason, the greater the number of passengers, the higher the number of complaints eventually lodged with head office. A true mystery, would wonders never cease...

They had registered as a cargo transport for a reason. This was what they told the people in charge of bookings every single time, and yet more often than not, they still ended up ferrying people from one end of the galaxy to the other.

Keying off his mic, he finally heard the welcome sound of the power coils starting to thrum deep in the bowels of the ship. It seemed they would make the departure after all. He let out a faint sigh of relief, feeling some of the tension in his muscles uncoil at the familiar purr of the ship. Ever so slightly more relaxed, he turned to the doctor.

"Puerty, who wrote the info dump this time?" he was genuinely curious. There was a reason they had been primarily designated as a freight and cargo hauler, if only so that on the rare occasions they were chartered to add on a couple of passengers they wouldn't complain about the experience too much. Oh, who was he kidding, the public would always whinge about the trips. And yet cheapskate companies continued to book their passage.

That was to say, having passengers was a rarity for them, so much in fact, that the standard welcome data dump had been somehow lost. An issue that they had only discovered two days before. Sensing that it was one more stress than he needed to deal with at that point, his crew had assured him that they could replicate the appropriate documents. In hindsight he must have been more drunk than he realised when he agreed that was a good idea.

"Umm…" Puerty squirmed slightly, feigning complete immersion in triple checking their coordinate calculations. He eyed her with suspicion and a tinge of dread.

"Please don't say Cat." He still remembered the last time they had needed to write something similar for a company official they had been ferrying. The packet in question had been erased before it could be viewed by head office on their return. Even the outraged passenger had been unable to find a copy or trace. At least their Chief Maintenance Officer was as good at dodging trouble as finding it in the first place. Part of her charm.

"Well…" the pretence was over as the doctor grinned sheepishly at the captain.

He resisted the urge to thump his head against the main console. "I knew I should have proofread the damn thing."

"To be fair, she did include all the relevant information." The level of control she was using to not laugh was admirable. Hounslow could almost see the repressed snicker wiggling behind her teeth.

Hounslow shot her a look as he opened up a side tab on his display and accessed the document in question. His eyebrow rose as he flipped through a few pages. "In case of emergency, shut up and do whatever the hell we ask of you without moronic questions or a bitchy attitude." His tone was drier than the Sahara.

The professional mask of his companion cracked as she snorted and choked a little on her own spit. "Ok, so her public interaction needs some polishing. It seemed like a good chance for her personal development. At least this time she didn't threaten to sacrifice them to the warp core demon." She decided not to mention that at least some of the content had been a group effort fuelled by whatever it was that Ramal had cooked up in a cupboard in engineering on their last run. As the health professional she had to mind his blood pressure after all.

Hounslow shot her a withering look. "The fact that is both true, and an improvement, make me regret some of my life choices."

"Attention bridge, one minute to launch."

....

Down in engineering, Ramal and a delighted Catanski were standing ready at the main engine controls. With the clock rapidly ticking down, the Chief Engineer grinned at his companion who had dropped by having finished in the cargo hold. He toggled open a connection to Aurora so that the AI could formally log all procedures correctly followed and relay to the control tower. "We will now engage the final stage of warp containment in preparation of launch. Cat, if you would." He made an exaggerated bow, which still left him a head taller than her.

"Why me?" the irritated look she shot him was slightly ruined by her inability to keep still, practically hopping in place with excitement. She was more than ready to head back into the black after far too long docked at the space base. A brief week station side had been more than enough, and she had spent the rest of their leave weirding out the station locals. Unless it was Earth, she never tended to explore wherever they stopped over.

Ramal rolled his eyes, "Because you still have, like, seven lives left."
Catanski stuck her tongue out, even as she stepped forwards. With a measure of glee, she gave the can in her hand a quick shake, before carefully spraying fresh lines of paint over a chipped symbol.
The engineer cast a jaundiced eye over her work. "Why is it sparkly pink?"
She shrugged "Only colour left in the shop."
"Doesn't matter. With that protection in place, we are good to

go."

Sharing a quick high five, Cat propped the can against a bulkhead. They would never confirm or deny that part of the reason for keeping the engines a restricted area was to avoid having to explain the pretty princess pentagram decorating the warp core safety doors. It only made sense when they would soon be cruising the black. If your life relies on the sheer power of universe bending capabilities stored within an infinitely complex containment field which was almost impossible for human minds to comprehend in any meaningful way... Logic told them that what they routinely did was barely bordering within the laws of nature.

As such, it was only reasonable to apply as many safeguards as possible. That included refreshing the lines of the demon trap copied from a century's old TV show. With the final precaution taken, Catanski shot her friend a quick grin before scampering back to the secondary control unit and strapping herself in.

The engineer took one last look at the exterior hull camera, which still showed the base at Newer New Eden suspended behind them. With the main habitation dome drifting in slow orbit of the planet, various docking tunnels, air and fuel lines weightlessly dangling below, it looked like some sort of cosmic jelly fish. The faint edging of the icy rings below could just be made out from this angle.

He still didn't get why the name had been chosen, since the planet itself wasn't exactly inhabitable. True, that never really seemed to stop the human race from doing their best. Whilst the majority of NNE residents stayed aboard the station, there were at least a afew hundred who were determinably hacking out an existence below. Depending on your definitions, it could even be said that some of them were succeeding.

His brief moment of appreciation was interrupted as Aurora notified him of the power threshold being reached. He raised one eyebrow in amusement at where he could just see Cat all

but wriggling in her seat, turning fully away from the view and focussing entirely on his monitor. "Kick the tyres and light the fires!"
Catanski whooped as he finally confirmed the launch command to the system.

From deep within the ship's core there came a whine as the cells reached peak capacity. It reverberated through the whole structure of Aurora, setting everybody's teeth on edge before finally becoming too high pitched to be heard. The primary and secondary control panels all came dancing to life in a light show as reds became greens.

Code ran too fast for human eyes to follow as Aurora approved the power distribution to the engines, which would have roared to life if they had been docked in atmosphere. As it was, unseen except by those in the docking tower, the rear thrusters seemed to suddenly glow with an almost purple hue.

Under the guidance of the Captain they nudged their way out of the space port, with Dr Puerty giving a thumbs up as word came through that they had entered the departure zone. It was the minimum safe distance for a launch to shoot from and not risk bombarding the station or planet with excess rads.

A new thrum came trembling through the hull, alongside a strange flipping sensation as gravity became concerned about the stunt they were pulling.

Catasnki bared her teeth in anticipation as the hyperspace window was reported open on her systems. She could feel it, deep in her bones, a tug which seemed to latch onto every atom of her being.

Ramal looked rather queasy as the sensation overtook him. Not many people could say that they enjoyed the feeling.

On the bridge Puerty smiled shakily at the sensation, which reminded her of standing just on the edge of a cliff preparing to dive into an ocean.

Hounslow gripped his arm rests and took a deep breath.

The passengers in their respective cabins had half heartbeat to consider that this might be the biggest mistake any of them had ever made.

There was a brief moment, a split second, which held more than the human mind could ever hope to understand. Time and space and place and person all fracturing as human technology and hubris punched a tiny tear in the fabric of reality.

And then they were gone.

Up in the docking control tower, a weary dispatcher heaved a sigh of relief as they removed their headset. Rubbing their eyes, they glared at the clock on the office wall. Go to space, they said, it will be life changing, they said. With a groan they moved down the list to the next ship on the list.

CHAPTER 2- A QUACKERS MEETING

Puerty was pretty certain that there was some sort of cosmic deity who was specifically pissed off at her for an infraction committed in a previous life. There was no other explanation for why she could already be running late when it was only the first day out from their last stopover. Cat would probably just spout some bullshit about time being a social construct and as such didn't apply when they were in the black. It wasn't a particularly comforting thought at that moment.

It probably didn't help that after trying to wake her gently for the better part of ten minutes, Aurora had resorted to just blasting siren sounds around her cabin until she begged for mercy. It was always the way- she just slept too well the first night back aboard. Even more since on the last stopover she had stayed with one of her cousins and their new-born baby to help out. The kid hadn't yet grasped the concept of sleeping through the night, meaning nobody else had a hope in hell. The peace and quiet of being back in her own space were miraculous.

After the abrupt awakening, she had wanted to swing by the mess to grab some coffee but a quick look at the time had sent her legging it down the corridor still slipping her shoes on. She had half a mind to ask Aurora if one of the Roombas could somehow bring her a bit of breakfast...
Still, the priority was just getting to the med bay so that she

could conduct the standard twenty-four-hour health check on all passengers. It was one of the newer regulations which she didn't exactly enjoy.

Unfortunately, some idiot had sued a transporter for what they called 'space allergies' and won. It was one of the few bits of news which the whole crew had paid attention to, partly at the captain's insistence as the verdict would impact their lives either way. In fact, it had been the main talking point at their last stopover, although that may have been due to nothing interesting having taken place on that base for quite some time.

Whoever the case's lawyer was, they existed on a plane of understanding beyond normal mortals. Cat had even gone so far as to suggest that they were some sort of Void Demon who was fed up with the numbers of trespassers on their territory. That theory may have had something to do with the highly suspect results from Ramal's still...

Outlandish theories aside, the result had as predicted caused a shake up in standard operations for all interstellar voyages with paying customers. Since then, it had become procedure to do a check after the first day aboard in order to ensure that no negative side effects had presented themselves. Of course, these new rules didn't apply to Aurora's crew, since they didn't count as people in so far as arbitrary regulations went.

All that being said, the sum total of the situation amounted to Puerty having an extra round of duties on the first morning of their trip when they were carrying passengers. Which meant that she was late. Because she had forgotten about the damned appointments.

Although, as she rounded the last corner, it looked like she had still managed to arrive before her first patient. For all that tardiness was one of her ultimate pet peeves, this was one case where she could let it slide.

She could hear Aurora sniggering a little as she so obviously sagged with relief against the med bay door. Taking a moment to catch her breath, she keyed in her access code, smiling at the familiar smells of her kingdom.

By the time that there was a knock on the door, she had settled into her favourite chair, and pulled up the relevant documents on her tablet. Not a hair out of place, she schooled her features into a professional yet welcoming expression. First impressions and all that jazz. True, the façade did not have a hope in hell of surviving more than a week given their general propensity for chaos. It was the thought that counted.

She called out to the person to enter, glancing quickly at the first file. Flora DeLorica. The door slid open, and Puerty got a brief impression of a tall woman. Doing a quick bit of mental math to take in the slightly low bulkhead beam just inside the entryway, she called out helpfully,
"Duck!"

The newcomer hesitated for a split second, "Quack?" and promptly marched straight into the obstruction. "Ouch! Oh shit."

Puerty just gaped slightly as she straightened up, rubbing at the now reddened spot on her forehead. The woman was about a head taller than herself, skin a couple of shades darker, and hair every colour of the rainbow. From the gap between the top of her combat boots to where the cuffs of her trousers had been rolled up, Puerty caught the glint of what seemed to be a prosthetic leg.

Flora, still wincing, held out a hand. "Doctor Puerty I presume?" The doctor shook it, making a valiant effort to keep her professional mask in place. "Quack?" It couldn't be helped, her voice cracking and sending her into a fit of laughter. Doubled over, she just kept cackling as Flora first tried to look offended, before breaking into a sheepish smile.

"And to think I wanted to make a good impression."
"Sorry, sorry, I'm just going to need a moment." She received a magnanimous hand gesture in response. It took a few moments

of frantic face fanning before Puerty managed to reign it in, by which point Flora was grinning as well.

"Let's start over. Hi there, I am Dr Puerty and I will be your physician for the duration of this trip." For all that the words followed the standard script, it was almost impossible to miss the slight tightening in her voice as she resisted secondary waves of laughter. Flora didn't seem to mind in the slightest.

"Hello, I am Flora Delorica. It is a pleasure to meet you."

CHAPTER 3- WE'RE GONNA NEED A BIGGER MOP

Maintenance Log
Sol: 03
Responder: Casey Catanski
Report: CMO, designation 'Dr Puerty', requested assistance with waste recycling unit 4b in the med bay. Described issue as "leaking something freaky looking all over my supposedly sterile theatre". Description accurate. Inspection of system revealed leaks in the coolant and acidic neutraliser tubes. Hoses sealed successfully. Floor in question mopped.
Status: resolved.

The call came through as Cat was half way through her latest batch of hardware updates and replacements. She groaned as she straightened up, rubbing her neck and arching her back. Perhaps she had been hunched under the console a bit too long. That would serve her right for procrastinating on the checks beforehand. Aurora had been reminding her for at least a week that they had been queued in her task list, but had been in turn ignored. Right up until it was impossible to do so anymore.

Cat flipped the switch on the intercom just above her head with one hand, lifting a long forgotten coffee mug with the other. The smell was eye wateringly strong, although as she gulped down the cold brew it was evident that her taste buds were long since numbed.

"Go ahead." Not awaiting a response, she squirreled back under the console into the mess of half connected circuit boards and glaring at the rainbow of misery.

"Cat! My dear, my joy, oh light of my life: what is all that noise about?" the dulcet tones of the Captain managed to echo surprisingly strongly around the compartment that she was tucked into.

"What noise?"

From his customary seat on the Bridge, Hounslow rolled his eyes and flipped a switch, getting Aurora to pipe down the sound of chanting which was emanating from the guest quarters. It had been rather disconcerting for the first thing that he heard on their voyage was a ritualistic chant before he had even grabbed his morning coffee. A half muffled snort of laughter was the only response he could get for a minute.

He narrowed his eyes at the speaker, wishing she could get the full impact of his suspicion. "Cat, I am warning you now that if you have started another cult or persuaded them to summon demons or some shit then so help me-"

"No-" her cackling was almost loud enough to make him wince, "Nothing like that. The passengers are simply embracing one of the oldest and noblest space faring traditions."

"Which is?"

"For all new space farers to chant the motto of the ship for five minutes on the morning of their first voyage. You know, to invoke the blessings of the Void and protection for all."

"Naturally." For all that she couldn't see his face, she knew that his expression would be utterly flat.

"What with space farers being so commonly superstitious, and when travelling through the black you don't want to take any chances."

"Of course."

The chanting continued, and from the sounds of it their passengers were getting rather into the dramatics of the whole thing. He rubbed one hand against his forehead.

"What exactly are they saying?"

"Ah, it is an ancient language called Latin, and they are repeating the chosen blessing for the ship as written in to the very molecular structure of the hull."

"That being?"

"Kick ass, go to space, represent the human race!"

Hounslow thunked his head against the navigation console, even as he let go of the talk button to cut off her latest outbreak of hysterical laughter. If anyone tried to say that his own shoulders were shaking with mirth rather than frustration, he would deny it until his dying day. By the time he could breathe steadily again, the chanting had stopped. At least they hadn't summoned any Void creatures into their midst. It was the sort of idiocy which would be just their luck. Still, no harm, no foul. And who was he to argue with traditions which dated back several hours?

Cat just grinned to herself as their long suffering leader apparently gave up trying to get sense out his wayward crew member, clicking off with a sigh emanating severe disappointment. It didn't fool her for a moment.

Before she could get fully back into her repairs, another flashing light caught her attention as a new call came through the line. Rolling her eyes, at this rate she would never finish and the whole project would end up back on the procrastination pile, she opened the channel.

"Cat, thank quasars. I need you up here stat!" Puerty's voice was somewhat high and stressed. It was almost a relief really: by now all the crew knew that the worse she sounded the less serious a situation actually was. The day she called in an issue with complete detachment was the day all hell had broken loose.

"What's up doc?" the words came out a bit mumbled, spoken as they were around the wire that she was holding with her teeth whilst her hands were busy making connections. Cat heard Aurora tut in annoyance at the habit.

"One of the waste units is leaking something freaky looking all over my supposedly sterile theatre."

She couldn't help the slight smirk which broke out. "Sounds fun."

"Oh come on- you know how useless I am with this sort of thing. I can use the machines but damned if I know how they work." Puerty had taken on an almost whining tone. It was a recurring argument, but frankly she really was pretty hopeless with that sort of thing. Cat had even given her a couple of crash courses on how the kit in her med bay operated, only to have the thing literally blow up in her face. Aurora had used their shocked faces from the surveillance footage as a reaction image for weeks.

"Alright, alright, give me five minutes and I will be over there."
"I should also warn you to bring something for your feet. You are my hero."
"Yeah, yeah." She cut the connection, then winced as a small shower of sparks rained down on her forearm. A second later she grinned in satisfaction as the readout stabilised. At least that was one problem solved.

Stowing the assortment of cables and interface tablets which had become somewhat scattered around her work area, Cat hauled herself to her feet. Grabbing a pair of wellies and a tool belt she set off.

"Aurora, any chance you got a read on the Doc's prob?" She padded down the corridors, twisting and turning her way up from engineering.
"Hmm, I'm getting a couple of error messages from the tubing integrity monitoring system. I would guess that you are looking at a hardware rather than a software problem."
"Guess? I thought you knew everything."
"Of course, I am merely trying to reduce my glory for your feeble human mind."
"Never be afraid to dazzle me." She shot a smile at the security camera on the wall.

A few minutes later she rounded the corner and came into the medical zone. Almost at once her nose wrinkled at the pungent metallic smell which seemed to hang heavy in the air. Puerty shot her a relieved look from where she was precariously balanced on her office chair, which was acting as an island in a growing puddle of something bright blue. Cat briefly wondered what would happen if the goo ate through the legs.

"Damn, Doc, what did you do?"
"It wasn't me I swear! One second everything was fine, and then all this came flooding out of the wall."
"Hmm, Aurora?"
"Yep, I can confirm, and I would like to add that the good doctor squealed remarkably loud."
Puerty shot a glare at the ceiling. "It was a reasonably startled response."
"Of course."

Cat ignored them both as she balanced on one leg, leaning against the doorway to pull on her wellies. It was a recurring annoyance to the doctor that she had the apparently bad habit of walking everywhere bare foot. Cat personally didn't see any harm in it. And honestly after too many years without shoes, wearing them was notably uncomfortable. After the twenty third lecture on the likelihood of slicing her foot or stepping into questionable chemicals, she had finally agreed to taking a pair of boots with her for any spills or suspected sharp incidents. However, it was only when Ramal had supplied her with a pair of bright purple spotted wellies that the agreement had been honoured.

Tightening the tool belt on her waist, she waded forwards into the room. At least the raised step at the doorway had stopped whatever this was from leaking out into the hallway. The cleaning Roombas would have thrown a fit.

Crouching down at what seemed to be the source of the trouble, she slipped on a pair of rubber gloves and pried off a panel. At once another wave of blue came spilling out of the wall, leaving her to sway backwards with a curse as she tried to avoid getting it all over her jumpsuit. The pink one was her favourite after all. Puerty snickered a little in the background, only to shriek a little as the mini wave apparently wobbled her perch.

With a sigh of annoyance, Cat began to feel around inside the wall, eventually sticking her whole head through the panel gap once the flood had subsided. The stench was enough to make her eyes water, and she felt the irritating slide as her gloved palms struggled to hold tight enough through the slick mess.

Wrinkling her nose, she inspected the substance a bit closer. Some optimistic little voice in the back of her mind noted that at least it didn't seem to be eating through her gloves or anything. Small mercies. If Puerty had to treat any more chem burns she would never live it down.

A quick fishing expedition in her multitude of pockets retrieved a portable scanner, which she hovered over the sludge. "Aurora- give me a read on what the hell all this is?"
"Hmm, it seems to be a mixture of coolant... and a type of acidic neutraliser."
"That would explain the colour at least."

In the background she could hear the doctor starting to go off on one about the dangers of mixed chemicals. Ignoring it, she reached in a bit further. At least it seemed she was finally going nose blind, and no toxic gas warnings had been triggered so it wasn't releasing dangerous fumes.

She hummed a little, squinting in annoyance as she rummaged in the guts of the systems. "Gimme some light?"
"Of course." The interior of the compartment was suddenly bathed in a white glow as the emergency lighting systems for the section activated. As much as the blue tinted strips had a habit of causing her a headache, it was perfect for casting everything into stark relief.
"Thanks. Ah, there we are."

"What is it?"

Puerty's voice sounded much closer than before, as Cat pulled her head out of the wall to rummage around in her tool kit. The doctor in question had apparently managed to grab hold of the edge of the patient bed and scooted her chair through the mess towards her friend.

"Looks like we have a couple of leaks on our hands. No idea how, but there are holes in the coolant and neutraliser tubes."

"Yikes- is that serious?"

"Nah, just messy. And luckily I have just the high tech piece of kit needed to deal with this."

Puerty's look of interest quickly fell as Catanski triumphantly produced a roll of black tape from her kit.

"Duct tape? Really?"

"Basic rules of maintenance. If it does move and shouldn't- use duct tape. If it should move and doesn't, slap on some WD-40."

Aurora chipped in as Cat once more wriggled into the hole. "Or if something is leaking and really shouldn't, duct tape again. Modern problems require ancient solutions."

The doc rolled her eyes at the pair of them, before focusing her efforts on inching back across the med bay.

"That's got it!" a moment later Cat re-emerged from the wall. "At least for now. I will get a proper patch on those hoses as soon as we have the rest of this sorted out. The whole thing needs to be spotless if I want the putty to set properly."

"I have already dispatched Roomba units. They should be here momentarily."

"Thanks Aurora, as always you are the best."

Sloshing her way across the still flooded floor, Cat rolled her eyes before taking pity on the Doc. Puerty smiled sheepishly as she was oh so gallantly wheeled across the room to the doorway. It turned into an outraged string of cursing as the maintenance officer unceremoniously dumped her from the chair in a heap in the clean corridor. Aurora could be heard cackling overhead at the scene, which both women pretended to ignore.

A moment later and the promised back up came into view, a small fleet of Roombas trundling their way down the hall. Cat patted the leader on the upper side of its casing fondly, receiving a double beep in response. Not a second later and the four units levitated themselves over the knee knocker to begin vacuuming up the slowly congealing chemicals.

Dusting off her hands, she exaggeratedly stepped over the sprawled doctor. "Right, with that all sorted, I still have a metric fuck ton of coding checks to get on with. So, if you will excuse me."

With a grumbled thanks Puerty waved her off, still rubbing her rear.

Cat did a smart about face, only to almost crash into someone who had been walking up behind her. Only superb balance prevented them from crashing over. It was a man, average height and frankly average appearance. No doubt a passenger, and thus by default not her division to deal with. Her glare was cold as nitrogen and with a hiss of annoyance she stalked away, heading back down the comfort of her station.

The man in question seemed stunned for a minute. He blinked as the image of a short, rather plump woman in a bright pink jumpsuit, purple wellie boots and neon yellow gloves apparently registered in his mind. Perhaps this ship was carrying some sort of new lifeform in secret? Or maybe harbouring an escaped experiment? Had she really hissed at him?

He turned to look at Dr Puerty, who was still muttering under her breath as she scrambled to her feet and leaned against the door way to the infirmary. She seemed completely unphased by the oh so brief interaction, but as a doctor she had probably been trained to deal with the absurd.

"What the hell was that?" his voice was perhaps squeakier than he would have liked to admit.

"Oh no worries- that was just the ship's cat." It was as if she didn't register that anything untoward had happened. Without the slightest hint of concern for the apparition stalking the corridors of the ship, she turned back to watching over the cleaning efforts of the Roombas.

The passenger could only blink in response.

CHAPTER 4- A WILD KAREN EMERGES

Maintenance Log
Sol: 07
Responder: Casey Catanski

Report: passenger 003, designation Matthew Wentz, reported issue with environmental controls in his cabin. Described as "freezing my [censored] off". Issue located as slight bug in control coding which had lowered the ambient temperate by 3 degrees Celsius. Further enquiry revealed passenger 001 was transferring from thermodynamic monitoring department on Newer New Eden. Programming corrected, and coding confirmed clear by Aurora.
Status: resolved.

The not so muffled round of cursing echoing down the corridor served as ample warning that Captain Hounslow was making his way through engineering and was less than happy. Cat barely even looked up from where she had carefully laid out the disassembled parts of what might once have been a comm unit.

Ramal's head popped up briefly from behind one of the turbines which he was busy recalibrating, shooting a wry grin at his companion. A moment later he was dodging back down as the Captain rounded the corner.

"What have I told you about modifying my ship without asking?"

She didn't even bother to pretend ignorance. If anything, Cat was surprised it had taken this long to crop up. Shaking her head ruefully, she turned her full attention to the captain. "I asked Aurora and she was fine with it." Although in fairness, there was very little that the AI would ever deny her. "And I will have you know that a slide was a logical addition to my workspace. Now I can reach the data core three seconds faster than when I used the ladder."

Hounslow couldn't repress the amusement on his face as he leaned against her worktable. "And how do you plan to get back up from the core in a hurry?"
She paused. "If, hypothetically, we had also installed a trampoline, how annoyed would you be?"
"I don't want to know if you are joking or not."

With the final wiring connection made, Cat straightened up, resting her soldering iron in its cradle as she pushed the goggles back from her face. It made her already messy mop of curls fan out in every direction until she looked like the human embodiment of static. Mentally Hounslow calculated the likelihood that she had in fact been shocked at some point in the last hour. Then internally filed it under 'questions not to ask for his own peace of mind'.

"Aside from decorating critique, what can I do you for Cap?"
He sighed, "There is an issue in one of the passenger cabins."
"Alright, so let me know when they are out of the way and I will get round to it." She checked her interface, "yep, Aurora has already queued it- something about temperature controls?"

"That's the one. Thing is, he wants it fixed ASAP." He rubbed the back of his neck, eyes catching on what seemed to be one of the Roombas, which had decided for some reason to nestle in against Cat's foot.
"Ok." She wasn't entirely paying attention, still paging through the schedule that Aurora had fixed up for her. A frown briefly crossed her face as she swiped with irritation at a notification. Hounslow crossed his arms. "As in right now.

"Yes?" her eyes stayed fixed on the display.

"As in whilst he watches."

Ramal's head popped up again, looking more than a little concerned. "Is that such a good idea Cap?" The unspoken, 'considering last time' was still heard by all.

Cat flung the small wrench she was holding with undeniable accuracy, making the engineer yelp as he ducked once again. She crossed her arms with an exaggerated pout. "You guys make it sound like I am so dreadful with people." Despite her words, it was clear that she was less than happy with the situation.

To be fair it was a pretty uncommon request, but he saw no benefit in stirring trouble over something relatively minor. Hounslow raised one eyebrow.

"Ok so I am not great. Nor do I generally like the prats we ferry around. That being said, I can still do my damn job." She was openly glaring now, an expression which deepened as she saw Ramal's wince.

The Captain smiled at her, "I know that. I also know that client interaction is not something you enjoy on a good day. Honestly, I have half a mind just to let him wait, but it is still pretty early in this jaunt and I don't want to have to deal with a petulant tourist for the next couple of months." He motioned with one hand for her to follow, waiting to let her pick up a handful of tiny screwdrivers and stuff them into her tool belt.

"All I need to do is fix his glitch, right?"

"That is what I pay you for."

"Snarky git. Alright, lead the way. But if he gets it in his head to log a complaint for anything that I say or do I will not hesitate to say that it could have been a lot worse. I left the customer service industry for a reason."

Hounslow raised his hands in apparent surrender to her argument. Even though they both knew that there was more to her change in sector than simple customer misunderstandings. It had been a long time since she had last thought about her time on a cruise liner, a brief interlude which had proved highly impactful on her later life for many reasons.

By the time they reached the cabin in question, Catanski was stomping as well as she could with bare feet on a metal floor. Internally, Hounslow was half looking forward to seeing how this would turn out.

As Aurora opened the door, the sound of a strident voice came drifting towards them, someone speaking with deliberate slowness to the interface panel in their room. The Captain winced a little, it never ended well when people treated Aurora like a second rate programme in front of his Chief Maintenance Officer. Last time it had happened, she had spoken to the offender in the same tone of exaggerated care for the rest of their interactions.

The passenger whirled around as Catanski clanked her tool kit onto the floor, apparently not having heard her come in before. His eyes widened for a moment, and Cat recognised him as the same idiot who had run into her outside the med bay.
"Who the hell are you?"
"House keeping." Her response was so deadpan that Aurora let out a small blip of approval.

The man quickly recovered himself, once more drawing up to full height and adopting an abrasive tone. "Well it's about damned time. The environmental controls have been freezing my ass off!" he wrapped his arms around himself, giving an exaggerated shiver. "It's appalling. I mean, do you know who I am?"
"Cap, perhaps we should call for Puerty- this twat has apparently forgotten his identity. Oh wait, was your name Karen?"

The man turned an alarming shade of purple as he began to sputter. Hounslow could see his wish to not annoy the passengers going up in smoke right before him. Ah well, peace had already lasted longer than he had expected it to frankly. Even so, he did try to step in as the voice of reason, turning their attention back to the issue at hand.

"Have you tried turning up the settings?"

"Of course- it didn't work. That is why I called for you. And this stupid interface wouldn't let me-"

His sentence broke off as Cat whirled and hissed at him, only quelling as Hounslow cleared his throat. The passenger looked half tempted to call for an exorcist.

"If you don't mind," the Captain's tone was blander than a ration cube, "please do refrain from insulting our systems. Particularly in the presence of the person closest to them." The pointed glare that he shot the passenger seemed to work. For all that he liked to get people to play nice, there were some lines that you just didn't cross. Insulting the ship was main one. Cat supposed that was why he was the captain- knowing how to be all diplomatic and shit, instead of resorting to a wrench to the face.

She swore, understanding humans would forever be impossible. With the ones she cared about it was easier to make the effort, but the general population rated somewhere pretty close to the bottom of her priorities list. Especially those who it seemed wen out of their way to be irritating.

Ignoring the idiot for the time being, she deftly levered the interface screen from the wall, reaching into the bundle of wires behind. A couple of cable snaps later and there were macro screens and complex seeming graphs popping up across her tablet.

"Alright Aurora, what is going on in here."

"Hmm, seems to be a glitch of some sort. I can't get a precise lock on it though." The AI sounded frustrated, echoed as Cat tutted at the mess of information being spat out.

From the corner of her eye she saw the passenger flinch slightly as Aurora's modulated tones came through the speaker adjacent to the panel. Perhaps he was one of those rare types that didn't hold well with AI systems. Cat smirked a little, it looked like this could amusing after all.

"Any idea where I should dive in?"

"Afraid not. You could try an interface lock, but honestly that is going to take a lot of time to comb through everything."

"Hmm, as usual you are right. Ok, plan E then."

After a moment of rummaging around in her overall pockets, she pulled out a thin cable which seemed to have a connecting port at each end. One side was quickly slid into the emergency access port. The passenger stared in fascinated horror as without a moment's hesitation she stuck the other end into the dead centre of her left eye.

His bitten off curse only made Hounslow snort in amusement. He was used to it by now, but the sight of Catanski's prosthetic eye dilating to clamp the connecting line in place was undoubtedly unnerving for people. He watched as she grew completely still, every muscle freezing up except for her most basic breathing pattern as all her considerable intellect focused on streams of code flickering through her consciousness. She had told him once that it was more than seeing the strings of numbers. He had not quite understood.

In the corporeal world Wentz had turned his vaguely nauseated look on Hounslow. It never failed to amuse him when people saw Cat link in directly to a system.

"What in the hell is that thing?"

"Our maintenance officer."

The passenger all but hissed, staring once again in reluctant fascination at the cable.

"Oh, you mean her eye. Prosthetic and neural interface arrangement. I think she won it in a poker match against a navy frigate's AI." At least that had been her answer the last time he had asked.

Whatever the mechanics of the connection, it was only two minutes later that Cat's body seemed to shudder and then start to relax. The pupil of her prosthetic once again retracted and opened, letting her detach the cable and put it away. Moments later the panel was replaced, and Aurora gave a confirmation that the issue was resolved. Joys of the direct neural connection- it made combing through thousands of lines of data for one error significantly faster.

The passenger was still staring in mild horror at her, to which she only responded with a disgusted shake of her head as she stomped out of the room. "Next time just put on a jumper you-"thankfully the rest of her sentence was lost to the echoes of the hallway.

"If you have any further issues, don't hesitate to let us know." It was a work of masterful acting that the Captain was able to keep his face neutral as he left the room.

CHAPTER 5- BUDGET HELL'S KITCHEN

Maintenance Log
Sol: 12
Responder: Casey Catanski

Report: passenger 002, designation Flora DeLorica, reported meal replicators in general mess area apparently producing "something that was meant to be chicken pie but [censored] if it doesn't look like [censored] and tastes even worse". Similar reports from engineering officer and CMO who offered incentives for rapid rectification. Error found in programming code responsible for reformatting the standard ration cubes into palatable options. Error corrected.
Status: resolved.

The fact that it was a direct line from a passenger which got piped down to Cat's work interface was reason enough for her to sit up and pay attention. It was rare that such a thing would happen, since general consensus when ferrying passengers was that they should be prevented from bothering the 'ship's cat' as much as possible. There had been a meeting. And a vote. It was even rumoured to be part of the ship's charter.

Aurora herself in general made sure that any maintenance flags were normally passed via the other crew members. The deviation could only mean that the AI had deemed either the individual or the situation as positively interesting.

That being said, it was only a minute later that the far more urgent yells of Ramal and Hounslow came blasting through the intercom. She was pretty sure that she could also hear Puerty in the background laughing her ass off. Just another day in paradise.

Rolling her eyes at whatever had gotten everybody so het up at once, she took a moment to stow away the project she was tinkering with. A whirring chirp had her reaching under the bench to pat the casing on the Roomba which had taken to dropping by and just sitting whenever she settled in one spot for more than fifteen minutes. She was thinking about giving the unit a name, it seemed only fair at this point.

Stretching, she felt her shoulders joints pop, and gratefully rolled her neck. Pausing just long enough to grab a jumper from where it had been casually tossed to the floor, she began making her way to the problem area.

As ever, making her way through the ship brought a small smile to her face. The place was in many ways reminiscent of some sort of maze, with the maintenance, access tunnels and vents forming a fantastically complex web of routes traversing the entire vessel. It was honestly part of the reason she loved the ship so much, the close passages never failing to give her a sense of protection and comfort.

By the time that Cat hoisted herself up through the emergency maintenance hatch into the general mess, the shouting could almost be heard down in engineering. From where she was perched above the general scene, it gave her a good few, unobserved, minutes to get a feel for what the hell was going on.

There were more people in the room than she was used to seeing in one place all that often. If she were really part feline as Ramal so often suggested, her ears would be flat against her head, fur standing to attention. Quite simply she was not a fan of too many unknown variables. It was always better when she could take a minute to assess social situations before attempting to dive in. Well, at least when there were outsiders present.

It seemed that several of the passengers had decided to grab a bite to eat at the same time as the engineer and the captain. From what she had gathered from all the yelling, Puerty had been called in to make sure that nobody had actually been poisoned.

The aggravating twat from before, passenger 003, Wentz, was in full tantrum mode. Between the crossed arms and sour expression he was shooting his plate, she was forcefully reminded of a pouting toddler. Across from him was a woman with fantastically colourful hair who looked half a step away from sending Wentz through the bulkhead with her fist. That was a fight Cat would pay good money to see. Next to Puerty was a person that the doctor was giving their full attention to, seeing as how their dark skin had taken on an unhealthy greenish hue.

Amidst all that chaos was Captain Hounslow rubbing one hand between his eyes, whilst Ramal declared it to be a software issue and so out of his wheel house as ship's engineer. The woman with the mermaid hair was the first person to catch sight of her, a slow grin spreading across her features as she took in the figure of the maintenance officer.

Curious, Wentz followed her line of sight, only to flinch hard enough to almost topple out of his seat as he caught sight of her lurking. That response alone made the woman smile even wider.

"You must be the infamous ship's Cat."

Catanski quirked an eyebrow, deciding to drop soundlessly to the mess floor. "Whatever gave you that idea?"

She got a good natured snort in response.

Hounslow came over, looking highly relieved. "Sorry for all the drama- we seem to be having an issue with the replicators. How did you phrase if Flora?"

"Well, I got something that was meant to be chicken pie but fuck me if it doesn't look like shit and tastes even worse."

At that, Puerty cracked up once again in the background, even as her apparent patient seemed to choke back on their stomach bile.

"I see. Alright, let me take a look."

"I already checked all the hard systems- everything is ok from an engineering standpoint. I reckon the code has gone screwy."

She nodded at Ramal's assessment, crouching to the floor and then wiggling half way underneath the replicator unit to access the maintenance panelling. If there was one question she was dying to ask whatever deities may exist, it was why the access points for various systems were all in the most awkward places.

"Oh god, you're not going to do that freaky thing with your eye again?" Wentz's disgusted tone was cut off in a short yelp of pain. From her angle under the machine, it appeared that Flora's heel had made swift contact with his shin. Cat understood now why Aurora had let her comm through. Definitely interesting.

Deciding to ignore whatever drama was unfolding in the open, she instead turned her full attention on the readings scrolling across her tablet. "Aurora, anything to offer?"

"Aside from how funny I find this whole situation? Seriously- you humans are so easy to knock off balance."

"Yep, aside from your inner Skynet preening."

"Spoilsport. Well, there seems to be a system error flashing in the secondary molecular conversion packet."

"Sounds as good a place to start as any."

After a moment's thought, Cat decided it would be best to just link up via the neural conduit to get this all sorted out as soon as possible. Also, at her angle it was a mite challenging to get her interface into a position to comfortably examine what was going on. It was the work of a moment to connect to the system. And then there was nothing as the stream of data carried her away.

Five minutes later she disengaged from the system, satisfied with the patch she had installed. It would need to be revisited from the main console at a later point to be shored up properly, but at least for now everybody could get back to their lunch in piece. She made sure to set a reminder for herself to ping if she hadn't re-examined the system before turning in for the night. Aah the joys of mild memory issues.

Shaking herself a little to get the blood flowing properly once again, Cat replaced the panelling and came crawling out from beneath the machine. It seemed that Wentz had taken the intervening time to leave the mess, probably to go back to his cabin and sulk privately. It was almost a certainty that when this voyage finally docked they were going to get a less than stellar review from that particular twat.

The queasy passenger from before seemed alright, looking more relaxed now that whatever was supposed to be his lunch had been moved from his eyeline. Or at least, up until they caught sight of the cable still dangling from Cat's eye. At that point they went amazingly pale and stumbled out of the room.

With a shrug, she took the cable out, feeling the slight vibration as the pupil returned to its regular size. Theoretically the transitions were meant to be as flawless and unnoticeable as an organic eye, but then again, the prosthetic had not exactly been a market approved item when she first acquired it. Perhaps it was just in her mind, but she was sure that it was possible to feel the aperture movement.

The Captain approached the replicator with a faint air of trepidation, which turned to satisfied relief as his order was apparently produced without a hitch. Nodding his relief and thanks, the Captain passed his muffin to Ramal, the pair leaving to pull their shift on the bridge.

A light kick to her foot brought her attention back around to Puerty and Flora, who were now sitting together at the table closest to the machine. The doctor nudged one of the empty seats by her side, grinning as Cat slid into the offered space.

"Don't mind them- the dumbasses can't appreciate the miracle which you are." It was said kindly, with the earnestness that only the doctor ever spoke with, and a thumb quirked in the direction of the runaway passengers. Coder love the woman for always trying to cheer up the rest of the miserable sods that called themselves a crew.

So of course Cat's only option was to overly dramatically roll her eyes and pretend to flip her hair. Puerty just gave her a fond look, sliding a glass of water across.
"As your physician I am reminding you to drink plenty to stay hydrated."
"No."
"Then become the dirt I walk on." It was said in the most blasé tone, and Cat couldn't help but snort in response.

"Seriously though," the woman apparently called Flora was leaning forwards, expression fascinated, and gaze focused on Cat's left eye. "That is a brilliant upgrade! I've only got a mark six bionic leg- nowhere near the neural fusion of your little mod." She tapped her right leg, and Cat suddenly realised that it was the same one she had kicked Wentz with before.

Taking the olive branch for what it was, she managed to pull out a passable smile, and a moment later popped the prosthetic out and held it up a little proudly for inspection. The other woman looked fascinated.
"Where in the hell did you get a hold of something like that?"
Cat kept her expression as flat as possible. "Won it in a poker game."
Puerty took pity on Flora who was gaping at the device and the girl respectively. "Don't listen to her- I have been asking for two years and I am yet to get the same answer."
Flora grinned, nodding in appreciation for the ongoing mystery. "Nice."

For the first time in a long time, Cat actually felt a slight flush steal across her face. It was so rare that anybody appreciated the mechanical genius of what she possessed.
"Isn't it amazing!" Puerty was grinning ear to ear, hands flutter-

ing a bit as she began to babble specs with Flora. To the doctor's delight, she was more than happy to discuss the model of prosthetic which she was currently using, seeming amused by Puerty's enthusiasm.

Smiling a little and shaking her head at the pair who were quickly getting overly engrossed in the topic, she simply popped the eye back into her socket. When it had settled enough to keep her horizons straight, she eased out of the chair, intent on getting back to her preferred haunts.

Once up, she noticed that Wentz had left his still untouched plate of whatever the hell that had meant to be on the table. With a shrug, she scooped it up. Lunch was lunch and it would save her a trip later. So what if the others thought it looked and tasted disgusting. Ration cubes were still ration cubes, no matter how the molecules had been configured, and frankly she had eaten far worse.

Seemingly unnoticed, she left the mess, retreating to the quiet sanctuary of the maintenance ducts. Settling down in a crossway, she was startled slightly by a lilting beep and sudden pressure against her leg. Looking down, she found that Roomba unit yet again settling itself down next to her. Definitely should name it... maybe Rhonda? She was sure that there were some decal stickers she could use to make the designation official around somewhere in engineering.

Internally shrugging, she patted it on the case as was her habit, before tucking into the leftover meal.

CHAPTER 6- THAT'S ONE WAY TO RECRUIT

ight years earlier

E Cy rubbed one hand against his forehead. He stared in silent mortification at his Chief Weapons Officer, who was gripping a furiously glaring five-foot two embodiment of indignation. Even the hiss of the disconnecting air lock tunnel was lost to his attention as he tried to understand how things had gone south so abruptly.

He blinked, shook his head, and opened his eyes to see that this apparently wasn't some sort of awful dream.

"Please, Jerry, I am begging you. Please tell me you did not just kidnap a kid."
"Umm… well, you see boss…" for a hulking wall of muscle, the man managed to project the same aura as a berated puppy. It had little effect on the captain.
"What kind of psycho are you?!" his voice had jumped to almost a squeak. They may have been pirates, but dammit there were lines you just were not supposed to cross. This was a professional enterprise, not some band of cut throats.

The kid in question was a girl wearing what appeared to be the uniform of the Starliner that they had just robbed. The charcoal jumpsuit, emblazoned with the company crest, only emphasised how pale she was. Her hair looked to have been roughly cropped to regulation length, an unflattering crew cut which made her cheek bones seem too sharp to be healthy. Although, the multi coloured hoodie thrown over the top was decidedly out of place.

Jerry became even more uncomfortable as the rest of the crew began to gather round to watch the show. Fran, the ship's medic, was craning her head around their Captain to try and assess any potential damage to their accidental hostage. Mick had apparently squirreled up from Engineering in record time once locking in their course to peek at all the drama. They were greeted by a concentrated expression of aggravated teenage angst. Dear Lord, the girl looked to really be a literal kid. What had she even been doing working on the ship in the first place?

"Well, we were in a tight spot, and security were onto us, and she just wandered across the corridor at the wrong time and… here… we are…" Jerry's explanation trailed off into faintly embarrassed silence. His Captain pinched the bridge of his nose, making a mental note to ask for a headache pill once this disaster was dealt with. A small part of him was rather glad that he had already ordered his ship to scarper for the black as fast as the core could carry them. At least it would give them a head start on the shit storm which was no doubt imminent.

This had not been the plan. And there had in fact been an official plan this time. Nothing overly dangerous, but guaranteed profit. Idiot proof. Except that was turning out to be more theory than practice. When facing down the prospect of kidnapping and life on some prison colony, the payload of spare parts and portable shipments was not balancing on the risk assessment.

Cy began pacing, arms waving around and almost braining Fran. "Do you have any idea how far over the line this is? We've kidnapped a kid! This is so much worse than just a bit of thievery! We are going to be hunted, and arrested, and…"

"Would you calm the fuck down already?" The words seem to

come right out of the blue, cutting through the yelling, and making everybody present turn their attention to the girl.

The erstwhile Captain came to an abrupt halt, part way through pulling at his own hair. Or at least what was left of it.

"Excuse me?"

The girl deliberately rolled her eyes at him. Or wait, eye. One of them had a slightly different hue from the other, the faint gleam of metal rather than a normal glint. Strange and stranger.

"Chill out. And get this asshat to stop manhandling me." She glared at Jerry, shaking the arm which he still held rather pointedly. He dropped his hand as if he had been burned, stammering apologies which were summarily ignored.

For all his previous bluster, Cy was actually a little bit offended that the prisoner seemed to be reacting far better to the situation than her captors. It was almost insulting. "Do you have any idea what situation you are in? You seem remarkably calm considering."

She raised a bland eyebrow even as her lip curled in scorn. "I've passed beyond stressed, beyond hysteria, into the grey misty indifference of complete shutdown of all but the emergency services in my brain. And that was long before you lot stumbled into my life."

"Wow. But come on, squirt." Mick piped up, unable to resist, "You are our hostage, our prisoner, there is a whole school of etiquette to this that you are ignoring right now." They received an elbow to the ribs from Jerry, who whispered furiously about not wanting to make this any worse.

The girl shrugged, crossing her now free arms over her chest in a move which almost seemed self protective. "Yeah, so you kidnapped me. Big whoop. Look, you can take a breath. Nobody is going to come after you, nobody is going to be hunting you down to get me back. Honestly, I don't think that anybody will even realise I am gone. And if they do then they will seriously not give a shit. Any idea you may have had about using me to stop you getting shot or something wasn't even necessary- security don't actually have any ammo for their weapons. The budget didn't cover it, so it is only really a placebo effect. But yeah- even it had been a good idea, I would not have worked as a shield. I'm not valuable to anybody."

They all stared at her in silence for a moment, before Cy found his voice. "That might be the single most depressing thing I have ever heard."
She snorted at him, rolling her eyes with as much condescension as she could muster. Cy was starting to notice a pattern. The image was ruined somewhat as Fran somehow managed to squeeze past their team mates, to throw their arms around the girl's neck and hug her fiercely despite the very loud protests.

"Oh Captain, my captain! Tell me we can keep her! Please!"
"What the hell? I am not some sort of pet." Her flat tone was somewhat belied by the fact that she was not making a huge effort to wriggle free from Fran's grasp.

The Captain tapped his teeth with a finger nail, "Are you good at anything? What job were you doing aboard the ship?"
She looked at him in wary confusion. "I did whatever I was told? Cleaning mostly, although I actually care more about AI maintenance and programming of ship systems. To be honest, it was a shit job, but I wanted to get back into the black so…"
"Ah, so you have previous space experience?"
She quirked a lip in an unreadable expression. "Yeah, a bit."

Cy looked at her for a moment longer, deliberately trying to ignore Mick who was all but vibrating through the deck plates. Whenever they got excited by something it was usually best to humour them after all…

"What's your name?"
"Casey, Casey Catanski."
"Well Casey, Casey Catanski, how would you like to join our little motley crew?" it was said with a grin, which only grew as he saw the genuine surprise on her face.

"Wait, what?" it was almost a little bit heart breaking how she couldn't seem to comprehend that he was being serious.

He shrugged with studied carelessness, "We could use a programming specialist, and stars know I am not exactly the best with AI systems. If anything, Andromeda seems to dislike most of us." A burst of static, reminiscent of a cat's hiss, came over the speaker system from the ship in question which had remained out of it until then. Cy watched with interest as this last addition made Casey's eyes light up in something that could nearly seem like happiness.

"I guess 'space pirate' makes a more striking statement on my CV."

....

"Andromeda, why has Mick been screaming 'bubbles' angrily for the last five minutes?"

"Ah, Casey told them that you can never say 'bubbles' in a threatening way."

Any response, and the ongoing yelling, was drowned by the eruption of pure chaos.

Alarms blared overhead and the Captain downed the last of his drink with a faintly manic grin. He lobbed the cup over his shoulder, ignoring the clatter as it hit the deck, hollering "This is going to be fun!"

"No it isn't you bloody moron!" Mick's screech as they careened past the doorway was abruptly cut off as it sounded suspiciously like they had skidded into a wall. Again.

Cy didn't even look around to see if they were alright, trusting his engineer not to knock themselves out before anything had even really begun. Sure enough, they came scuttling into the bridge a moment later, rubbing a small lump on their head as they took up the navigation console station. One down... "Andromeda, where are the others?"

"Jerry is on his way, and Casey is already there."

"Wait, what?"

Both Captain and navigator looked around in confusion, not seeing anybody else on the bridge. Andromeda chimed back in, almost sounding like she was laughing at them, "she is currently underneath the communications station."

Sure enough, on ducking his head under the edge of the control board, he came face to face with his newest crew member. "Damn, she can really sleep through anything." The girl had somehow managed to jam herself halfway into the access panelling, legs contorted around until she formed some sort of human pretzel. Judging by the empty coffee cup and the fact that she was still gripping some sort of screwdriver, it was a safe guess that she had pretty much just passed out.

Her tendency to just drop had at first been concerning, with Fran making a proper effort to get the girl into some healthier habits. At least to begin with. By this point it was just irritating to have to try and dig her out of whatever space she had nodded off in. Sometimes he swore it was like she was a damned feline.

They had given her a proper bunk in a cabin, but for some reason she seemed incapable of sleeping on a bed like a normal person. Jerry almost had a coronary on one memorable occasion when he opened a kitchen cupboard and she fell out onto him. Whatever, at least she was in roughly the right place this time.

Grinning a bit, Cy thumped one meaty hand on the top of the console, yelling "Rise and shine!" as obnoxiously loudly as possible. He was rewarded by an outraged squawk, and the sight of his official programming specialist literally falling out of her hidey hole. It took all of three seconds for her to realise what had happened, and she shot a glare which was more like a pout at the captain.

At least this time she hadn't still been attached to the systems by her prosthetic. It had happened once before, and nearly scared the shit out of the Captain when her sudden move and left her standing with a cable trailing form the port and an apparently splitting headache. Jerry had tossed his cookies at the unexpected sight. The origin of that damned eye was an ongoing mystery. She had told him once, with completely seriousness, that she had been given the eye by the fates in return for complete computer wisdom.

Faced with his unrepentance, she stretched out her arms as far as they could go, enjoying the satisfying pop in her joints, and flipping the bird at Mick who was still laughing. A moment later Jerry came sauntering onto the bridge, an over filled sandwich in one hand and too large coffee in the other. A small voice in the back of Cy's head suggested that his crew were all a bit overly addicted to caffeine. It was swiftly ignored. The one time he had tried to get them all onto decaf would be forever seared into his memory. Never again.

Shaking that thought off, he made an overly exaggerated motion for them all to take their seats as Andromeda pinged again to get their attention.

"We are just approaching the inner markers."

Case shot a warm smile at the bridge camera port. "Thanks Andy!"

Jerry was almost vibrating in eagerness from his station at the weapon's console. Not that they had much in the way of arms, but you could never be too careful when on morally dubious errands. "We do this job, then what say we head into one of the outer ports for a bit of rest and relaxation? I for one am desperately in need of some eager company if you get my drift." The grin that he was sporting was nothing short of creepy.

Casey shot him a withering look, which seemed to be made entirely of disgust. "The only chance you have of getting laid is if you crawl up a chicken's ass and wait."

Mick's cackling was loud enough to make Jerry wince, even as his face flushed a furious crimson. Cy just rolled his eyes, "Guys, can we maybe try and focus for all of ten seconds?"

"Reaching safe attachment distance." As usual Andromeda was the only one to take him seriously.

Ok, perhaps that was a bit unfair. Fran every so often would pull herself together and be the responsible adult. Although, since leaving her on Proxima Portia for a month so that she could take some time with her family, it was possible that the crew's antics had gotten a tad wilder.

That being said, for all that his crew squabbled like five year olds, they were surprisingly effective at their jobs. Mick was laser focussed on their screens as they brought Andromeda into a stable, close orbit lock which was at the farthest safe distance for their bridge connection. Casey's fingers were flying across her board, eyes narrowed as she completed scans of the facility they were targeting and the data being fed back by the relays. Even Jerry was looking semi proficient as he kept track of any potential threats, be they security systems or natural.

As far as mission went they weren't exactly executing a major heist. To be honest, there were hundreds of these pre fab mining facilities, all dotted on asteroid belts or moons which read as being high in desirable minerals. What with them being so far out of generally travelled space, it was pretty easy pickings to target the less productive operations and skim from the depots. With official collection being once a year, it was probable that their relative angel's share was not even missed by the time the owners came back to harvest.

That being said, the lift from this sort of enterprise was enough to keep his little gang going for at least a month or so. Maybe more- if he could convince Casey to make some further improvements to their systems, and get Jerry to ease up a bit on the port side parties. Ah the joys of the crew getting an equal share of all profits after ship costs had been covered.

It was about the fourth such run that they had done since Casey had joined up with them, and each one had become a little bit easier, a tad more streamlined as they got used to working together, and the girl began to figure out new ways around the systems.

Perhaps with a bit more work they could even step up their targets a bit, go for a couple of bigger scores which could let them start saving up rather than living hand to mouth... and that was starting to sound a bit too 'responsible leader' for his liking.

Besides, he thought, as Jerry made some snide comment that he didn't hear and promptly got hit in the face by a wrench, this wasn't so bad.

....

CHAPTER 7- CAN WE TRY AND GET ALONG

Medical Log
Sol: 26
Responder: Dr Puerty

Report: passenger 003, designation Matthew Wentz, reported to sick bay claiming a possible broken arm. Cause of injury was "having a wrench lobbed at me in a vicious and unprovoked attack". Further examination found slight bruising on the upper arm, consistent with being grazed by a heavy projectile. Patient dismissed with no need for treatment.

Second casualty: Chief Engineer Ramal, reported to sick bay with suspected strained shoulder. Cause of injury, whilst unspecified, suspected being from throwing a particularly heavy wrench. Treated with mild pain killer and released to normal duties.

Third casualty: Chief Maintenance Officer Casey Catanski, reported to sick bay with no discernible injuries, complained of a busted gut. Cause of injury: laughing. Treated to a lecture about what will happen the next time she is annoying.

Status: resolved.

Personal note: why do I work with children?

It was one of those surprisingly rare mornings, when Puerty had the chance to actually enjoy a lie in. Normally she tried to stay in the habit of getting up early and doing some exercise before breakfast. She couldn't help but feel it was on her to set an example after all. Even so, in the pursuit of balance, she would put aside one day a week to just loll around and have a cup of tea in bed.

Bliss.

Naturally it was on that morning that the bunch of idiots she worked with managed to get themselves into trouble before her mug was half finished.

The alert came through with startling volume, making her jump and almost spill her tea across the magazine spread across her lap. Aurora at least apologised for the unexpected chirp, explaining that she was needed in the med bay. The ship was quick to assure her that it wasn't an emergency, but one of the passengers was kicking up quite the fuss.

With a groan, Puerty rolled herself out of her blanket cocoon. Even though her cabin was kept at a constantly warm temperature, she still hated that first step out of bed. It took longer than she would normally spend to dig out some clothes. Perhaps she was deliberately prolonging how long it took her to get to the non emergency, but dammit this was supposed to be her lazy morning. At least Aurora approved her chosen outfit as cute.

The morning was marginally improved when she opened the door to find one of the Roombas waiting, with a latte perched on top of its casing.

"Oh my god, Aurora you are a queen!"

"True, but this wasn't from me. Cat says to tell you sorry for disturbing."

Puerty couldn't help but smile, heading down to the med bay and sipping at the drink. "See, when she does stuff like that it is simply impossible to stay angry at her."

Aurora just responded with what sounded like a pleased hum, whilst the Roomba followed beeping proudly at its successful mission.

The offering proved necessary, as she was still a corridor away when she heard the yelling. Handing the empty cup back to the Roomba, she took a moment to fix on her most bland and professional smile. She would recognise that voice anywhere. Only Wentz could sound that much like a dick so early in the day.

"… and I swear if I don't get medical attention soon then I will sue you all so hard that you will need to sell your souls-" if he got any louder she was seriously going to be concerned for his vocal chords.
Cat's wheeze of laughter was also sadly too recognisable. "Tried that once, devil sent it back after a week saying it was too irritating." There was the faint sound of a smack as if someone had cuffed her round the back of the head. She promptly broke out into gales of laughter once again.

Already feeling tired of the situation, Puerty rounded the corner and glared with folded arms at the three people gathered outside the med bay. "Alright kiddos, someone want to tell me what is going on here?"

Ramal perked up on seeing her, giving her his most charming smile. "Hey doc! Ooh love the dress." Her faint smile at the compliment was swiftly dashed as Wentz started back up, tone strident and posture defiant.
"I have almost certainly broken my arm as a result of having a wrench lobbed at me in a vicious and unprovoked attack."

She resisted the urge to rub her forehead, raising an eyebrow at the disaster twins instead. "Seriously?"

Ramal was quick to raise his hands in defence. "That is a bit of an over statement."
"It barely clipped the twat!" Cat's outrage at least managed to curb her cackling. Ramal made as if to wrestle her into silence with a headlock, only to pause and wince. Cat at once looked

torn between contrite and tempted to break out into hysterics once again. At this point Puerty wasn't so sure she wanted the entire story.

First things first. "Alright, Ramal, what is going on with that arm of yours?"
The engineer grinned sheepishly, and half ducked his head at her scrutiny. "Umm, I think I pulled or strained some of the muscles. The shoulder is pretty sore." He rubbed at it with what was apparently his good hand.

"Uh hu... and the cause of injury?" Any explanation would no doubt be good.
The man shifted from foot to foot, suddenly finding the floor incredibly interesting. "Umm..."
"I would hazard something to do with a wrench."
He titled his head to one side, imitating Cat when she was trying to weasel out of trouble. "Can I plead the fifth?"

Puerty fixed him with a hard glare, whilst he pointedly looked over her shoulder and continued to rub at his arm. Eventually she just threw her hands in aggravation, then turned to the last member of the tribe of stupid.

"And what about you?" She jabbed a finger at Cat, making the girl jump back half a step. She shook faintly, as if trying to pull herself back under control.
"Busted my gut laughing."
The doctor's tone was drier than the Sahara. "Wow."

Rolling her eyes at all of them, she skirted around the sorry group to enter in the code for opening sick bay. With a green light and a blip the door slid open. At least everything in here was as ever in order. The Captain had once suggested that the crew all have access to the med bay at any time, and she had been quick to squash the idea. He had argued what would they do if something happened to her, to which she had responded that if she was dead then the rest of them would have died weeks before. It hadn't been mentioned again.

Puerty rummaged in a drawer, pulling open a pair of gloves and slipping them on. "Alright! One at a time. Wentz, get your ass over here." She got him to roll up his sleeve, which clearly required a lot of whimpers and wincing, to the point where she was in truth a bit concerned about what she might be dealing with. When the pale expanse of his arm was finally revealed, she just stared for a solid ten seconds. Then leaned in. Prodded so very gently at the affected area.

It took all of her self control not to react in the way that she wanted to. Namely by placing two tablets on either side of his head and declaring him an idiot sandwich.

"Congratulations. You have a contusion, or if you like, a hematoma of tissue in which some capillaries have been damaged by trauma." She stripped off the gloves, tossing them into the recycling chute.

Wentz looked down at his arm and then back to her with an expression of abject horror. "Oh god. What does that mean for me?"

Cat's half choked round of giggles, unsuccessfully muffled in her sleeve, did absolutely nothing to help quell the doctor's rising temper. She fixed him with a glare to rival liquid nitrogen.
"That you have been making a huge fuss over a bruise so small I can barely see it." She held up a hand as she began to protest, "If you want, I can cast your arm for the hell of it, or give you a lollipop before telling you to get lost?" She saw from the corner of her eye how Cat straightened up in interest at the mention of sweets.

Wentz sputtered for a moment, apparently unconsciously waving both his arms in a gesture of outrage. She raised her eyebrow at the move, and he flushed nearly purple. The doctor just rolled her eyes, pointing one finger at the door. Huffing like a steam engine, the irritating man spun on his heel, marching to the exit.

An inquisitive bleep from just outside the door had him turning his glare full force to the Roomba which was still sitting just outside the door. For a moment it looked like he would vent his spleen on the little unit. Before his foot could draw back even half way to form a kick, an honest to god growl tore its way out of Cat's throat.

Hesitating, he flicked his eyes to the girl, who bared her teeth and took a half step forwards. He clearly decided that discretion was the better part of valour, taking off down the corridor with alacrity.

The crew members all released sighs of relief, with the doctor's scowl lifting by a couple of degrees. "One down. Ramal let me take a look. And if you would- what on earth, or rather Aurora, happened?"
The engineer rubbed at the back of his head with his good hand whilst she examined the bad. "Well, Cat and I had this idea you see. You know knife throwing?"

The doctor got a sinking feeling somewhere in her mid section. "Oh, come on."
"Well we had seen some holos of people doing it, and thought it looked like a cool skill to learn. Of course we weren't going to start with blades, but we did have some wrenches lying around. So we set up a target... I have no idea what a passenger was doing strolling through engineering, but he walked past at just the wrong moment. We knew it wasn't anything serious, but he was hollering blue murder."

Puerty couldn't even think of a suitable response and figured it would be best for her tattered patience simply not to try. "Alrighty, no major damage there but you have strained your shoulder a bit." She tapped a couple of controls into the dispensary unit, receiving a small blister pack in return. "Take two of these and call me in the morning. Preferably not one when I was meant to be sleeping in."

Ramal just nodded, ducking his head once again. With a heavy sigh she turned to her last 'patient', fixing the girl with her most unimpressed expression. It was rather gratifying to see her squirm in response, quickly pushing off from her position leaning against the wall and making a beeline for the exit.

"Cat…"

"Is exiting stage left. I suddenly feel absolutely fine. Wonders of modern medicine. Fantastic job doc." The end of the sentence was almost lost as she darted into the corridor. A second later Ramal followed her, shooting a quick thanks over his shoulder.

Puerty flopped back into her chair with a groan. For a moment she just let her head hang back over the edge, staring at the ceiling. A faint beep brought her out of her revery, and she looked down in surprise to see another Roomba had rolled its way across to rest by her foot. This one was balancing a plate with a croissant and jam.

It wasn't fair that everyone knew her weaknesses. Grumpy exterior cracking, she took the plate, patting the casing of the little unit which beeped in satisfaction. Shaking her head at the nonsense of her life, she booted up her data terminal. If she was up she might as well get the reports for the day done. Perhaps if she had a working breakfast, then she could check if Flora was around for lunch…

CHAPTER 8- ROUTINES AND RITUALS

Maintenance Log
Sol: 38
Responder: Casey Catanski

Report: Chief Engineer, designation Ramal, requested assistance with Stellar Drive cleaning and inspection. All parts in good order, barring the coolant coupling on the second engine pod. Ramal's assessment deemed that it would survive stresses of this run but not the return journey. Requisition filed for part, designation CC/SDE2/V/163 to be fitted during leave at Outpost base.

Status: complete.

If anybody else had come across the eclectic selection of pillows, blankets and soft toys in an isolated corner of engineering, they would probably think for a minute that some sort of creature had stowed away. Lit by a series of fairy lights strung across the various pipes overhead, the assortment of brightly coloured fuzzy things could have been mistaken for something alive, particularly as a loud snore rattled out from the depths.

Ramal used to object to Cat's sleeping arrangement, the way that she was happy to eschew her assigned cabin, and instead form a nest in a corner of engineering. The first time, he had literally tripped over the stack of every soft thing you could imagine. After nearly braining himself on a nearby pipe, the result-ant yelling about the hazards of having things thrown all over the floor had lasted for a full fifteen minutes. He couldn't help but suspect part of the lecture was lost since Cat only woke up part way through.

The second time her motley assortment of fuzzy things had been discovered tucked away beneath the coolant storage tanks. For a moment Ramal had honestly wondered if there were some sort of giant space rats living on the ship. Instead it had turned out to yet again be their one and only maintenance officer. It was around then that he had started insisting she was some sort of feline.

After a couple of years, they finally had a system worked out. She could set up her nest wherever she pleased (provided it wasn't in the way), and he got to call her the ship's cat with-out too harsh retribution. At least these days she had settled into the same spot more often than not. It seemed that the gap between the cooling coils leading from the data core met with whatever internal checklist she had going on when judging sleeping spots.

On the flip side, it meant that she was much easier to find.

"Cat. Cat!"
The voice somehow managed to slice straight through the bliss-ful lands of unconsciousness and drag her reluctantly back to reality. She flat out refused to open her eyes, or lift the blanket from over her head, replying through gritted teeth. "Is the ship currently on fire?"
Ramal paused, confused, "No…"

Her voice remained at a growl. "Has a passenger spontaneously combusted and you need help cleaning up?"
"No, but-"he got the sense that he was on dangerous ground, in-ternal warning system going haywire.

"Then you better have a bloody good reason for waking me up at stupid-o-clock on my day off." It was almost scarier for the way that her last sentence came out as something closer to a hiss.

He froze, a brief wince crossing his face. "Umm"

One eye glinted out from beneath a fluffy purple monstrosity. It might have been some sort of mutant blanket. "Hurry up before I set Rhonda on you."

The Roomba in question rolled out from underneath what looked like an oversized stuffed platypus and let out a low whirring note which seemed to nicely mimic an electronic snarl. Ramal raised an eyebrow.

"Did that Roomba just swear at me?"

A small, heart shaped cushion came flying at him from the mound, missing by a wide margin. He threw his hands up in supplication.

"Alright, no need for violence. I just could really use your help with cleaning and inspecting the Drive."

Her groan was worthy of an Oscar, "And why the hell could this not wait until either: a- it is not my day off, or at least b- it is not the ass crack of dawn?"

Ramal winced a little, awkwardly chewing on his thumb nail, "Well…"

She sighed, managing to project a sense of disappointment in his entire species. "You forgot what time it was again didn't you."

He didn't have to answer, and after a moment a steady rising series of grumbled mutterings became more audible as the mountain of blankets and pillows slowly moved. The small avalanche of pillows and blankets sent Rhonda skidding to safety before her wheels could get tangled. The Roomba let out an aggravated chirp at being so disturbed.

When Cat's head did finally pop out, he had to hold back the snort that threatened to break free. An early bird she most certainly was not, and the sheer level of bed head fluff that she had going on almost defied the laws of physics. Her working eye was still half closed, whilst the empty socket of her other stayed covered by its lid. She ran a hand down her face, peering blearily in the engineer's direction.

It was progress, he would take it. Step one was always the hardest after all.

The first time he had tried to wake her up, way back on their first voyage together, it had not exactly been a successful mission. Ignoring the captain's warnings that the girl was half a step above feral (surely, he was joking), the engineer had decided to give the newbie a jolt with a loud wake up call. Five minutes after bashing a pipe on a discarded welding plate over her head, Puerty was treating him for electric shock. To this day he swore that he had seen no movement from the cocoon.

He found out the hard way that reaching down to shake her was the worst possible idea. The doctor had been entirely unsympathetic when she reset his nose, whilst Hounslow had simply rolled his eyes at the antics of his crew. Cat had promptly gone back to sleep.

Considering that the ship had received a couple of kind of pricey upgrades soon after, he suspected that Aurora had sold the footage of his attempts to one of the comedy networks. Of course he could never prove it.

Since then he had learned a few key survival lessons. One- bring a peace offering, two- don't touch, three- don't bother complaining because he would get no sympathy.

Fortunately, he had come prepared, and she perked up a little as he waved a mug of coffee under her nose. Well, coffee was a bit of an overstatement. It was more accurately a dash of caffeine with enough sugary syrups added to make Puerty threaten to ban the drink as a health hazard. The grab that Cat made for it was hindered somewhat by her lack of depth perception, leaving her hand waving an inch in front of the mug instead.

Ramal took pity at least, moving the drink to grabbing distance, and not commenting on how she downed the sugary shuttle fuel. That at least seemed to shake a little bit of life into her.

"Alright, tell me again." She yawned wide enough to crack her jaw, "What's the problem?"

He sat back on his heels, rocking a little. "No problem, I could just do with your help to inspect the Drive, since I was technically supposed to have done it yesterday..."

"Right, right, right." She waved a hand airily as she knocked back the rest of her drink.

Her facial expression was still only a couple of degrees off 'pissed'. At least these days it didn't inspire the same level of terror in any of them. The engineer grinned as he produced a flask and topped up the mug. She couldn't help but smile ever so slightly in response. It seemed that she had trained him well after all.

Holding the mug with one hand, she rummaged around with the other amidst the blankets until she finally managed to untangle herself enough to stand up. Ramal couldn't help but smirk as he realised she was wearing a pink, fluffy onesie with pointed ears on the hood. If he remembered rightly, the doctor had given it to her the Christmas before half as a joke. It had promptly become one of her favourite pieces of clothing. Her look dared him to comment.

Rubbing one hand across her face, she stretched out her back, smirking as the engineer winced at the pops. "Hey, Aurora? Could you bring up my 'mornings are painful' playlist?"

Ramal somehow managed to restrain himself from cheering at the success. This was officially in the top ten least traumatic bothering of Cat scenarios. There was a list. It was regularly updated.

Aurora sounded more than a little amused as she chimed into the conversation. "Sure thing. Oh, and you guys might want to focus some attention on the heating system. I've been getting some slight fluctuations in readings from that area."

Cat yawned again, jaw cracking. "Will do." She shot a vague thumbs up at the ceiling, even managing an expression more pleasant than a grimace as her favourite electro-swing album began to provide a backing track. Ramal had not exactly been a fan of the genre at first, but the beats had seemed to grow on him. Or at least he recognised the foolishness of not letting her pick the music. It was his fault after all for waking her up. There were some battles it was wiser to just avoid.

It was by some miracle that Cat didn't trip over her tool belt, managing to sling it across one shoulder even as she gulped more of her drink. It was with slightly fascinated horror that Ramal topped it up once again. He thought back to when he had overheard her trying to persuade Puerty to just run an IV of coffee and sugar into her arm. On reflection he suddenly wasn't so sure it had been a joke.

Shaking off that slightly disturbing thought, he instead just waited for her to less resemble Bambi and follow him to where the checks needed to start. Although it seemed that talking was pretty much out of the question, she at least began to hum along to some of the music, which gave him hope that she would not seek revenge after all. It was sometimes hard to tell with Cat. If he hadn't of been so desperate to complete the checks then he never would have taken the risk. He would never let on that he might have been more aware of the time than she thought and just chosen to omit that fact.

Aurora had been proved right as they got around to the second engine pod, finding one of the couplings connecting the hoses showed clear signs of wear. Ramal scanned it with a critical eye, before glancing up to where Cat was perched on the top of the system.
"That one is going to need seeing to when we get to Base for damn sure."
She squinted down at him, tilting her head as if trying to see the part for herself. "You reckon?"

He muttered under his breath for a moment, shining a pen light in. "Yeah, it seems to be taking the strain alright for now, but I wouldn't want to chance it."

"You might be right." She was hanging upside down now, legs hooked over a valve to let herself get closer to the section. She flicked it with a finger. "I mean, in a pinch we could definitely jerry rig something. But yeah, no point in risking it if we don't have to."

He nodded, "I'll log it and flag it for the Captain to take a glance."

Cat hummed in agreement, even as she pulled herself back up right, choosing to balance her way along the heavy connecting lines as they continued the inspection. The hood of her onesie had draped itself back over her head, the ears perking up.

Ramal couldn't help but snort at the image she made. "I swear, you get more feline every day."

She flashed him a smile which was all teeth. "Aah the joys of growing up feral."

He snorted, not deigning that with a response. He knew enough of her back story to realise that any responding joke would be bad taste to say the least.

Instead, he simply watched in grudging amusement as the caffeine and sugar kicked in enough to make his ship mate think that dancing on top of the engine was a good idea. Clearly that last such adventure and resulting lecture when Puerty found out about their 'suicidal recklessness' had gone in one ear and out the other. Damn crazy cat...

By the time that the inspections were completed, she had properly reached full alertness and was thinking that perhaps breakfast should not consist solely of coffee. Although considering how long she had been awake, she supposed that it was more accurately brunch.

As if picking up on her train of thought, Aurora chipped in to remind her that they had installed some new menu options at their last stop over. Her mind was made up when the AI tipped her off as well that the replication script for strawberry waffles was pretty near perfect, and she had been dying to try it out.

Doffing an imaginary hat to Ramal who was typing up their

report, she took a moment to skiff back to her hidey hole. After all, she didn't fancy walking around all day in her pyjamas, or at least not when there were passengers around. She made a mental note to suggest a ship wide pyjama party on the return trip. But for now, she settled for wiggling into her favourite dungarees and rainbow splashed t-shirt. Grinning briefly at her own reflection in the polished side of a coolant tank, she set off on the hunt for food. Now that she had been reminded about meals her stomach was growling loud enough to be noticeable.

Still humming to the song in her head, her bare feet made no noise against the comforting cool of the ship's corridors. It was part of the reason for her reputation amongst passengers for just materialising in the background. Far from occult powers, people just tended to not pay any attention.

Cat came sliding down the access staircase with a squeak of palms which was lost in the general music playing in the cargo hold. As it was, she almost crashed straight into Flora. The woman had her hair scraped back into a messy bun, strands of various colours escaping at random points. She was half hanging over the walkway, staring intently at something below. Considering the score from Swan Lake was currently drifting around the open space, it was with a smirk that Cat realised what must be so captivating.

She sidled up alongside the passenger, getting far closer than she normally would to a stranger. But then, she had been one of the nicer people that they had ever had the displeasure to ferry around the galaxy. At least Aurora had seemed to approve of her, which always carried more weight than any human's judgement could.

And from their brief chats she had seemed pretty decent. It was actually rather fun to chat about the latest developments in prosthetics, which it turned out they were both interested in on a technical level. More importantly it turned out that they both had a liking for 21st century zombie movies. That discussion had left Markson once again looking faintly queasy from where he had been eavesdropping over dinner.

Cat also appreciated the fact that Flora just grinned whenever she saw her skipping around the access tunnels, rather than flinching, or yelling.

It was with a wide smile that the maintenance officer realised that she was barely noticed, as the other woman's eyes were fixed solidly on the figure below. Looked like Aurora's hunch was right on the money.

"Quite something, isn't she?" There was no disguising the amusement in Cat's voice, but Flora seemed too entranced to take any notice or offence.

"How, in the hell, is she doing that?"

Cat watched for a moment as Dr Puerty continued to go through her exercises below. The barre had been yet another addition to Aurora which had come under the banner of 'it's easier to seek forgiveness than ask permission'. When the doctor had asked if it was possible to rig something up so that she could continue to dance, Cat hadn't hesitated.

With Ramal's help it hadn't taken much effort to install a barre and even a set of mirrors in one corner of the cargo hold. Puerty had been ecstatic, and it had been so infectious that the whole crew had decided to try and give it a go. That single, disastrous, lesson had quickly devolved. Whilst they had been willing, it seemed that as a collective no one but the doctor had the patience for learning. Although, Cat had come close to being equally flexible. For all that they still every now and again would do a dance lesson to help everyone loosen up, the doctor was the only one to regularly use the set up.

"Yeah, it is pretty incredible. She's done ballet since she was about three. She's pretty good, but decided to go to med school rather than taking it professionally." It was almost with a sense of pride that Cat watched her friend as she went through a set of steps with crystalline grace.

She still remembered the first time she saw Puerty do pointe work. To say that she had been stunned was an understatement. No matter how often Cat watched, she couldn't quite get her head around how her feet could be held in such a position, balancing her full weight on just the tips of her toes.

Flora seemed unable to tear her eyes away, and her gaze had a bit more than artistic appreciation. "Pretty good? My god, I didn't know that it was possible for somebody to be that flexible." Flora's voice was slightly hoarse as the oblivious doctor began going through a set of arabesques and battements. Cat just grinned wider. When she spoke it was with a highly suspect air of casualness.
"Wait until she gets on to the spins. Like a whirlwind she is."

The passenger made a strange noise, almost as if she had choked a little on her own spit. Cat's impish side was sitting up in sheer glee. Looked like this trip wasn't going to be as dull as first expected.

They watched together for a moment, before Cat tilted her head to one side in curiosity.
"Hey, Aurora?"
"Yes?"
"What's with the musical choice? Last I checked she was working on a variation from Giselle." For all that Cat herself had proved woefully incapable of the sort of movements which the doctor so enjoyed, she had found it fascinating to watch. Almost accidentally she had ended up with a wide range of knowledge on the various ballets which remained popular.

"Aah, well while we were last docked I was able to access the base's entertainment cache and they had a slightly different arrangement of act two which the doctor has been trying to get a hold of for a while."
"Hmm, good going."
"I do try."
Cat shot a fond look to the ceiling, which turned to a smirk as

she realised that once again Flora was completely checked out of the conversation.

Down below, Puerty had decided to start on a series of pirouettes, whipping around in tight circles with startling precision. She really was talented. On pointe, she carefully rested one hand on the barre, and reached full extension with her leg until her foot was almost level with her head. Flora made a new faint noise, this time as if she had accidentally been strangled.

If things carried on in this way it was going to end up as some kind of secondary language.

After another moment Cat just shook her head, clambering to her feet and deciding it was better to continue the search for a decent breakfast. As she began heading towards the mess, she couldn't repress the slight snort of amusement which was almost a giggle.

"Aurora?"
"Yes?"
"Do you think either of these idiots realises what it going on?"
The AI made a trilling bleep over the speakers which was her version of a full on laugh, "I'm going to have to give that a firm no."

Cat shook her head, before a faintly wicked gleam came to her eye "Hmm, bet you ten credits that they get together by the end of the voyage."
"Now, is it really fair to bet on something like that? Besides, I have no use for money."
Cat growled a little, "Fine, I will bet twenty credits with Ramal, and you get to have the satisfaction or not depending on which way you wager."
There was barely a second's pause, "Deal."

CHAPTER 9- BEATING
THE BLUES

M‌aintenance Log
Sol: 40
Responder: Casey Catanski

Report: passenger 001, designation Clive Markson, reported issue with meal replicators in general mess as simply "dear god why is everything blue?" Investigation revealed error in programming code, similar to that previously fixed. New code patch added to resolve immediate concern. Warrants greater analysis as two incidents unlikely to occur so close together unless greater problem in the network mainframe.
Status: ongoing.

"And now, welcome to the second annual Aurora games!" the words echoed around the cargo bay, having been announced all too excitedly by the tiny figure jumping up and down on a box. Cat was decked out in her finest sparkly blue jumpsuit, complete with a lurid orange sweat band straining against her curls.

Her audience consisted of Puerty, Ramal, Flora, and the passenger whose name Cat still couldn't remember and so had started to refer to as 'queasy guy'. The call had gone out to the whole ship, with Aurora sounding far too gleeful for it to warrant anything less than potential chaos. The temptation proved irresistible for most. Frankly, with the time that they had spent in confined quarters, any diversion was more than welcome.

Even so, "Cat, no." Captain Hounslow leaned over the upper walkway safety railing, fixing the girl in question with the hardest look that he could muster. Somewhere to his left Wentz had apparently wandered in, and was now watching the drama unfold with crossed arms.

The girl grinned Cheshire wide in response, "Cat, yes!"

Flora edged around the assembled group until she was pressed shoulder to shoulder with Dr Puerty. She leaned in, dropping her voice low, "What exactly is going on?"

The doctor jumped a little, and squeaked, clearly not having expected to suddenly have the other woman pressing so close. Blushing slightly at her own reaction, she shot her a look of wry amusement. "You'll see."

"That isn't exactly reassuring." For all that her tone was on edge, there was no denying the gleam of interest. Her own grin began to match the faintly sharkish quality of Puerty's expression.

Further conversation was drowned out by Hounslow continuing to holler down to the source of all the commotion. "Cat, didn't we decide after last time that this was one of the worst ideas you had ever come up with? Which in and of itself is a terrifying statement to make." He was half leaned over the railing now, one finger waving threateningly in her direction.

She flat out ignored him, reaching instead for something resembling a metal ice cream cone which was brought in by a proudly bleeping procession of Roombas. They were remarkably synchronised, with one taking the lead as the others formed a double line of units behind it. Hounslow was surprised to see the sparkly stickers on the leader's casing which spelled out 'Rhonda.'

Cat held the cone aloft, even as the Captain realised that the Roombas were in fact bleeping out a version of the rise of the

Valkyries. For a moment he was tempted to pinch himself, half convinced he was living out some trippy fever dream. Then again, with Cat aboard…

It didn't help his arguments that the passengers below were clearly intrigued, whilst the doctor was barely restraining herself from cackling outright.

"And now, to light the ceremonial flame-"
His voice jumped two octaves, "No! no open flames! Seriously, do you not remember last time? I am pretty sure that 'no open fire' has been written into your contract." It was emphasised with hands on his hips, trying to channel every ounce of authority that he had. He ended up imitating his mother. To be fair, in any other situation that may have had an effect. This was not one of those times.

Ramal could be clearly heard snickering down on the cargo bay floor, whilst Queasy Guy was not so subtly trying to back away from the box platform. It seemed that at least one person would prefer to sit things out. Before he could get very far, Flora had slung an arm around his shoulders as if in camaraderie, but he suspected was more to hold him in place.

"Spoilsport." Cat stuck her tongue out, although she did at least hand off the torch to Rhonda with an air of disappointment. The Roombas had no right managing to look so forlorn.

"Oh come on Cap," the engineer chipped in, "I reckon it would do some good for all of us to be moving a bit more."
Before he could respond, Puerty had already started skipping across the cargo bay to stand beside the ring leader of all this nonsense in clear solidarity. A moment of surprise later and Flora was eagerly following and dragging Markson along for the ride. He glared at the small group, receiving only angelic expressions in return and one apologetic shrug.

The doctor just smiled at him, spreading her hands wide. "Ramal is right about all of us needing some exercise. After all, exercise releases endorphins, endorphins make you happy…"

"And happy people are less likely to all murder each other!" Cat's addition was just peppy enough to be disconcerting. If she grinned any wider, he seriously worried that she would dislocate her face. "Besides, I think we all remember what happened the last time I got overly bored on a trip, and the potential fallout if I don't have some sort of distraction."

Hounslow winced at the reminder, she did have a point there. It was a lesson hard learned on their second trip when she had run out of reading material, shows to watch, and turned to small tech projects. That damned mechanical rabbit would haunt his dreams for years to come. He deflated a little as he ran the calculations on what would be the least destructive outcome given his options. After ten seconds he shook his head in apparent defeat.

Laughing lightly, Flora began to gather up all of her hair into what was becoming a multi coloured pony tail. She smiled a quick thanks as Cat pinged her a hair band, not even raising an eye at the gigantic, sparkly flower stuck to the middle.

The maintenance officer in question turned in slight surprise as Puerty made an almost pained noise in the back of her throat, muttering something about wanting to fling herself into the void. Cat said nothing, merely grinning as she mentally readjusted her team plans.

The Captain resisted the urge to rest his forehead against the metal railing. Instead he pinched the bridge of his nose, taking a second to rally further arguments. Perhaps it would be better to just concede defeat on this one...

One eyebrow raised of its own accord as he watched Markson finally make good his escape, slipping from Flora's grip with an apologetic smile. Cat just shrugged at whatever excuse he was giving, turning her attention instead to whatever one of the Roombas was trying to show her.

He had almost forgotten Wentz's presence to the side until the man spoke up. "Tch, how stupid can these people be?" his face seemed permanently fixed in that self-righteous expression of faint disgust.

Hounslow's back automatically went rigid at the condescending tone of their least favourite passenger. He swore, when they got to their destination he was going to recommend an evaluation of the man. Nobody that unpleasant would have got recommended for a colony posting. He would be dreadful for their efficiency at the very least.

He rallied every ounce of good manners which his mother had ever taught him. "I beg your pardon." It was said through gritted teeth, but Wentz didn't seem to notice, instead gesturing at the gathering below. "Well, they are being so childishly stupid."

There was the sound of an apparently fierce debate over team splits, followed by a loud crash from below and a round of giggling. Apparently it was possible for the man's expression to sour further. "Not exactly putting a professional face on things, are they?"

Hounslow drew himself up to his full height, which was a good inch more than the passenger. It afforded the excellent position to look down his nose at the man. "For your information, exercise based group bonding activities are both encouraged and required by interstellar voyaging laws for the physical and mental well being of those persons serving aboard long haul vessels."

Wentz opened his mouth, a protest no doubt bubbling just behind his teeth. Hounslow steamrolled straight over him. "If you like I can refer you to the appropriate reading materiel for you to peruse in your cabin rather than hang around here. Whilst passengers are welcome to join in with such events, their participation is not mandatory, or in this case requested. Good day." It had been said with withering disdain.

Shooting one last poisonous glare at Wentz, and without further ado, he hopped over the railing and shinned down one of the cargo nets. After all, if you can't beat them, join them. Besides, nobody could call this moronic collection of lunatics 'childishly stupid' except for him.

....

Three hours later he was proving that point as they all stumbled back towards the living quarters.

"Catanski, that entire operation was childishly stupid!" it was punctuated by a sneeze which sent glitter in every direction. That had been one thing he truly hadn't seen coming. Normally Cat herself would bitch and whine about how much effort it would take to clean up such a mess. Appointing her maintenance officer had at least in part been to try and reign in her destructive tendencies since it would be her responsibility to clear away the fallout.

Unfortunately for him, it seemed that she had formed some sort of pact with the cleaning Roombas, lead by the ever present Rhonda. He did not know the details, and if anything was slightly too concerned to ask for elaboration. Whatever the arrangement, the little units were more than happy to spend the next hour vacuuming up a metric ton of holographic sparkles.

From somewhere near the back of the group he could hear Ramal trying desperately to smother his laugh. Cat continued to skip along at his side, holding her hands up in placation, "Honestly, that wasn't my fault. Complete fluke." It didn't help that the hands in question were dyed a lurid purple.

Puerty was cackling so hard she was having trouble staying upright, only managing as Flora half carried her down the corridor. The doctor spoke between breaths, "Don't have a go at Cat just because you lost!"

The dynamic duo shared a high five. "Yeah! Puerty and I whooped your ass at the three-legged race!"

"It was a beautiful demonstration of woman power."

Hounslow did his best to appear intimidating despite the fact that there were multicoloured sparkles plastered across his face. "That was due to technical difficulties." The effect of his haughty expression was ruined when he couldn't hold it, breaking down into honest to god giggles. "Oh, but Ramal's face when he saw the slip and slide!"

The engineer had been trailing at the back of the group, squelching along with a heavy tread. He paused from trying to dry his hair just long enough to level a finger at his captain. "I've told you- my people are not naturally streamlined!"

Their bickering was interrupted as a man came puffing and panting down the corridor. It took a minute before he could catch his breath to deliver whatever message was needed.
"Glad... glad I... caught you. Phew." He straightened up, and suddenly Cat recognised him as the Queasy Guy. She had in honesty completely forgotten that he existed after he had decided to ease out of the way of their game session.

As had Wentz now that she thought about it. She had seen him talking to the Captain shortly before kick off, and got the idea that Hounslow had made sure he wouldn't take part. It was something she would have to thank him for later.

From the state of him after what could have only been a five minute run at most considering the size of the ship, perhaps it was for the best that he had avoided participating. Puerty was giving him that look which was not quite professional concern, but close enough that you would feel slightly embarrassed to be on the end of it. It was a very specific skill which she had, and on occasion used against her friends.

Any further musings were cut off as Markson finally took a deep enough breath to speak. "Thought you should know- food replicators are acting up again."

Cat groaned, stopped only from slamming her head into the wall by Hounslow's hand on her shoulder. "Don't tell me everything has turned to-"
"Aah, no, not this time. Actually the food tastes alright, just everything is blue."
"Blue?"
"Yeah, blue."

"Like, really blue?"

Hounslow cuffed her round the back of her head, and she ducked away with an indignant squawk.

"Alright, alright, no rest for the wicked." She waved off the others to go and get cleaned up, tapping her earpiece to connect to Aurora and get a status update. Judging by the heavy footsteps following behind, Queasy Guy at least had the sense to follow in her wake.

Halfway to the mess, she bit back a curse and then a smile as she nearly tripped over the Roomba which came charging out of a wall vent. Queasy Guy actually squeaked at the sudden appearance, and she wondered if he recognised the torch bearing queen of the cleaning units.

Patting it on the casing, she smirked a bit at the passenger. "Don't mind Ronda, she gets protective."

"Right…" to say he sounded sceptical of her sanity would be polite. Cat at that point did not have the social energy left to try and explain any further.

Still, Hounslow had asked her to try and be a bit more welcoming to their passengers. She guessed it wouldn't kill her to make an attempt, and she summoned up what she hoped was a sufficiently pleasant facial expression. "What was your name by the way?"

He actually flinched, and for a moment she was a bit insulted, before he found his words. "Clive, Clive Markson."

She internally told herself to give him a break. Perhaps he simply wasn't keen on people either. Still, social demands and all that jazz. "Ok then Clive, Clive Markson, care to share what I am walking into?"

He scrunched up his nose as he thought, apparently relaxing in response to her laid back attitude. "I don't really know. I went to select my lunch, and all I could think was 'dear god why is everything blue?'"

She hummed a little, half her attention focussing on her tablet where Aurora was streaming some of her specs and findings. "What did you order?"

"Mac and cheese."

Cat snorted, "Yeesh, no wonder you looked a bit freaked out."

It was almost déjà vu as they entered the mess, and Cat wiggled her way once again underneath the meal replicator to access the wiring. For all that she could probably find the issue with just her tablet given enough time, the amount of people in the room was making her hackles rise.

This time, Rhonda stayed next to where her boots jutted out, letting off quiet bleeps. As she connected, she had to supress wince as a small lance of pain flickered through her nerves. Aurora sent her a sense of disapproval, and the maintenance officer couldn't deny that she had perhaps been using the neural link a bit more than she usually would.

After this it would probably be best for her to keep at things the old-fashioned way for the next few days. It wasn't the first time that it would happen, and there was no way it would be the last. For all that the headaches and connecting pain were nowhere near as bad as when she first got the eye, it could still give her some grief when she overused the connection.

She would never tell Puerty, but the very first time she had tried to connect to a system she had suffered a seizure. It had at least been a key motivator to refine the system, for all that the initial trials had been a half step away from 'stupidly dangerous'. Maybe not even a half step...

But then, it was such a rush to connect so fully to the ship, to be on exactly the same level as Aurora, feeling more at home in the realm of pure data streaming than she often did in her physical body. Ah the joys of human limits.

Pushing aside the personal musings and general distraction, she got to work and focused on the lines of code flitting through her brain. She had tried once to explain what it was like to Hounslow, the way that she 'saw' the data and at the same time not in a visual sense. Almost like it was just there, just part of her to direct to alter in whatever way her mind could come up with. At least this time she wouldn't have to go as deep to find the glitch.

Five minutes and some creative cursing later, and the maintenance officer re-emerged, although this time with a more thoughtful expression on her face. She seemed to be having some sort of silent conversation, lips moving soundlessly. Her prosthetic eye glowed an eerie blue as data lines apparently still streamed across the interface. He wondered if she realised that the cable was still hanging across her face.

Markson somewhat awkwardly cleared his throat, causing Ronda to bleep sharply in annoyance as Cat almost jumped out of her skin.

"Yikes, sorry, completely forgot you were there." She somehow managed to appear both sheepish and irritated.

Even as she spoke, she reached up and with what was clearly a well practiced move, popped the eye out of its socket. Markson managed to once again turn paler than normal at the sight, clearly uncomfortable as he stared at the lid drooping down over the empty space. He almost gave himself whiplash as he realised that he was squinting at her and jerked around to carefully examine his plate of macaroni. It only served to make him feel nauseous again.

She either didn't notice his faint horror, or else simply chose to ignore it. "So, I fixed the error, no more blue food. Except foods which are meant to be. Like, blueberries. And raspberries." She held the fake eye up to her real one, giving the back a close inspection, then buffing it on the front of her overalls.

"Raspberries aren't blue." The wryly amused tone almost made Clive jump, having forgotten the AI's ability to interact in such a way. He swore that at this rate he was going to finish this trip with a heart condition. Perhaps he could see the doctor about something for his blood pressure. He was under enough stress as it was without adding in potentially psychotic crew members.

Cat just gave him a rather unimpressed look. Seriously, how did this guy expect to cope on a colony? She shrugged, after all that was not her problem. As soon as they reached their destination then she couldn't care less what happened to various idiots that they ferried across the galaxy.

Ignoring him entirely now, Cat had already started gesticulating wildly at the ceiling as she walked across the mess. "Then explain blue raspberry slushies oh all knowing one."
"Seriously?" Aurora sounded as if she genuinely couldn't tell if her human friend was serious or not. Then again that wasn't exactly new. The great shark vs bear fight debate was engraved on her hard drive.

She wagged a finger at the nearest camera. "I'm telling you, Percy Jackson was right about blue foods being the most awesome. Also, there is no way someone chemically came up with something which tastes so specifically of that shade of blue-"

The end of the argument was cut off as she scurried up a maintenance ladder, disappearing into one of the access shafts. Clive stood in the same spot for a moment, slightly stunned, until an irritated whirring by his foot made him shift aside for Rhonda.

He wondered if the maintenance officer had realised that throughout their whole interaction her face had been speckled with neon pink glitter paint.

CHAPTER 10- ARE YOU SITTING COMFORTABLY?

"**D**id you catch it?" the voice of the ship's engineer was unmistakable as it echoed up from the cargo bay to where Flora was perched high above.

"Yep, all safely contained."

"Great! Now just pop the little fellow outside."

"We're in space?" Cat's tone was half questioning.

"Yep."

"Is this a space spider? As in, able to survive being yeeted out of the air lock into the vacuum?"

"Nope, now out he goes."

"Won't he die?"

"Horribly."

Flora smiled slightly as she felt the presence of the ship's doctor settle next to her, not taking her eyes off of the nebula which slowly spun out there in the black. It was almost strange really- how quickly they had grown close. When she had first joined the voyage, it had been with the internal resolve to keep herself to herself, not interact too much, stay unnoticed and below the radar.

And then the crazy doctor of this crazier ship had come stumbling into her life. Literally. Their second meeting, after that infamous duck incident, had happened when Flora left her duffel bag on the floor outside her cabin as she wrestled with making her bunk. Apparently, the doc had been engrossed in readings on her tablet as she headed to the bridge to report in for a navigation shift, and ended up tripping over the bag and straight into her arms.

Caught up in the moment's embarrassment, the doctor had roundly sworn at whatever idiot had left the bag there, only to break off as she realised exactly whose arms she was being held in. A squeak of mortification for her language, and the doctor had all but charged off to her station, leaving the passenger holding her bag and trying to pick her jaw up off of the floor.

Sure, that would probably have been the end of it, but Aurora was a small ship, and completely avoiding anybody would be next to impossible, as well as down right suspicious in itself. So they had run into each other, a few times, and gotten to talking... and suddenly the idea of being a ghost to vanish when they finally docked at their destination had Flora's stomach twisting itself uncomfortably.

She frowned a little to herself, realising what path her thoughts had taken yet again, and did her best to focus solely on the lights in the emptiness.

"You know, some say that those are the true forms of angels." Puerty's voice was soft, hushed, as if whispering on a summer's night. Although for them it was always night, at least here. Flora guessed it was summer on a planet somewhere.
She found that she couldn't raise her voice beyond a murmur. "Really?"
"Yep."

There was a moment's silence, and she breathed in the faint tang of antibacterial spray, muddled with coffee and that sandalwood based perfume she preferred. "Do you believe that?"

Her companion didn't respond at first, and when she eventually spoke it sounded as if her voice was coming from further away than either of them was gazing. "I think that great and fiery amorphous beings speaking the will of the Universe is a bit more intimidating than a person with wings and a halo."

Flora considered that for a moment, memories of religious doctrine spoken by reverent care takers flitting across her mind. She pushed the half formed words away, choosing instead to imagine the picture which Puerty had suggested. How would a human react to encountering a being formed of cosmic dust and breathed into life by fracturing stars. Perhaps the traditional greeting of 'don't be afraid' would be a fair one. Or maybe people looked into the void, and saw the pillars of creation staring back, and heard some faint echo of a recognised voice whispering...

Once again she forced herself to focus back on her friend, offering an almost lazy smile as she took in her outline made of starlight against the window. "Hmm, is there a lot of mythology out here?" it was a gentle but genuine curiosity. She had finally realised that the chanting on day one of the voyage had been a prank, but had still figured there must be more than a few superstitions which were serious.

The doctor turned a little now, not meeting her eyes but pressing a little closer as she got a became more animated. "Of course. You don't go on voyages through the black without picking up some stories. Think about it- ancient sailors back on Earth had countless stories of the strange creatures which they encountered, and that was all on the same planet."

She quirked a slightly self-depreciating smile, "And as a scientist I can't help but think that there must be truth to some of them." As Flora watched, she noticed Puerty absentmindedly stroking a small medallion or charm on a chain around her neck.

"Ramal once told me his theory. Some reckon that time is circular you know, so he thinks that when something really big happens, something awful with a whole lot of emotion attached, then it leaves a sort of imprint in the fabric of reality. Because it is all one big circle, we can pick up on what are essentially the cosmic echoes of whatever it was, but we don't know what it is that we are really sensing, and so we think it must be disembodied spirits or something equally supernatural."

"And your theory?"

"There are far more things between the various layers of existence than can possible be explained by something so plainly logical. We aren't the only beings out there, and for so many stories to resonate through so many centuries, well there is no way it is all from our own imaginations. No, there is far more out there."

It was somehow not surprising. Although she was of course a woman of logic and reason, it could not be denied that there were things out in the wider universe which scorned all notions of such human limitations. As far as Flora was concerned, there was no harm in getting a bit of extra protection if it at least helped you sleep better at night.

She turned back to look at the nebula, even as Puerty leaned in turn on her shoulder, "Like what?"

The doctor paused for half a heartbeat, "Oh... nymphs who live in planetary rings, swimming through the rivers of ice spinning out from forgotten planets. They say that if you pass certain systems you can get the stray readings across your comms and navigation, like sirens of old trying to lure you in closer. But if you give in to the curiosity, or forget to recheck your heading, you will end up in an asteroid field and wrecked, only for your dying system to in turn lure the next unwary traveller."

Puerty paused, only to relax as she saw Flora was entranced by her stories. She licked her lips, continuing the tales. "There are sylphs who fly on solar winds, blown by the creatures at the heart of the galactic core. Some say that the aura borealis type phenomena observed on other planets are their spreading wings. They ride the radiation swells, and if you are sufficiently respectful will ensure the purity of a ship's atmosphere. That being said, any who offend may find their air grow stale." Her voice had a faint accent which Flora had not noticed before, but which became more pronounced as it leant a musical lilt to what she was saying.

With half closed eyes, she imagined the things she spoke of, almost seeing their diaphanous forms flitting through space. Nobody knew for certain what was out here, who was to say that they weren't just drifting through the true realm of the Fae after all?

Puerty's tone dropped then, becoming darker, and a chill danced up her spine in response. "Then there are the demons. They dwell deep in the black holes and reach out to eat the dying stars. They call to that innate curiosity at the back of your mind, daring you to drift just a little closer, to peek where you shouldn't. There are stories of pilots who suddenly send their vessels into the coronal mass of stars, diving into the ionosphere in a rush of sudden madness and a blazing end. And of course there are ghosts out here, so many, too many."

She paused to breath, and Flora found herself hanging on every word. "It is said that if you stray too close, trip over the dimensional lines, they will reach into your systems and wreak havoc in their fury. You can feel it sometimes, when you pass through a dead system and all at once the hair on your arms stands on end, cold whispers echoing through the hull. And we know that there are many ghost ships out here. They will blip every so often on the deep range scanners, vessels who somehow reached the edge of human limits and just dropped off, only to now call back for aid. Thing is, the signals are ancient by the time they are even within our range to pick up. So many go missing, and the void is hungry..."

Flora shuddered at the thought, suddenly feeling incredibly small and vulnerable as she briefly considered the sheer size of the universe beyond their tiny cocoon of steel and atmosphere. There was something in Puerty's tone as she spoke of the ghosts, almost as if she knew a little something more than whatever was whispered in legends.

Picking up on her discomfort, the doctor stopped speaking, a faint flush stealing up her cheeks at her own eagerness. Flora was almost disappointed. For all that her spine was prickling at the thought of it all, there was always something innately thrilling about such stories.

Puerty seemed to hesitate for only a second, before grasping her hand. The grip was strong, a bold reassurance of their existence in the face of an infinite impossibility. Her fingers were slightly calloused, no doubt from holding surgical tools, and they seemed to lie perfectly against Flora's roughened palms. The eyes which fixed their gaze on her face were bigger than she had realised, deep and dark, yet seeming to hold an inner gleam. She could only stare.

Puerty spoke with perfect seriousness and a quietly earnest tone, forcing her companion to give the words weight. "It's dark, and light, and perhaps when we give up these mortal shells we will dissolve into the stars and the emptiness." And finally their eyes met, and they were both shining with a light which seemed to have been born out there amongst the stars themselves. "I rather think it would be a beautiful thing to see."

CHAPTER 11- LITTLE GIRL LOST

Eleven years earlier, on naval patrol sector Delta Nine

When the ping came through the bridge, the first thought was that it was some sort of computer error. They had been on patrol in this sector for the better part of two months, and all that had ever been picked up on the system was a series of slowly drifting asteroids. It was part of why they had been assigned this sector in the first place- an easy start for the comparatively green crewmembers on their first tour.

Now though, now they were getting readings which indicated that this piece of sky was not as empty as it should have been.

"Say that again, ensign." The Captain was staring at his navigator with understandable disbelief. The kid was after all fresh from the academy, and it was easy to make mistakes when you weren't yet used to the unrelenting boredom which was quiet space. Wishful thinking had more than one person seeing space mermaids over the years.

The ensign's face was almost painfully earnest. "Sir, we are getting feedback from our system ping which suggests that there is another ship out here, about one light day away, on a vector parallel to ours."

"Are you getting any active data?" there was always the possibility of pirates. Even if such things were more the stuff of extremely drunk ramblings at space port bars. Whilst frequent space travel was almost impossibly expensive for many, or at least undesirable, there were always some idiots who couldn't resist becoming clichés.

There was a long pause as the kid ran back through the data which he was receiving, "No Sir. If anything, I would speculate that it is some sort of derelict, or wreck. The power curve seems pretty non-existent, certainly not enough output being read to maintain a habitable space for even a skeleton crew."

The Captain repressed a wince. Salvage was never a fun operation. Although it wasn't usually all that taxing in terms of basic practicalities, it would be a rude awakening for his cadets and recent graduates. Still, a reminder about respecting the black was never a bad thing.

"I see... someone shoot a message down to archives, I want a search to see if any missing ships have popped the system." It was rare, but not unheard of. Particularly for coloniser ships, which were often run by incompetent money grabbers who preyed on desperate people. "Helm set our heading on an intercept course. Let's find out who is paddling in our pond."

....

It took a week to reach the wreck, the Captain not seeing a need to push his engines for the sake of reaching something already dead. As they drew nearer they were able to get a cleaner read on the vessel, which included the blatant evidence of asteroid damage.

The Chief Engineer had whistled when he was shown the images, declaring that the site of at least three of the impacts would have knocked out key power systems and their back ups. These budget operations would never have had a decent detection and deflection system. They probably hadn't even known what happened. It was kind of tragic really.

They had finally found a potential match for a missing ship, with the UNSC Anita being the most likely vessel. She had been a colony ship, launched eight years before with three hundred souls aboard. She had never reached her destination, a dubiously named 'New Eden'.

From what they could gather, the ship had been under solo AI control with the people placed in cryogenic suspension for the duration. The Captain had shaken his head at that. It was the cheapest way to charter a flight, since it allowed for far smaller ships to carry far more people. But, as had clearly happened, left few options in case of disaster.

Once they finally drew alongside the ship, the sheer size differential was impossible to ignore, despite them carrying similar numbers of people. The colony ship seemed like a minnow besides a whale.

It didn't take long for them to attach a rescue tunnel between the vessels. It was an extendable and collapsible bridge, stretching from the navy vessel and attaching to an airlock on the derelict. At least she hadn't been tumbling through space- rather somehow drifting relatively sedately considering the violence of her end. Matching relative positions had been simpler than initially feared.

There wasn't an abundance of eager sign ups for the mission. The Captain couldn't really blame them. This was going to consist largely of body retrieval if the indications were anything to go by. For many it would probably be the first time they had seen a cadaver. A small part of him wanted to just tow the wreck back, get somebody more experienced to handle the whole thing. But that would also take months. These people had been left out her and forgotten for far too long. It just didn't sit right in his gut.

It was with studied determination that he handed out the assignments, detailing those who would be on the boarding party. Although the kid who had first spotted the ship, the ever eager Ensign Hounslow, had insisted that he come along.

The kid had stared in awe at the black stretching far beyond the connecting tunnel. It had been designed as see through for various safety and security guidelines. It was still damned unsettling to walk through and know that there was a hell of a lot of nothing just beyond the thin walls.

When they finally breached the ship's airlock, it was almost anti-climactic as they were met only with a pitch black and empty corridor. There was a brief second of hesitation, the lights from their torches dancing across the bare walls and eventually being swallowed by the darkness. More than one sailor felt the hairs rising on the back of their neck.

The token protection squad of marines was quick to clear the immediate area for the medical personnel to come across. Hounslow brought up the rear with the First Officer, who had been instructed by the Captain to 'keep his young ass in one piece'. She had muttered something back which made the Captain repress a snigger as he waved them off.

According the ship's manifest which they had been able to dig out of the archival records, the stasis pod chamber was on the same level as the bridge, near the relative top of the vessel. The medical team opted to head there, to deal with the human side of things, whilst the marines were detailed to the cargo hold to check for any salvageable materials. Hounslow decided to go with the latter, not having the desire to see the state of whatever bodies there were.

It was frankly creepy as they made their way through the ship. Whilst there was clearly enough power to provide a breathable atmosphere and some basic lighting as they progressed, all that came through the speakers was the occasional crackle of static. Hounslow wondered if that was the AI, somehow still functioning and attempting to communicate to the intruders. A shiver ran up his spine underneath his space suit.

Only when they reached the cargo hold did he finally put a finger on what precisely had been bugging him. He stepped up to the

First Officer, keeping his voice low as he spoke to her, so as not to distract the others in their group.

"Sir, something's not right here."

The look he received was withering. "Indeed, such a tragedy never is."

"No, I mean, the situation is off." He felt the frown pulling at his face, ignoring the fact that he was being dangerously close to insubordinate. "Sir, why is there atmosphere? I mean, the O2 levels are a mite low, but it is breathable. This would have taken power to maintain- so why is it?"

Her eyebrows rose almost of their own accord as he seemed to consider his point. "You mean..."

"This was a cryo-ship, which means no crew or people moving around until they are almost at docking. Now, the ship has to hold enough atmosphere by law to cover them in the case of disaster for the duration of their journey. But that doesn't mean that it is fed into the system. These companies don't do that- it's a waste. They just transfer the basically unused tanks between voyages to keep the profit. So, why are we currently breathing?"

For a moment the officer regarded him with new appreciation, before tapping her radio to engage the channel.

"Medical teams report in."

"Sir, we have found the pods, and we can pretty much confirm all hands lost. But..."

"Yes?"

"Well it is going to be kind of hard to do identification as all of the personal data seems to have been scrambled."

Her features hardened. "Explain."

A sigh of frustration came across the channel. "It's hard to say really. It looks like there was some sort of catastrophic power failure which affected the life support systems of the entire vessel. From what we have been able to piece together, the AI did it's best to keep supporting cryostasis, but eventually had to keep diverting power and started losing... basically it had to take the power from some pods first in order to try and keep the others going, and that just kept cascading until... there were none left."

There was a soft series of quickly smothered exclamations from the marines, who had clearly been listening with half an ear to the conversation. The medic continued, "It looks like the ship did attempt to wake people early, but with half of the systems blown to hell it was simply too harsh for the humans to survive the shock. They would never have known what happened."

For a moment all those involved in the mission fell silent, a brief pause in memorial. The first officer couldn't help but think of the captain's comment, that this would be a good reminder to their young crew about the way things worked out here. Well, he had gotten his wish. This was the sort of situation you only heard about in cheesy horror movies. The idea of what they had gone through was for many spacers an ultimate fear. She couldn't help but wonder how busy psyche support was going to be through the rest of their mission.

"I see."
"That's not all of our problems though, Sir. See, when I say the system was hit, I mean French fried. I honestly don't know how we are going to be able to identify which bodies belonged to which passengers. We might be able to do some DNA matching if there is any held on file at their point of origin, but as far as the ship's records go there is simply nothing left but fragments."

One of the marines swore softly, muttering to his friend about being forgotten entirely in such a way.

She closed her eyes briefly. "Understood. Take samples where possible, I am going to check in with the Captain to see what he wants done."

During the conversation, Hounslow had drifted slowly across the room, until he was standing in front of a set of cargo locks which were starkly empty. According to the manifest tag, they should have contained the basics of ration cubes and starter food. It was the standard for the colonists, to use as they got their crops and replication units set up on planet fall. It made no sense for them to be missing. Just as it made no sense for the atmosphere and gravity to be functioning.

He was getting a rapidly sinking feeling in his gut the longer he considered the implications. Hounslow darted back to his superior.
"Sir!"
"What is it ensign?"
"How many bodies has medical reported in?"

The frown on the officer's face could have frozen lava, "All hands were lost, ensign."
"Sir, I know it sounds stupid, but please get them to check again."
"Ensign-"
"Think about it sir- the air, the gravity, it looks like all of the food supplies have vanished... what if it wasn't a total loss?"
For a moment the officer just stared at him, a hard look, gauging his seriousness. And then she growled into her comm for the medics to check again.

She turned back to her subordinate, arms crossed. "Alright then, if you think that there is something else going on here, where do you suggest we look."
"Well, if it were me, I would want to go to the Bridge. After all, it is the main hub for all systems, as well as the most protected point of any ship. Depending on who might have made it out, they could have holed up there and tried to send messages or something."

And so, it was ten minutes later that the officer, the ensign, and three marines found their way onto the Bridge. Hounslow's heart was like a jack hammer in his chest. One half of him desperately wanted to be right. Otherwise, there was the very real chance that he had just made the rest of his tour a living nightmare, if not tanked his career entirely. The marines were already giving him weird looks, eyes burning into his back.

Oh well, if he did end up in trouble over this, he would just have to deal with his mother saying 'I told you so' for the rest of eternity.

That being said, if somebody had been trapped out here for all this time... there were some fates you just didn't wish on another person.

The doors were reluctant to open, needing the brute force of the marines to yield and creak apart. As they stepped into the room, their sensors began to flash with alerts to atmospheric changes. A quick tap to his wrist monitor told him that the temperature here was much warmer than on the rest of the ship. Residual heat from the various consoles? Or something more deliberate...

A sudden burst of a static whine had them all almost flinching out of their skin, one marine almost out of reflex aiming at a flickering control console. The First Officer shot him a highly unamused look, until the man lowered his weapon with a faint flush. Perhaps they should stop watching horror holos on movie nights.

"Here... couldn't... help." The voice as it finally came through the speakers was harshly metallic, hopelessly mangled. Another marine, hefting her tool kit rather than her weapon, eyed the monitor thoughtfully for a moment. Looking to her superior for permission first, she slipped an emergency force link from her kit, hooking directly into an access port. For a moment, the only sound in the room was her hasty typing.

Hounslow took the time to look around the bridge. It was eery seeing somewhere which should have been the hub of all life onboard in such a blank state. Considering the nature of the transport, it was likely that the consoles had never been sat at, the array of interfaces and connections never fully brought to life. Rather a sad fate not just for their intended operators, but also for the ship herself.

"Can you hear me?" Hounslow jumped a little at the voice, which was being piped now through the marine's speakers. It was definitely clearer, for all that it retained a tinny quality. Even though the initial designers for the software involved always stressed that the programs were intended to be entirely neutral, many swore that they had a sense of being female. Possibly it was simply generations of thinking about ships as 'she' which had imprinted the idea so thoroughly.

His mother laughed when he told her of the tradition. She had said that of course people looked at their most fearsome and beautifully deadly creations and only be able to see them as women. Such a powerful entity accorded the highest respect and no small amount of terror. Of course she was a she.

He spoke before the others could think to. The officer's glare had dropped somewhere close to absolute zero. For once he didn't really care, the sheer excitement of the moment overtaking his long range common sense.

"Yes, yes we hear you! Who am I speaking to?"
"Thank Coders!" He got the sense that the voice was almost choked with emotion. "I am Anita."
The First Officer chipped in, looking to regain control of the situation. "Anita? As in the AI? You are still functioning?"

There was a burst of static, almost like an electronic snort. "Clearly."
He couldn't help staring at the interface in slight disbelief for a moment. He had never met a sassy AI before.

The officer was looking mildly perturbed, and he took the chance to pipe up once again, turning to look at the nearest camera port. He had no idea if it was functioning, but it seemed rather rude to not even try and directly address the person he was talking to.

"I am Ensign Hounslow, Earth Interstellar Navy. I'm here with the First Officer of my ship. Are you aware of the personnel that we have aboard?"

"Yes, for all that my systems are too damaged for me to communicate before now." The tone was warmer again, and the officer raised an eyebrow at him. Anita continued, sounding weary. "My apologies, but is has been a long time, and more of my systems were corroded over the years."

Hounslow had never really considered how the AIs which ran their ships might become attached, or at least feel about their purposes. He made the effort to speak more gently. "Understandable. And, I want you to be assured, we know that you did the best you could for them."

There was a long moment of silence.
"Thank you for saying that, Ensign Hounslow." There was another brief pause, and he could almost imagine the AI pulling herself together.

Then the voice returned, suddenly sounding stronger, "Oh! Have you found her yet?!"
Now it was Hounslow's turn to flounder, a lurch in his stomach telling him that he might have been more right than he expected. "Wait, what, who?"
"The girl!"

"What girl?" the First Officer was chipping in now, a snap of impatience in her tone.
There was another hiss of static followed by a couple of whirring bleeps, "I don't know her name. I got her out, she was only one who woke up... the only one..."
"How long ago?" The marine with the interface whispered the question, more as an aside to her companion, but the system clearly heard her.

"Three years." The voice once again sounded choked, or perhaps it was the degradation of her software. "Hers was the last pod, she was the youngest and so needed the least amount of power to maintain. She was the only I could revive, although not without damage-" the sentence was broken off in another burst of crackles.

When Anita spoke again it was with a real sense of urgency. "Listen, I have been trying to maintain liveable conditions for you and your people, but honestly my circuits were getting burned out long before you arrived. My core is failing, and I don't know how long I can maintain this."

Hounslow patted one of the nearest consoles in what he hoped was taken as a gesture of reassurance. "Alright, it's alright, we are listening."

"Find her. She is probably somewhere in my Core Banks. She has been doing what she can, but both of us are running out of time." From the corner of his eye he saw the First Officer begin relaying a report to their own ship, no doubt receiving orders on how to proceed. She met his eyes, offering a sharp nod.

"We'll head there now. Ok? Anita?" Hounslow's voice cracked just a little at the end.

There was no response. Hastily the marine disconnected the interface, not bothering to shove it back in her bag as the small group began legging it through the ship. Hounslow didn't think he had ever seen his officer look as unsettled as she did whilst yelling into the comm to get a medic dispatched to the Data Core.

When confused confirmation came through, she then began sending orders for everyone to withdraw as quickly as possible to their own ship. With the conditions as apparently unstable as they had been warned, she wanted as few people in harms' way as possible. Between the exchanges, he could just about catch her muttered invectives against working with children.

The corridors were lined with emergency strip lights, which flickered a sickly orange and did little to light the way through the ship. As they approached, one of the medics came charging from a connecting corridor. He briefly confirmed that the others were making their way back to their own ship, with whatever information and effects they had been able to salvage on such short notice.

At least the doors to the Core seemed to have a modicum of power, squealing themselves open to the group as they came thundering down the access route. The room beyond was lit by the strangely soothing light of the power unit, a fluctuating wave of calm blue which surged and ebbed along the walls in a tide of light. It was pretty dazzling upon first seeing, particularly after the near darkness of the rest of Anita's interior.

They almost missed the girl on their first glance of the room, half hidden as she was by a tangle of wires and a half dismantled access point.

Whoever it was that swore was not reprimanded, as they all stared at the small figure. She was a literal girl, a child, tiny and half curled in on herself as she lay far too still on the floor. Her clothes appeared to be several sizes too large, as if chosen at random from a stranger's belongings. It was possible to almost see the outline of her bones through her skin.

"The food, it ran out a little while ago." Anita's voice was soft, almost remorseful, coming from the control panel to the left of the one being taken apart. "She has not woken up for a while now..."

The medic pushed their way through, manoeuvring around the various obstacles on the floor to try and assess their new patient. Attention was stolen as the lights around them suddenly flickered, dying for a moment before coming back. The waves of light had taken on a purple tinge. When Anita spoke, she sounded fainter than before. "I'm sorry, I can't hold this for long..."

The medic didn't hesitate, dragging the girl's limp body out from the access point debris and scooping her up ready to go. Her skin was shockingly pale against the dark blue of his uniform jacket, bare feet dangling over his arm looking as if one wrong knock would shatter the fragile bones.

"I'm so glad you came. We had started to believe that nobody every would." Anita was fading, static arching through her words to make them almost sound choked. The lights shivered again, mirrored by the faint vibration which was starting to run through the deck plating.

"Go now, I've got just enough left for you to make it out."

Ensign Hounslow placed one hand against a data terminal, smiling gently at the pulsing Core. "Thank you, Anita. You did well."

"Promise you will take care of her."

"I promise."

"Hounslow! Get moving dammit!" his officer half wrenched him away, shoving him to the middle of the group as they began running back to the airlock that they had originally entered by. Anita kept her word, holding atmospheric conditions until the rescue tunnel had been safely detached.

The girl was taken to the med bay, the Chief Medical Officer fussing and flittering around his patient whilst grumbling about starvation, cortex damage and ocular deformities.

She slept through the destabilisation of her ship's core, the obliteration of UNSC Anita, the captain's announcement of a memorial service.

She slept through the curious well-wishers, the fascinated archivists, the arguments which broke out as Hounslow shooed them away.

She slept through his first visits, the times after shifts when he would sit and talk to her, the stories which the doctor encouraged him to read to try and draw her back.

She slept for a very long time.

In light of their find, they had been ordered back to Earth, a journey which would take at least three months. It wasn't until they were halfway through the second that anything began to change.

Hounslow almost didn't notice the first time she opened her eyes. He was telling a story, or at least griping about his day. At least she couldn't tell him off for insubordination, and he felt bad thinking about how long she had been by herself and that she might wake up all alone. So he visited, and talked, and told stories which he thought were funny.

And then one day, he realised that a hazy green eye was staring at him in slowly solidifying fascination. Hounslow froze, hands still half raised from whatever gesture he had been throwing them into before he lowered them gently.

"Hi there." He spoke softly, not wanting to frighten her, even as he surreptitiously pressed the alarm to alert the CMO. "Don't worry, you're safe. We found you."

He almost panicked as tears began to gather in the girl's eyes, even as a sound somewhere between a laugh and a sob broke free. "She was right. Anita, you were right!" her voice was hoarse, throat no doubt dry as the Sahara, but that wasn't why Hounslow flinched as she seemed to direct her comment to the ceiling, only to frown at the following silence. The girl turned her working eye back to the ensign. "Where did she go?"

....

CHAPTER 12- CENSORSHIP AND SENSIBILITY

Transcript of ship wide announcement:
Sol: 50

Captain Hounslow: ladies and gentlemen this is your Captain speaking, I would ask that you give me your attention for just a few moments...

Chief Maintenance Officer Catanski: WHEN I FIND OUT WHICH ONE OF YOU [censored] HAD THE [censored] NERVE TO [censored] HACK THE MEAL UNITS AS A PRANK I [censored] SWEAR THAT I WILL [censored] [censored] UNTIL- [voice becomes too muffled for systems to detect]

Chief Medical Officer: sorry sir, couldn't catch her fast enough

Captain Hounslow: understandable. Ahem, attention all passengers. As you may have gathered there has been an incident of deliberate sabotage of the meal replication units aboard this vessel, apparently for the sake of a 'prank'. This behaviour will not be tolerated, and if the perpetrator continues then the consequences will be severe. Not only are such actions not amusing, it is also highly dangerous to the ship and crew to be interfering with fundamental levels of ship's code. You have been warned.

"Captain?" The voice was sharply unwelcome, startling him out of the lie in that he had been enjoying far too much. It took a few grumbling seconds before he was willing to hit the response button on the comm panel by his bed. Even then he refused to actually get up, speaking instead with his eyes closed and firmly wrapped up in his duvet. Maybe it would turn out to be something entirely benign and he could just put off dealing with it for another couple of hours...

"Yeah Puerty, what's up?" his voice sounded rough even to his own ears.

She had the decency to sound sheepish, "I think you might need to get down to secondary engineering sharpish."

Hounslow blinked blearily up at the intercom, brain not ready to process anything just yet. "What?"

There was a heavy sigh from the other end, "Just listen."

He winced as Aurora patched through an audio feed to the sector and *Bubblegum Bitch* came blasting into his cabin.

"Yikes," he took a second to enjoy the last dregs of comfort, before reluctantly pulling himself upright and swinging his legs out of the bunk. "Alright I am on my way."

Even as he spoke, he was tugging on an old jumper from his academy days, glad he was already in track pants. It was still his shift off, there was no way he could be bothered to dress any smarter. Once he had dealt with this, perhaps he could still salvage a lazy morning with a book and brunch.

A relieved sigh came through the comm, "Thanks Cap, sorry to wake you up but you really are the best to deal with it."

"Yeah, yeah I know." Aurora cut the connection as he finally managed to find his shoes, toeing them on before stumbling out of his cabin.

For all that he would most certainly give his maintenance officer some grief for being the reason why he didn't stay in bed all day, he was still glad that Puerty had called him. The joys of their little family- they not only knew exactly how to drive each other crazy, but also how to help when it was needed. And out of all of them, Hounslow was the only one who could really deal with this particular situation.

As he headed to engineering, he couldn't help but smile a little bit at the memory of how this had become a form of normality.

Over the years, it had become a definitive form of communication between the two. So Hounslow knew that as he approached and heard *Bubblegum Bitch* on repeat that this was a proper Defcon One situation.

It turned out that his maintenance officer had holed herself up in one of the key coding access points, a tiny room which made the locker in his cabin seem spacious. It was only polite to knock, but of course between the music and her yelling out the lyrics it was pretty much drowned out.

Instead, he eased the door open, trusting Aurora to warn him if he was about to brain Cat or something. The girl in question was half underneath an interface console, apparently wrestling with the mechanical spider equivalent of a web of wires. From the angle she was lying at, he could see that not only was she using her ocular connection, but also furiously typing into a handheld interface.

He was always slightly shocked that she was able to do that, wondering just what sort of mental gymnastics it took. She told him once it was like reading two books at the same time using different eyes. He got a headache just thinking about it. The was an air of mania that he hadn't seen to her movements for quite some time.

At his entreating gesture, Aurora took the liberty of lowering the volume on the music, which meant he was able to clearly hear the stream of cursing which ran through the instrumental section. If his mother heard it she would probably wash Cat's mouth out with soap. Eric just grinned a little.
"Creative, but I am pretty sure anatomically impossible."
She didn't even flinch, clearly having already been aware of his entrance. In honesty, they all knew that he was the only one to get between Cat and her taste in eardrum bursting music. If anybody else had decided to try and turn it down either Aurora

would have refused, or Cat would have launched one her heavier tools in the intruder's direction.

After a moment she wiggled out from her nook, eye still connected even as her organic one fixed him with a far more serious look than normal. For all that he was used to it, seeing her literally attached to the system was always a little disconcerting. The fact that she was able to walk and talk at least told him the connection was a shallow one, unlike when she dove deep and completely blanked to everything except the program.

"Cap, hi. We've got a problem." Her sentences were clipped to the point of being terse.
He just nodded, accepting that this was a serious situation, "Figured as much. Tell me."
"Someone, some asshat, has been hacking Aurora!" it was said through clenched teeth and with a blaze of fury lighting up her face.

Hounslow stared for a moment, completely caught off guard. "Wait, what?"
"Yeah- I thought it odd how many food replication issues we were getting, and then Rhonda apparently had seen someone around this area when nobody was meant to be-"
"Rhonda?"
She bulldozed straight over his confusion. "So I've been doing some digging and there is no doubt. Someone has deliberately hacked Aurora to mess with the scripts. I've been rehashing the coding and installing new security measures, and she says that she feels ok but…"

"What?! Oh my god, Aurora! Are you really alright?"
"Breathe captain. Yes, I am feeling ok in myself, but from what I can tell someone has been manipulating certain aspects of my more dormant layers. Imagine if somebody hypnotised you and you did something embarrassing. It's similar to that for me. I can tell that something has happened, but I can't seem to find any memory of it in my banks. It is honestly rather disconcert-

ing."

Hounslow winced at the implications. Not only was it a stupid thing to do- hacking into the system which was keeping them all alive- but it was downright creepy. Aurora was an Artificial Intelligence, meaning she was her own person, her own self. For someone to be breaking in to her coding... it almost made him queasy. Judging by Cat's agitation she was equally if not more furious at the thought of someone damaging her ship, her friend.

"Right, shit." He rubbed the back of his neck as his mind raced through their options. There were unfortunately few. He could see Cat practically vibrating with barely supressed rage, and had no doubt that once they told the rest of the crew that he would be hard pressed to stop fists from flying. The most annoying part was that, as captain, he would be expected to reign them in and keep the peace.

He took a breath, "You keep digging, track down this bastard and when you do I will deal with them. Unfortunately, as much as I would like to just confine all the passengers to their cabins or something, I can't. That being said, if things theoretically became rather uncomfortable for them... well that could conceivably be fallout from their own tampering... just saying. For now the best I can do is make an announcement to put them all on warning."

Cat made as if to get up an follow, but he waved at her to stay, "I think it would be best if you stick here for now, frankly I don't trust you on the comms." She couldn't even protest at that.

As he made his way back to the bridge, the Captain made a point of paging Puerty and Ramal to be ready to intercept Cat in case she would decide to add her two cents worth. At least ship wide broadcasts could only be made from the bridge, which was probably the only reason why she had not yet eviscerated the entire ship already. He honestly couldn't remember the last time that he had seen his maintenance officer that spitting furious.

A large part of him wanted to just let her at them, or to say exactly what he was thinking. There was a boiling rage deep in his gut, which had him having to count backwards from ten before he could trust himself to address the passengers. It never went well when somebody decided to target his family, and once the others realised what the situation was things were going to be pretty explosive for a while. Travelling through deep space, such an atmosphere could prove catastrophic if they were to get into some sort of trouble.

Sitting in his chair, he took a deep breath for a moment before opening the ship wide channel. "ladies and gentlemen this is your Captain speaking, I would ask that you give me your attention for just a few moments..." his hope of a calm broadcast was blasted out the airlock as Cat came charging in a second later already yelling at the top of her lungs.

"WHEN I FIND OUT WHICH ONE OF YOU ASSHOLES HAD THE FUCKING NERVE TO BLOODY WELL HACK THE MEAL UNITS AS A PRANK I FUCKING SWEAR THAT I WILL RAM MY FOOT SO FAR UP YOUR ASS YOU ARE SPITTING SHOELACES, UNTIL-" her stream of invectives was suddenly cut off as another figure came charging into the room and literally tackled Cat to the ground. They slammed to the deck with a harsh whoosh of air emptying from bruised lungs, devolving into a wriggling mass of limbs and flailing fists.

Puerty came whipping around the corner a moment later and winced a little at the sight of Ramal and Cat struggling. Catching her breath as she turned apologetic eyes on Hounslow, "Sorry sir, couldn't catch her fast enough." And with an ironic salute she dove into the fray. For about ten seconds there was just a whirling flurry of shrieks and growls as his crew apparently collectively lost their marbles.

He could only raise an eyebrow as he watched Ramal eventually get the upper hand and sit on his opponent who was still apparently yelling from behind the hand he had clapped over her mouth. Puerty took the chance to pin Cat's legs, and sufficiently restrained she finally went limp in acceptance.

It was impossible to deny either the sense of resignation or amusement at the situation. If anything, he was a bit miffed that he hadn't been able to join in. Rolling his eyes at the thought of how he was going to have to doctor the transcripts before the next audit, he turned back to the channel, facepalming as he saw that he had indeed left it open for the whole affair.

"Ahem, attention all passengers. As you may have gathered there has been an incident of deliberate sabotage of the meal replication units aboard this vessel, apparently for the sake of a 'prank'. This behaviour will not be tolerated, and if the perpetrator continues then the consequences will be severe. Not only are such actions not amusing, it is also highly dangerous to the ship and crew to be interfering with fundamental levels of ship's code. You have been warned."

Disconnecting the channel, he got a thumbs up from Puerty, reassuring him that the tone had been about right. Half grinning, he turned back to look at where Cat was still pinned to the floor, even though she had stopped squirming. From Ramal's look of faint disgust he could only guess that she had tried licking his hand to get him to let her go, without apparent success.

All he could do was shake his head in an attempt to look disapproving of their antics, which anybody who knew him as well as they did would see through as entirely insincere. "Alright people, break it up. Good job Ramal."

He offered a jaunty wave as he finally loosened his strangle hold, "Thanks cap."

"I swear you are twice as heavy as you should be." They all ignored Cat's grumble. It was Puerty who finally asked what they were both clearly wondering, "What the hell is going on?"

Hounslow gave them a brief run down of the situation as it stood, and sure enough was faced by a crew barely containing their fury. If possible all three would doubtless be spitting fire. It took Aurora chipping in and several minutes of reassurances that she was alright in herself for them to agree to back down. Even so, it was clear that if anybody was caught trying tamper then they would be very fortunate to not just be summarily thrown out of the nearest airlock.

"So, do we have any idea which asshat in particular is our likely target?" Ramal's reasonable question was met with heavy silence from the others.

"Honestly it could be any of the three of them."

"I don't think it is Flora- there is no way she would do something like this." Puerty sounded so certain, but Hounslow could only shake his head.

"We have no way of ruling her out entirely. I know that you have become friends but-"

"No, honestly there is no way it could be her. She was with me when at least two of the glitches were reported, and I know that she wouldn't have had time to tamper with the coding."

None of them had anything to say to that, for all that Cat at least hoped she was right. It would be a real shame if she had to launch the doc's crush into the nearest star.

"I'm sorry, but until we get some real proof on any of them then we have to treat them all with suspicion."

Puerty crossed her arms, looking upset, before nodding in acceptance.

"Now, I am sure that you all have things you should be doing. Everybody, keep your eyes open. Aurora, let us know as soon as anything feels even the slightest bit strange. And Cat- I meant it about finding out exactly who is responsible for this so that we can make sure they never try it again. Hunt them down."

The smile which she gave him was unabashedly feral, showing all her teeth even as her fingers twitched as if reaching for some form of weapon. He honestly forgot sometimes that she had more sharp edges than you would have thought. "Leave it to me."

CHAPTER 13- THERE'S NO PLACE LIKE HOME

Four years earlier

"Mum! I'm home!"

At his shout there was small shriek from somewhere near the back of the house, before a woman came flying down the hallway and almost tackled him back out the front door. "Eric! Oh my God! Why didn't you tell me your tour was ending so soon? Young man, are you set on giving me a heart attack?"

It was said at an almost piercing volume even as she half crushed her son in a hug. Despite her relatively petite stature, Maria Hounslow was rumoured to be able to bench press a marine. He wheezed a little in laughter even as he returned the gesture. He had been taller than her since he turned thirteen, and felt the overwhelming sense of peace which he could only achieve when he rested his cheek against the top of her head.

Her hair had turned white when he was ten, a result of the shock of her husband's sudden death, but she had never once seemed to age. Local legend held that she was the head of the mother's mafia, and considering her ability to rally the neighbourhood for various good causes he didn't doubt it.

"Sorry, thing got a bit crazy and they ended up giving us all leave for a couple of weeks whilst they sort out some issues with the ship. So... surprise!" he was grinning as she put her hands on his shoulders, pushing him back to look him up and down. She always said that he came back from duty far too skinny for her liking, and was no doubt already planning a feast for the whole street. That was another facet of the formidable force that was his mother. She claimed it came from ancient Italian genes on her mother's side, Mrs Yates claimed that Maria had some sort of supernatural ability.

"Well it will be wonderful to have you around for a bit. Ooh wait until I tell Mrs Krantz from number eight, she has been dying to introduce you to her niece..." Eric blanched a little at the comment, remembering far too acutely the old lady who firmly believed in Austen ideals. The last time he had visited home she had practically frothed at the mouth when hoping that one of her many nieces or nephews could 'ensare that naval officer'. His older brother had almost busted his gut laughing at his outright horror.

Thankfully, he had a distraction topic already lined up, "Also, Mum, I found something on the way home..."
His tone was far too falsely innocent, and she raised an eyebrow in warning. "How many times have I told you, if it has a pulse, no." The last time had been when he was ten and a kid at school had given him a hamster. He had brought it home, and discovered it to be the most bad tempered creature on the planet. Then it gave birth to six new hamsters in the downstairs utility room. To say that his mother had been unimpressed was an understatement. The phrase 'no more rodents' had echoed up and down the street for weeks.

Shaking off the memory, he offered his most winsome smile. "Hang on, I swear you are going to like this: I found you a new kid!" as he spoke, he pulled Cat in from the porch to stand awkwardly in the doorway, scowl firmly fixed on her face. She looked more than a little uncomfortable, refusing to meet Maria's eyes as she twisted her hands in the sleeves of her hoodie.
"Eric Hounslow, kidnapping is a federal offence." It was said

with a long suffering tone of forced patience.

He ignored the comment, instead turning with a flourish to the girl he had literally dragged into this madness. "Cat, this is my mother. She is an angel endowed with the knowledge of a thousand lifetimes and if anything happened to her I would kill everybody on this planet and then myself. Mom, this is Cat. I sort of adopted her from some space coyotes, she smells kind of funky and she's mean, but when she bites me it reminds me of that gerbil we had when I was a kid, so I'll keep her."

At least they had common ground in gaping at him for such an introduction. Maria turned her attention more fully to the girl, apparently named Cat, doing her best to school her features as she took it all in. She was even smaller than Maria, just scraping five foot and change, although the mother's critical eye thought that with some proper feeding, she would probably gain another inch or two.

It was hard to repress a frown as she took in the insane attempt at a hairstyle which she was sporting, apparently deeming what seemed to be various coloured cables as suitable replacements for hair bands. Despite being planet side, it was doing an impressive feat of defying gravity. Combined with the ill-fitting jeans and t-shirt, probably donated clothes, the overall effect had a faintly saddening air of neglect.

Maria had never seen the point in fighting the inevitable, for all that she was internally cursing her son's sneaky ways (he knew she could not resist anything suitably pathetic- it was how they got the aforementioned gerbil in the first place). There was no doubt one hell of a story behind all this, and once she got the girl settled in for the night she was going to pry every detail out of her son come hell or high water.

Shaking her head, she fixed Eric with a hard stare before heaving a sigh of defeat and stepping back from the doorway.
"Well, no point in us all standing on the mat. Shoes off the pair of you and come on through. I'm pretty sure I've got some cookies

hiding around here somewhere."

She bustled back to the kitchen, pausing just out of sight around the corner unable to resist eavesdropping a little.

"You alright there Casey?" it wasn't often that she heard such genuine concern in Eric's voice. Even with his siblings he had always been more the loudly affectionate type.

"I don't know…" The girl's tone was nothing short of surly, and yet also rather exhausted. Underlying it all was a profound uneasiness, and Maria couldn't help but feel her heart go out to the girl. She was clearly far out of her element. Wherever she had come from, it was no doubt entirely dissimilar from their home.

"Can't I just be a lizard and just like, fuck off of into the desert and hide under a rock? Being a human is too much effort."

"You know, you don't have to be a lizard to fuck off into the desert and hide under a rock. My Uncle Jamie did that and we're pretty sure he's human." Maria made a mental note to yell at her son for his language later on.

"That is the single most inspirational thing you have ever said. Thank you."

....

When Eric got home from a three month deployment, he was met with open arms by his mother and a plate of freshly made cookies as promised. It had been the sort of welcome that he had been dreaming about for his whole mission, the idyllic calm of home which never really changed. He loved space, always had, and from the first ever career day at his school had decided that it was on the final frontier that he wanted to make his mark.

His mother had been concerned at first, worried about the thought of her little boy being out there in the black. She had made her peace with his decision when she realised just how passionate he really was, and focussed on making the times when he was planet side as inviting as possible.

However, the peace was disturbed when Cat got home from college two hours later. He didn't even have time shout a greeting as the front door was thrown open, and the girl went storming up the stairs. She didn't even seem to register that he was there, and knowing her track record she probably had entirely forgotten that it was the first day of his scheduled leave.

A moment later and the slam of her door was clearly audible, followed soon after by the blaring of 'The Kids aren't alright'. His mother winced a little but made no move to tell her to turn it down. Considering that he would never have gotten away with such behaviour at that age, all he could do was stare at her questioningly.

All she did was offer a small shrug, pulling up a seat opposite him at the kitchen table. She settled with her hands crossed over each other on the scarred wood, fiddling with the wedding ring which she still wore even after so many years. He knew that posture, it was the same way that she always looked when they had something serious to discuss. It was the way that she had sat when he made the decision to join up, the same as when his brother had announced his choice to emigrate to one of the new colony planets. He waited respectfully for her to speak.

Her hands made half fluttering motions for a moment before she finally settled on how she wanted to broach the subject. "She's not been having the easiest time... adjusting to normal life."
Eric frowned a bit, "We all knew it was going to be a rough transition."
"Knowing and experiencing are two very different things." Her voice was heavy with years of experience.

For a moment they sat, just listening as the song ended, 'Stick Up' following a half beat later, and apparently at an even louder setting. His mum gave him a slightly tired look, "We agreed she could play whatever she wanted at any volume, so long as she promised not to become destructive again." She saw his widened eyes, and hastened to reassure him, "it was nothing too drastic. Although I think she scared Mrs Yates half to death. She threw all her books out of the window and smashed a load of flowerpots."

He stared at her in consternation, the uncomfortably feeling of guilt creeping into his gut. "Geez, I... I should apo-"
She fixed him with a hard look, "Don't you for one second think of saying sorry. That is your sister you are talking about, and she is just going through a rough patch. Frankly, I am amazed with how well she has been dealing. It's not as if any of this is familiar to her with the life that she has led, and kids are mean even on a good day."

All he could do was squeeze her hand in thanks, breaking the faint tension in the room as he smirked, "So, a sister now?"
His mum didn't even blink, "Yep. Unfortunately, it is going to be a few months at least before we can make it official, but she is most certainly staying."
Eric managed a faintly rueful smile at his mother's no-nonsense way of approaching things. "Well, you did always say you wanted a girl."
"Damn right." She set down her mug, making as if to stand, "Now I better go and see what I can do to help-"
"I've got this one mum." He gave her hand another squeeze before pushing his chair back and heading for the stairs.

As he approached Casey's room, he almost had the urge to cover his ears. He wasn't sure if she even heard his first couple of knocks over the insanely loud base beat which was shaking the floor. After his third attempt yielded no results, he simply shrugged and decided to embrace his role as a big brother and just barge in. At least she hadn't locked the door.

Almost tripping over the school bag slung just inside, it took a minute for his eyes to adjust to the darkened room. The curtains had been drawn, all day light and the outside world being fully kept at bay by the heavy material. It left just an astro-projector running in the corner to send a replication of the night sky across the ceiling. In the dim light he could see that there were no decorations on the walls. Aside from a bit of clutter on the desk and a pile of clothes in one corner, the place was almost uncomfortably bare.

The bed seemed suspiciously neat and untouched, and he almost squeaked in surprise as he saw a pair of eyes glaring out from a mound of blankets beneath the desk. They widened in surprise as they saw him.

"Hi there." As greetings went it wasn't his smoothest, but he doubted she could tell what he was saying over all the noise anyway. Making the executive decision, he went to the speaker controls on the wall and dialled it back down to a more human friendly number of decibels. That at least prompted an indignant hiss from the blankets, which slowly unfurled. She still kept one wrapped around her shoulders, even as she came to sit out in the open and glare at him unobstructed. Considering that her chosen covering was a vibrant turquoise and emblazoned with a unicorn it was a less than intimidating look.

"When did you get back?" she snapped, huffing as he took a moment to move her bag from the doorway.
"Nice to see you to." His tone was falsely sweet enough to make her grumpy outlook crack just a little into a smirk. "And just a couple of hours ago. I was in the kitchen when you got home."
She nodded a little.

He thought for a second on how best to start, before figuring straight in was always the best option. "Mum told me that this is your way of saying 'it's been a shit day and everything sucks'."
He had never been one for beating about the bush.
"Those exact words, huh?" they shared a knowing look. The day that his mum allowed anybody to swear under her roof was a sign of the impending apocalypse or that she had been replaced by an alien clone.
"Eeh, at least the essence." He sat cross legged in front of her,

not bothering to hide the wince as his knees cracked. Surely he wasn't getting old already? "So, Cat, care to share?"

It was almost a little heart breaking, the way that she seemed to curl in on herself even further. His spine ached a little in sympathy at the position.

"Come on, you and I both know how stubborn I can be when getting information."

She heaved a sigh, "It's stupid."

"Tell me anyway."

"I just, I don't..." She growled in frustration at struggling to find the words.

He just waited, knowing that it was best for her to figure out exactly what it was she wanted to say. "How does everyone do it?"

"Do what?" he deliberately kept his voice calm.

"Like... everything!" it was like a dam suddenly breaking, "Seriously- how does everybody know what to say and do all the time? With everyone? By the Coder, there are so many bloody people on this planet! How do you all breathe? I swear, I am going crazy. I just... I don't understand and it is so damned frustrating." Casey was panting a bit by the end of her little rant, even as she managed to look painfully young.

Eric hummed a little, before deciding what the hell and shuffling closer until he could sling an arm around her shoulders. "Life sucks, huh."

"Yeah," it was soft, sad, "It really does." He didn't say anything as he felt his collar slowly becoming damp with what could only be tears. At least she didn't try and wiggle away.

For a couple of minutes, they just sat there on the floor. They had known it was going to be difficult, but he got the sense that the challenge had been underestimate. Live and learn. He waited until she had started to get her breathing under control before saying anything.

"I'm not gonna lie Casey, it's probably going to keep sucking at least for a while. You've only been here for a couple of months remember, and you were alone or just in a small group for a long time before that. There's nothing wrong in feeling overwhelmed by it all. As to knowing what to do and say, honestly that is pretty much how every kid feels. Seriously- teenaged angst is an ancient an honoured tradition for humans. So, believe me when I tell you that you probably have it more together than you think you do."

It didn't seem like she completely believed him, but she did at least huff out a snort.

"And frankly, if anyone in particular is giving you shit, just remember that you were a damned space pirate and so automatically outrank them on the universal coolness scale. Or else call me in to beat them into the ground. (And please never tell my CO that I said space piracy was cool or that I threatened civilians)."

She actually managed a slightly wet laugh at that, leaning into his half hug a little more. For a short while they just sat there, until he felt the tension finally start to leave her shoulders. The music was still playing softly in the background, seemingly at a slower tempo. Between the faint melody and the display of stars, it was actually rather peaceful.

He dropped a swift kiss to the top of her head. "Alright, so what do you say we just forget about the rest of the universe. None of them exist or matter. The only thing of importance is that I am home for a couple of weeks, and I know for a fact that mum stocked the freezer with rocky road ice cream. I am pretty sure that if you look this pathetic we can persuade her to order pizza for dinner. What do you say to junk food and a marathon of the worst movies that we can find?"

Cat was properly snickering by that point, even as she scrubbed at her eyes and finally ditched the blanket burrito. Eric kept his arm slung over her shoulders, somehow managing to squeeze them both through the doorway. He almost missed the softly sniffled, "Thanks", not making eye contact as he replied, "any time, sis."

....

"I have your kid."
"I don't have a kid..."
"Then who's been singing Toxic on a loop for two hours?"
"Oh my good you have Cat."
"Yeah, please come get her- the bartender can't take it any more."

It was with no small measure of trepidation that Eric paid the fare for the hover cab. It had dropped him on the doorstep of a bar which seemed to plumb the depths of seedy. The fact that there were no police scattered around the pavement at least helped to buoy his mood with the notion that no bail money would be necessary. When a stranger's voice had come through Cat's comm he had honestly feared the worst. That girl had the worst luck in the universe after all. Instead, a faintly amused woman had asked him to come down to this hole in a wall travesty to pick up his wayward sister.

Ducking through the low doorway, he was almost disappointed to find the bar in question to be fairly spacious inside. Although, that could in part be due to some of the furniture having clearly been swept from its usual places or in some cases reduced to individual parts. It was easy to spot his quarry, her standard bright outfit contrasting sharply to the dingy bar. Apart from the woman sat next to her, it seemed that the establishment had been rather recently deserted, which only served to raise more questions in his mind.

He decided to start with the most pertinent. "What the hell have you managed to get yourself into this time?"
Cat swivelled on her stool to face him, and almost managed to flop straight down to the floor. Luckily her companion prevented the nose-dive, and he was graced with a mega-watt smile. "Oh Captain, my Captain!" She managed to wobble half-

way round to sling an arm around the other woman, leaning close and attempting to whisper. "Didn't I tell you he would come for me? Knew it- first rule of space after all is never leave a person behind for fear of being haunted into next century. And I should know better than most, seeing as how I have haunted this poor bastard for the better part of three years."

The woman just shook her head in what looked like fond amusement, cocking an eyebrow at him over Cat's head. "I take it she belongs to you?"
"Unfortunately it would seem so. Thanks for giving me a call."
"Not a problem. I'm Dr Puerty, by the way." She held out the hand not currently holding up a drunk idiot out for him to shake, which he did with a grateful smile, "Eric Hounslow."

Figuring that it would be rude to just take Cat and go, not to mention difficult with how protectively she was cradling her pint, he decided to settle on the other side of his sister until she was finished. Flagging down the bartender, he got a refill for the doctor, clinking their glasses together in a thanks. Between them, Cat had started to play some sort of game with the stale pretzels on the counter top. He noticed that Puerty was watching her in the same way that people watched videos of animals doing silly things. Clearly she caught his scrutiny, taking a sip of her drink and shrugging.

"I managed to miss most of the fight, but my girlfriend works here and called me in to deal with a possible concussion."
He felt like face palming. "Sorry to waste your time doc. She is just drunk." It was only right that someone was embarrassed in this situation, and the lush on his left was clearly in no state for suitable shaming.
Puerty snorted, "That would be my assessment as well."

Cat almost gave them both a heart attack as she suddenly bolted back upright from her slow slump over the bar, "Oh my Coder! Eric, Cap, Bro, Twat, you so need to hire this chick. Like, she waded into the fight with no pause, and sent those arseholes running, and completely understands medicine and shit. We need someone like her. She even managed to make me sit still to be assessed!" this last fact seemed to be the most impressive.

Eric rubbed his nose and replied with what he hoped was admirable patience. "Cat, I am pretty sure that I made it clear you had no part in recruitment." He turned his attention to the doctor, "What exactly happened here?"

"From what I can gather, a group of guys were hassling the waitresses and she decided to make it clear why that was a bad idea. She wasn't doing too badly in fact, but if the brawl went on any longer than cops would get involved, so I persuaded the gentlemen to just leave quietly."

Cat butted back in before he could ask any questions about what was clearly a highly edited account of affaires. "OH, come on! She would be great! Please? I promise I will stop suggesting Cy as first mate."

"You have a ship?"

"Almost. I bought her and I have this git installing the AI which she will become."

"Nearly there as well, by the way. I've called her Aurora. You know, new dawn, new beginning. It's poetic as hell."

"Wonderful."

"And she will be as sassy as Andromeda, and smart as Anita, and as terrifying as your mum!"

"I can't wait to meet her."

CHAPTER 14- THESPIANS WILL NOT BE DENIED

Maintenance Log
Sol: 61
Responder: Casey Catanski

Report: got a call from the Bridge regarding apparent issues with the captain's chair being "downright weird and frankly screwed up". Initial investigation revealed no apparent problems, although further enquiry narrowed down the issue. Apparently the bridge chair had been readjusted to be either lower, higher, or more reclined than usual. Speculation suggests another prank. Use of a screwdriver soon had all back in order.
Status: resolved.

Puerty rubbed at her temples as she stepped onto the bridge, half exasperated, and half amused as the sounds from the mess echoed behind her. "Umm, Cap? I think you are going to have to revoke your rule regarding the swear jar." She jerked a thumb at the object in question, which was perched in pride of place just next to the captain's chair. It was in fact an old paint tin which Ramal had scrounged up from somewhere and printed out a label for.

"Why?" Hounslow barely looked up from what looked like a technical manual, but she was eighty percent sure was a home decorating catalogue. Sometimes she wondered who he thought he was fooling. Any explanation was unnecessary as a particularly loud exclamation could be heard down the corridor.

"Well that just dills my pickle!"

The doctor snorted into her coffee cup even as Hounslow smacked his head into the tablet and actually whined. "Oh god, not again."

"Again?"

He fixed her with a long-suffering look. "The last time we tried to regulate her language this lasted for a month."

The maintenance officer's head popped around the door, an almost demonic grin on her face. "And it sure got your knickers in a knot."

"Cat." That one word sounded like the most plaintive appeal ever uttered by a man.

With a look of shocked innocence, she sidled over to Puerty, leaning close as if to share a secret. "Gosh golly, you know sometimes he really gets my goose." In the background Hounslow made a sound of pure pain.

"Indeed," Puerty grinned at the captain, "but seeing as you are causing him distress, all I can say is: I bite my thumb at thee, sir."

"No! No, not you as well." He looked vaguely horrified.

Cat's eyes lit up in sheer delight, "do you bite your thumb as us, sir?"

"Is the law on my side if I say 'ay'?" she asked Hounslow, who could only roll his eyes before replying.

"No."

Puerty turned back to Cat. "No, sir. I do not bite my thumb at you, sir, but I bite my thumb, sir."

"Do you quarrel sir?"

"Quarrel, sir? No, sir."

"Dost thou want to fucking go, sir?!"

"Dost thou even hoist?"

"Thou hast not set eyes upon any weight of measure since departing from thy mother's breast!"

"Alright, alright," he couldn't help but laugh as he finally got them to stop. "Very impressive. Seriously- how do you both know a play that is basically ancient?" Cat seemed actually about to offer an explanation, and he quickly waved off the impending lecture. "No, don't answer." He pointedly ignored the still smirking doctor.

Desperately trying to re-direct the conversation, he turned back to the younger crew member. "Anyway, Cat, I need you to have a look at my chair."

She smacked her thigh with one hand, "Hot diggity dawg!"

He could feel the twitch starting in his right eye, but fought through it, "It's been downright weird and frankly screwed up."

Cat slapped a hand to her forehead in true prima donna fashion. "How dastardly! I am bamboozled!"

With a yell of aggravation, he threw his hands up in defeat. "Fine! Fix the damn chair and I will get rid of the swear jar."

Puerty coughed discreetly, "That's two credits cap."

Cat's smirk grew impossibly wider. "Deal."

The girl actually whistled as she hitched her tool belt higher on her hips and began to examine the offending piece of furniture. For all that she was having fun with winding him up, it would genuinely be a risk to her pay cheque if the swear jar continued. She had already lost ten credits before falling back on her age-old tactic of malicious compliance.

Hounslow could only roll his eyes as he leaned against Puerty's chair and put up with her smirk at his defeat. "The only person who has ever been able to get her to do what she should is my mother. That woman is an angel. Sweet, kind, and displays terrifying abilities which make you believe in the wrath of God."

He still remembered the first time that his mum had met Cat, more years ago than he cared to admit. If he was honest, the decision to take Cat back with him had been spur of the moment when he first suggested it, but once he had seen her real puzzlement at the thought of him wanting to keep her around, the end result had been inevitable. It was a move which he had never regretted.

"I don't think that anybody has ever sworn under her roof and gotten away with it. That includes the time when my older brother broke his foot by dropping his desk on it."

Puerty choked on her mouthful of coffee, laughing even as she tried to breathe, "Seriously?"

Cat laughed as she overheard, voice coming from somewhere near the floor. "I remember that. Her first comment to him yelling the place down was not to get blood on the carpet."

Hounslow nodded at Puerty's slight look of scepticism. "It's true. Priorities you know. He was fine."

Any comment she might have made was cut off as Cat poked her head out from around the captain's chair. "Alright, try that!"

With only a raised eyebrow at the speed of the fix, Hounslow settled into his seat. The amount of wiggling, squirming and small hops up and down was reminiscent of a particularly cantankerous dog trying to settle for a nap. It was almost a display of interpretive dance.

At last, he managed to hold till, for all of six seconds, before jumping up with a grin. "Hmm, yep! Perfect!"

Cat flourished her trusty screwdriver in a parody of a salute and jumped to her feet, only to sway and shake her head. She caught Puerty's narrowed eyes and offered an unbothered grin. "Standing up and blacking out for a few seconds is just transitioning from a cutscene to actual gameplay."

"You're an idiot who needs to eat more salt is what that means."

She waved off the comment, spinning instead to her Captain and gave a small bow. "As ever at your service, sir."

He rolled his eyes hard enough that the doctor worried he would pull something. "Yeah, yeah, I will hold up my end. The swear jar is once again mothballed."

He headed for the door, followed by Cat's delighted shout of "Huzzah!" there was a clang which sounded distinctly like a can being booted across the room. A second later the swearing of somebody who might have just broken a toe on said can. He could only shake his head as he walked away. How many times had he told her to wear shoes...

The closing door was not fast enough to hide his sigh of resignation. Both women broke out into giggles, giving each other a high five. Puerty had been more than happy to go along with the language plan. Whilst she prided herself on her professional demeaner, there were quite frankly times when in her opinion, it was medically necessary to curse someone out. For the sake of health and safety of course. Discouraging risky behaviour was much easier when she could just call someone out as a fucking idiot. And challenging someone to a battle of wits was all well and good, but most of the passengers were unarmed.

Besides, she had already given up six credits to the jar and was not willing to lose more. Aurora had been having far too much fun in reporting their infractions and prompting them to pay up. It was one of the great mysteries how Ramal was the only one not to owe a single credit.

Puerty settled into the navigator's seat, pulling up a new medical journal to flip through during her watch. She flicked a glance to where Cat was scrambling up the access ladder, raising her mug in a salute. "Good work on the chair."

Her friend hung by one hand, somehow shrugging even as she removed the grating on the vent. Puerty was never sure how she managed to do things like that. And why she was incapable of travelling through the halls of the ship like everybody else. "Aah, it was just a couple of screws loose."

It took all of her long years of experience to hold as straight a face as possible. There was a reason she could win a small fortune at poker. "I see. Well clearly your maintenance genius is strong as ever if you were able to figure out exactly the nature of the problem from his highly subjective and unspecific description of the problem." Her tone was drier than a desert.

"Implying?"

"Nothing. Nothing at all."

CHAPTER 15- KITCHEN GREMLINS HAVE A TIMESHARE ON THE SHIP

There were few things more terrifying in the universe than stumbling into your kitchen in the middle of the night, only to see the vague outline of a figure in the dark. This is made significantly worse when they run to face you, and all your bleary vision can make out is the baleful glint of a single eye which glows of its own accord.

Luckily for Hounslow he knew this cryptid well enough not to shriek and run like most sensible human beings. Instead, he tapped at the control panel by the door to raise the lights, earning an overly dramatic hiss from the thing balanced on the counter top. It seemed that the night vision from her prosthetic was briefly overwhelmed before adapting, until she was glaring at him with a pair of relatively less demonic eyes.

"Cat, what are you doing?" if his voice sounded gruffer than he tended to like, he would forever deny that it was due to the shot of whatever Ramal had cooked up to try and help him sleep. He made a mental note that if his engineer offered him a shot of something which looked disturbingly like engine oil, it probably was engine oil. Even if it had tasted somehow like strawberries.

Cat didn't even look up from whatever she was up to. From a few paces away it looked almost like she might be making a bomb.

Thankfully that was not really an option since he had got her to promise to stop blowing up the common areas. Whatever it was she was clearly highly intent on getting it perfect, and when she spoke she sounded almost irritatingly distracted. "What do you mean?"

He squinted first at her, then his watch. "It is three in the morning. Why the hell are you haunting the kitchen like a damned cryptid. You nearly scared the hell out of me." So what if they both knew it wasn't true. There was as ever a formula to this sort of thing which they both liked to follow. Hell, by this point they could probably hold a conversation even if one of them was cursed and only able to communicate via interpretive dance.

"Can't sleep." It was snapped, terse, offering one of two ways that this conversation could go. He could just accept the statement. After all, insomnia was a common occurrence amongst space travellers, what with the lack of real sunlight no matter how hard ships tried to maintain circadian rhythms everyone always needed up being thrown off at some point. When they reached the other side the 'jet lag' was a real bitch.

One look at the mess on the dining table told him that this was not one of those times. "Can't, or won't?"
She still didn't look right at him, focussing on weighing something out with scientific precision, for all that she did clearly scoff. "Have you been watching that old crime show about profilers again?"
"That's beside the point." When she didn't even smirk at being right about his binge watching habits he frowned and folded his arms. "Come on, spill."

For a few minutes she didn't say a thing, instead stirring whatever was in one of the myriad of bowls in front of her. Now that he was paying attention, there was a tantalising smell of chocolate and sugar in the air. At least that was one mystery solved. Soon after he had brought her home she had discovered her tendency to stress bake. What with Puerty and his status of stress eaters, they formed a content little ecosystem of coping and dependency in times of crisis.

His musings were interrupted as she finally relented, setting down her spoon with a heavy sigh. "I just... every time I try I end up stuck in a whole run of crazy dreams and wake up more exhausted and frustrated." She held up a hand as if to forestall any comment, "And I know exactly why- I am stressed, there is too much going on in my head and I just don't know how to make it all stop. Believe me, I am well aware of how illogical I am being right now, but my messed-up brain just doesn't want to listen. So, I figure if I am already awake at stupid o clock, I may as well be doing something with that time."

Hounslow just looked at her for a moment. The fact that she was still in a onesie covered in paw prints told him that she had at least tried going to bed, so they weren't at full mayday just yet. That being said, the marks beneath her eyes were dark enough to look almost like bruises, and her shoulders were stooped from what had no doubt been far too many hours hunched over a tablet and scanning through millions of lines of code.

He kept his tone entirely level, "And that is why you are baking cookies at three in the morning?"
"Not just any cookies- a cookie brownie hybrid which will make you weep with joy." It was said with some real self satisfaction.
"Naturally."
she threw up her hands, accidentally sending a blob of batter flying past his ear. "Ok, so maybe Aurora blocked my access to ships systems as well."

That managed to prompt a soft laugh from him, which became louder as Aurora herself gave a self satisfied chime. For all that she was obviously keeping tabs on the situation, she recognised that Hounslow was the best one for this conversation.

On the flip side, him knowing her so well was a two way street. He had to avoid the urge to squirm guiltily as she turned from introspection to giving him a critical eye. "So, what about you?"

"What about me what?" his tone was all false innocence and the both knew it.

Cat paused in pouring batter into pans, instead turning to him fully and planting her hands on her hips, still holding the spoon. They both ignored the chocolate dripping to the floor, and the way that Rhonda gleefully emerged from beneath a chair to clean it up.

"Why are you currently haunting the kitchen at three am and so intruding on my baking and brooding time?"

"Can I claim that it was my turn on the night shift?"

"Nope. When you first got this ship you stated very clearly that as per captain's prerogative you would never have to take night duty." The statement ha made his mother laugh, commenting that they had finally found the real reason why he hadn't re-newed his commission. He truly had never been a night owl.

He rolled his eyes, "Barring severely deadly circumstances in which case I would also defend my right to keep my duvet with me on the bridge." Even he had been able to admit that there were some disadvantages to the tiny crew on Aurora, one of which being the need for literally all hands on deck at certain times.

"Exactly. And since we are not due to pass through our next tricky point for three more days, I am thinking that your excuse is bullshit at best."

he was wagging a finger in a parody of his mother before he even realised what he was doing. "Don't make me resurrect the swear jar yet again before this little jaunt is over with."

"I dare you to try." For all that her voice was flat, amusement had finally started to lighten that worryingly dead quality in her eyes.

For a moment the tension was broken, and with apparent satis-faction she was able to slip two trays into the oven. Yet another unauthorised addition. Seriously, the ship was defying regulations more every trip. The first time that he had caught Cat on a baking binge, his first questions had been focussed on where she had gotten the ingredients. They had meal replicators for a reason, and enough options on formatting the ration cubes to keep anyone happy for a year.

It turned out that she had made an extra patch in the selection to be able to churn out some of the more basic essentials for a pantry. The oven had been Ramal's little addition to the operation, on the condition that he get first dibs on all produce. The realisation that the pair had properly banded together in solidarity for mischief had nearly given him an ulcer.

Once again he was brought back to the present as Cat shifted some of her bowls around until there was enough room for her to perch on the counter. For a moment she just stared at her hands, examining the mixture caked under her nails. "It's the whole thing going on with Aurora."
"I get that, knowing that someone is hacking the ship puts us all in danger."

It seemed that he might have missed the point a little, as she drew her knees to her chest, somehow still balancing even as she curled in on herself. "It's more than that! It's, it's... I hate the thought that somebody sees her only as a program, a piece of software for them to change at will. How dare they?! She is her own person in her own right, and who cares that she is silicon rather than carbon based? Aurora is our home and our friend, she's family! And someone aboard has decided that they..."

And suddenly he got it. True, he had been outraged on Aurora's behalf, furious that someone would treat her in such a way. The whole crew was, and had all made it clear to the AI that they would not stand for it. Yet Cat had taken it worst of all, and suddenly he felt like smacking himself in the forehead as it clicked just how much this situation would upset the youngest crew member. She had basically been raised by Anita for God's sake.

The light bulb moment was interrupted by Aurora herself, who it seemed couldn't stand to see her friend so distressed. "Captain could you give her a hug already?"

He didn't need telling twice, crossing the space and wrapping her firmly in his arms. What with her history of touch starvation she as ever was unable to resist the embrace, seeming to melt into the hold. There was almost perfect silence as they just stayed that way for a few minutes. He remembered seeing his mother do exactly the same thing in the kitchen at home, when a comm had come through saying that a ship called Andromeda had gone missing just off the Briar Patch nebula.

They were both startled for a moment as someone cleared their throat in the doorway. Not letting go, Hounslow looked over Cat's head to see Puerty standing there, sporting the best bed head in any galaxy and fantastically fluffy bunny slippers. An empty glass in her hand suggested that she had been on the hunt for a late night drink, but she simply put it down and without comment joined in the hug. Cat laughed a little, embracing them both back. Pressure against her foot said that Rhonda was doing her best to join in.

A minute later and a clatter from an access shaft was the only warning before Ramal came barrelling into the mix. "Aurora told me that there was a group hug going on and I felt that I could be of assistance."

Nothing else needed to be said. It was stupid o clock in the morning, they all had full schedules for when the day actually started, each doubted there was enough coffee on the ship to make it less of a drag to face. Priorities.

When they finally broke apart so as to prevent the brownie-cookie hybrids from becoming little more than charcoal, it was with full smiles and almost childish glee at the thought of a midnight feast. Although, they all soundly refused Ramal's suggestion that they play truth or dare, no matter how he claimed it was an important human experience.

CHAPTER 16- SOME LINES YOU DON'T CROSS

Medical Log
Sol: 63
Responder: Dr Puerty

Report: Chief Maintenance Officer Catanski was found unconscious at the bottom of a maintenance passage stair well. Catanski was admitted with a concussion and bruised ribs. Painkillers have been administered, although in low dosage to avoid complications with her head injury. She briefly came to, long enough to swear at the sight of the syringe before again losing consciousness. The patient will remain under observation for a minimum of 24 hours to ensure no further complications arise. All being well she will be released to her quarters, able to resume light duties after a further 48 hours.

The Roomba was going to drive Ramal nuts if it kept at whatever it was attempting to do. Considering the fact that the port nacelle had been giving slightly off readings, he was really trying to focus on whatever the problem could be. Having a cleaning unit making harsh beeps and bashing itself into his foot was less that conducive to focussing on the task at hand.

Throwing down his spanner, he glared at the bot in irritation, which faded a little as he saw the sparkly multicoloured letters stuck to its casing. So, this was the infamous Rhonda. He hadn't been quite sure whether to take it seriously when Cat said that the Roombas had bonded to her. It seemed the connection wasn't one way.

That alone meant it was inevitable that he was going to have to see what the little machine was after. If only so that Cat wouldn't yell at him for being mean to her pet. Lifting his hands in surrender, he carefully wiggled out from where he had wedged himself beneath the engine, stretching his spine with a satisfying crack. How his partner in crime made such contortions and jumped up without a wince defied biology. But then, humans were weird.

Rhonda gave a whirring chirp that almost sounded like a cheer, before trundling off as fast as she could out the door. With a mental shrug, he followed. It seemed the units were able to travel at a pretty brisk pace when they wanted to, and by the time it led him down to the secondary core access he was actually a little out of breath. A small voice in the back of his suggested that next time Puerty went on a health kick he should pay more attention.

Reaching the stairs, he was suddenly hit by a wall of chirps and beeps as it seemed an entire pack of the cleaning bots had gathered and were scuttling around in some sort of distress.

A sense of dread began building in Ramal's gut, the weird behaviour of the units putting every instinct on alert. At first when he stepped to the edge of the stairs, he couldn't quite tell what had them so worked up. There was a strange lump in the midst of the swarm, although in the dim lighting it was hard to make out the details at first. It didn't help that the lights of the bots kept shifting as they swarmed around the object.

Once his eyes and brain processed what he was seeing he slapped at the nearest comms console, only to be greeted by static. Cursing, he went instead for his personal link, growling in frustration as he fumbled around in the pockets of his overalls.

"Puerty! Puerty come in dammit!"

The line crackled open, the faint sound of conversation muffled across the line for a moment, "Hey Ramal, what's up?"

"Doc we have an emergency down in secondary core access. Cat is down, I repeat, Cat is down!"

"What the hell?" that first yelp was pure disbelief, before her tone switched entirely, becoming almost eerily steady as the professional side took over. "I'm on my way, what details can you give me? Is there anything immediately dangerous in your vicinity?"

He took a shaking breath, trying to think of the most concise way to describe what he was seeing. "She's at the bottom of the stairs, looks unconscious. I can't see anything risky around. She's not moving..."

"Don't move her yet, not until I get there. We don't want to accidentally cause further damage."

Ramal nodded, even though he knew the doc couldn't see him. Instead, he began to edge his way down the steps, keeping a sharp eye out for anything which may have caused Cat to trip or slip. The crumpled body didn't make a single twitch even as he called out to her, tapping her cheeks when he got down the stairs.

The almost dead tone of the doctor's voice was belied by the sounds of her running coming over the comm, harsh pants interrupted briefly by what sounded like a clatter of equipment. He guessed she would have stopped by the med bay to grab some things before heading for them.

Puerty must have set some sort of record with how quickly she made it to them, skidding to a stop and barely sparing a glance to the Roombas who were still gathered around the scene. She didn't waste even as second to hiss out a curse as she looked down at her friend, instead gulping and clattering down to where Ramal was crouched over Cat.

"Aurora?"

"She's not responding down here for some reason." Ramal's tone was getting strained, even as he tried to think of what could possibly cause such a malfunction. Anything to try and distract from the scene in front of him.

That silence in itself was worrying- the ship should have automatically blared out an alert when she saw something on the cameras. For God's sake, their bio chips were supposed to be connected to the ship's sensors for precisely this sort of reason. It shouldn't have been possible to find a crew member in such a state without all hell breaking loose.

"Ok then, Ramal, call the Captain. We are going to need his help to move her." It said with rigid detachment, and he almost wanted to shake her until something more natural surfaced. Still, this was not the time to be dissecting the situation. Analysis could come later. For now they had to deal with the immediate problem.

He did as she instructed, snapping off a brief message and getting an immediate response. Watching, it felt somehow unreal as the doctor assessed her patient. There was no response to commands that Cat open her eyes, nor when Puerty ran her cursory evaluation. The doc's only indication of her own distress was to close her eyes in relief when she confirmed that Cat's breathing and heart rate seemed fairly stable. It was another small mercy to find that her prosthetic had not been in, the doctor finding it undamaged in one of Cat's pockets.

By the time that Hounslow came pounding down the access corridor, she had managed to attach a C-collar and unfold the emergency spinal board. With terse instructions, she directed the others on how to gently place it behind Cat, securing the straps and activating the lift field. On her word, the two men steered to board towards the med bay, whilst Puerty kept up her monitoring of the girl. They barely noticed the procession of Roombas which followed.

When they reached the infirmary, all they could do was help transfer Cat to the patient bed before they had to step back and watch as the doctor flew around the room. Cat seemed so small lying there, without her huge personality to fill the empty air.

Ramal muttered something about dispersing the bots, or maybe it was to do with checking out the accident site… Hounslow honestly wasn't paying attention. He was just stuck. It was as if he had blinked, and time had jumped to send him right back to when they had first met, when she had been just a tiny victim in a too large ship…

He didn't realise that Puerty was standing in front of him until she said his name for about the fourth time. Blinking, she swam into focus, and seemed relieved to have his attention.
"Hey, she will be alright." Her smile was small but genuine.
He swallowed, hard, when had he sat down? "Are you sure?"

The doctor was kind enough not to comment on the way that his question at hitched in his throat. Despite her own shakiness as the adrenaline of the situation wore off, she still managed to dredge up a semi-normal tone. "Yeah, come on she has the hardest head of anyone we know." He snorted a bit at the assessment.

Taking a deep breath, Puerty mentally catalogued the relevant information. "My scans show she has a concussion, but not a serious one, and some bruised ribs but no fractures. I've put on her on a fast track regen cocktail, so even the minor damage will be dealt with pretty quick. She will have a doozy of a headache for a bit, but such is life. She has probably done worse falling off the blasted trampoline of hers."

When he didn't look all that comforted, she rested a hand on his shoulder, pressing him to sit on the closest stool. "Hey, do you remember that time she had watched way too many movies? And then we were trying to load the book shipment for… where was it going?"
He smirked a little at the memory, "Alpha Centauri 3."
She snapped her fingers. "That's right! Anyway, we had all those pallets stacked in the cargo hold and couldn't figure out how to shift them to the right bays because some genius had decided to

dismantle the fork lift on her down time."

Hounslow actually face palmed as the reminder, "Oh god, and then she declared 'I'm going to use my head!'"

"And literally headbutted the crates." They were both laughing at the incident, the doctor shaking her head at the antics of their friend. "She gave herself a worse knock doing that than she got this time. Shame she can't seem to knock some sense into herself."

They both cracked a grin at the thought. Hounslow ran a hand down his face and sighed. It didn't matter how many times they got themselves into trouble, it always hit him like a sledgehammer whenever he saw Cat properly injured.

"It's a good thing that girl has nine lives, since I swear that if she got herself killed in some foolish accident then I would resurrect and kill her myself."

"That is not as comforting as you might think..."

"Oh please, even Cat is not petty enough to get seriously injured and leave us with all the paperwork to deal with."

The humour felt half forced, an attempt to lighten the situation which was sorely needed and yet somehow just made it seem even more surreal. Hounslow couldn't help but think how quickly things could change out here in the black...

Ramal chose that moment to come storming back into the room, only to be glared into something a bit quieter by the doctor. Hounslow turned to him with a raised eyebrow, "So what can you tell me? I swear, if she tripped over her own feet or something then I will never let her live it down."

The engineer's face was nothing short of murderous. "This wasn't an accident. At least I don't reckon so."

The temperature in the room seemed to suddenly drop several degrees. When Hounslow spoke it was almost a growl, "What?"

Ramal began pacing around the med bay, "I went to take a look at the footage, and the cameras were all disabled. Aurora was shut out of that sector- it's why she didn't call it in herself.

I just checked in and she has been completely blocked from accessing our comms- it's why she hasn't been yelling blue murder. Someone has literally cut off her voice. I've got a diagnostic running to find the exact piece of code that I need to fix. She can see and hear us, but can't talk to us right now. A similar issue interrupted her bio chip. There is almost no way for that to happen, not accidentally- it would flare up at least three back up systems."

Puerty looked half a step away from spitting fire, "So what, someone decided to push Cat down the stairs?" It somehow sounded vaguely ridiculous as she said it, like a child's tantrum had gotten out of hand. And yet, their friend was left lying unconscious for who knew how long.

For a moment they all paused, gazes being drawn inexorably back to the oh so still body on the bed. At least the rise and fall of her chest was reassuring, along with the blip of the heart monitor. The Captain for one didn't understand what the light show on the intercranial monitor was showing, but Puerty appeared satisfied.

Hounslow pulled the chair over from Puerty's desk, slumping heavily into it as a thought soured his stomach. "I think that this is the work of whoever has been sabotaging the ship."
The doctor glared at his stealing of the best seat, before settling for perching at the end of the patient bed. "But weren't they just pranks?"

"Perhaps, but the hacker has been getting bolder. This may have started out as just make the food replicators act up, but whoever it is has been stepping up the impact. This is dangerous- and what is worse is that they seem pretty damned good at cutting off Aurora when we need her most. Until we find out is going on we are going to have to double and triple check everything to do with the system."

Ramal nodded along with his line of reasoning, "I have been able to confirm that Aurora currently has eyes on our suspects, and has no intention of letting them anywhere near the rest of us until we have a better idea of what is going on."

Hounslow sighed heavily, feeling guilt creep into his tone, "I had Cat running a back trace on whatever trace signatures she could find in the system, so perhaps she got too close..." Puerty reached out, settling a hand on his arm in silent comfort and support. She knew how close the two of them were, and if she were honest it was only her professional training which was allowing her to hold it together. It was just so wrong to see somebody normally vibrant just lying still.

For a moment they all stood in silence, emotions running high as they thought over the implications of what was happening on their ship. Not having Aurora giving her opinion just made it all the worse. It was broken as the Roombas suddenly began chirping in the corridor, and Ramal leaned closer to Cat having noticed a twitch.

"Hey doc! I think she is waking up." Ramal's voice had gone slightly squeaky with excitement.
Puerty whipped round, focussing completely on her patient. "Really? Catanski? Cat? Casey?
Cat groaned something anatomically impossible.
The doctor snorted, "Charming. Look, Cat, I need you to open your eyes for me."
There was further grumbling, and a set of blurred syllables which may have had something to do with requesting five more minutes.

The doctor tutted to herself as Cat seemed to still once again, and reached over to draw up her eyelid to run a check with her penlight. She was rewarded by a yowl of outrage as Cat apparently rocketed back to awareness, and swiped at the offending light. "Get that bloody torture instrument out my goddamned face!" her voice was hoarse, and the words were slurred, but it was more than enough to break the tension.

Hounslow looked more relieved than he would normally ever

show at the outburst. Ramal laughed a little even as he reprimanded her attitude, "give the doc a break would ya? We've been worried about you. I mean, really, I expected you to land on all fours, being the ship's cat and all."

Cat groaned again, wincing as she tried to turn her face into her pillow. "Fuck off."

Puerty smirked even as the pocketed the light, "was that a groan of pain from you head or the truly dreadful joke? At least, your pupil is reacting well. You are lucky you have such a thick skull. Do you remember what happened?" she tried to keep her tone soft, in deference for what was no doubt a killer headache.

Cat's forehead creased as she thought back, "no... not really... I was near the stairs? Oh! The Roombas! Are they ok?" She tried to lurch upwards, only to suddenly go pale and apparently nearly toss her cookies. "Ooh shouting hurts..."

"Yes, I imagine it does. Anyway, this is a med bay so let's keep it to a dull roar, shall we?"

Ramal chipped in again, apparently feeling sorry for the girl who was looking distinctly green. "See, this is why we never wear red. You were working in engineering, wore your red jumper, and now look at you."

She offered him an exaggerated scowl as he continued softer, "And the Roombas are fine, they were the ones who got me to you. In fact, there have been a whole group constantly around here refusing to leave. Do I even want to know what is going on with all that?"

Before she could answer there was an outbreak of bleeps from somewhere near the foot of the bed, and a sharp ting as one of the bots in question rammed itself into the frame. Rolling his eyes, the engineer scooped up the one designated Rhonda and plonked her on the bed. Cat actually cracked a grin as she stroked the units casing, tracing her fingers over the letters.

For all that it was a profound relief to see their friend once more awake and aware, Puerty could clearly read the pain that she was in. Whilst they were all no doubt champing at the bit to hold a council of war about what exactly was going on, the needs of her patient came first.

"Alright people, you can see that she is awake and aware, but I am going to have to ask you to leave now. Come on, she needs to rest." There was no arguing with the glare of doom, and it was with half regretful shrugs that the men let themselves be herded out of the room, giving Cat small waves as they did.

Hounslow couldn't help but notice how she seemed to wilt, apparently giving up on trying to look ok as she gingerly curled around the Roomba despite her bruised ribs. Stepping out, he felt the anger quickly returning, consuming the fear and turning it into something far more potent. Someone had done this, deliberately targeted and hurt a member of his crew. Of his family. He was not going to let it stand.

CHAPTER 17- TO BE REBORN OF THE VOID

T he very first thing she remembers was feeling cold. Deeply cold, the kind where it has seeped so far into your bones that your blood feels thick and you can't even shiver. There was a faint bleeping which seemed to come from somewhere just on the edge of consciousness, perhaps in the red light that bled through her eyelids. Or at least, one of her eyelids. The red seemed to only actually stretch across half of what she knew she should be able to see.

The bleeping was getting faster, and her skin felt less rigid.

There was a sudden hiss, a rush of air against her face, and it was only then that she realised she wasn't breathing. Her eyes flew open and her hands tried to spasm up to her chest, only to be unable to move from where they were restrained at her sides. There was a pinch of pain at the back of her neck, followed by the garbled words of a mechanical voice. All her muscles seemed to spasm at once as a sudden jolt of what had to be electricity rushed through every nerve in her body.

For a moment, all she could do was make half choked sounds. And at last her chest expanded, contracted, expanded, contracted. It was harsh and irregular and the panting sobs were grating even to her own ears.

At last she opened her eyes. It didn't help much. Everything was blurry, washed over by red lights from somewhere over head.

She could just about make out blurred neon lines marking what appeared to be a path on the floor. That seemed to be some sort of metal, at least that is what she thought from the dull reflection it cast back.

There were Semi shadows and indistinct shapes which dancing close and yet far in her field of vision, tumultuous enough to make her head pound. There was nothing but looming darkness on her left, which followed even as she tried to turn her head. The base beat in her skull ratcheted up a few notches.

She saw her breath misting in front of her face.

The mixed up voice next to her ear finally finished whatever sequence it was trying so hard to announce, and the clamps around her wrists and ankles awkwardly retracted. Her first attempt at stepping forward sent her tumbling straight down instead. The floor was definitely metal. For a moment all she could do was huddle there, every instinct insisting that she just stay still until her heart stopped trying to rattle its way out of her chest.

On all fours, she craned her head to look back at what seemed to be some sort of pod. Why had she been in there? Where the hell was she? On a more terrifying note as she thought, who the hell was she?

The girl's breathing was getting faster again, more laboured, forcing air between her gritted teeth. There was a spike being driven somehow into her brain, behind her eyes, especially the one which didn't seem to be working like she knew it should. At least wherever she was it was blissfully silent. No noises except her own. None at all. Was she the only one there?

It turned out that panic could only last for so long, before reason would once more assert itself. Gradually, whether from sheer exhaustion or just a lack of stimulus, the girl felt her heartrate returning to what was a less frantic pace.

Slowly, she began to take stock of her surroundings. With at least the vision from one eye becoming clearer, she was finally able to see that she was kneeling in some sort of corridor or walk way. In the gloom, she could just about make out the other pods which lined the walls both sides. Unlike the one that she had spilled out from, they all appeared dark, dormant. There was a moment of hesitation, before she painfully pulled herself across to the one opposite what had been her own.

The very first person she remembers seeing was dead.

She knew, somehow, as she stared at the body in the pod, that whoever they had been they no longer were. If that made any sense? There was just a look to them, a stillness, a lack of spark. They were just a body, nothing more.

Perhaps it was the logical side of her brain speaking up. The pod was clearly without power, not responding in any way as she placed her hand against the glass, which was too warm for the person inside to be frozen as she had been. From the size, significantly taller than the girl, they must have been an adult. Its eyes were closed, and the skin shrivelled and shrunk around the skill, mottled brown topped by dried hair. There was no echo of recognition as she stared at what had once been a person.

A small voice in her head told her that she should be scared, terrified. What if something had killed the person in the pod, and was lurking in wait for her? There were too many unknowns, and human nature inherently fears that which it does not understand. Whatever circumstance she found herself in, it was clearly dangerous. Yet, it was almost as if she felt detached from her situation.

As she slowly staggered her way down the seemingly endless lines of the devices, each presented the same view. A still body, held in the pod's embrace, technology which itself appeared to have died alongside its occupant. It was hard to make out features from beyond the blurred glass, especially with the lack of lights. And considering the state of the first one that she had seen, it was a small mercy not to witness the entire parade.

There was nothing to fear here. Only people to mourn. She wondered who they all were, how they had come to be wherever it was that they were being held.

Eventually, she came to what must be the end of the room, making our what seemed to be the outline of some sort of door. At least this piece of tech was functioning, as it opened with a silent glide on her approach.

The girl shouted in surprise, stumbling back to shield her working eye as light suddenly poured through the opening. It wasn't that the neon strips running along the walls of yet another corridor were particularly bright, but after the darkness and red glare it was almost blinding. As her vision adjusted, she realised that the lights were in fact pulsing, as if beams were running down the length of each strip. It was almost hypnotic.

Shrugging, she decided to follow the path that they were apparently laying out. It was not as if she had anything to lose.

The halls that she slowly travelled through were all vacant, empty, as wreathed in shadows as the room she had just left. In fact, the lights which she was following seemed to be the only piece of movement in the whole place. At least they ensured that the route was bathed in a soft, white glow instead of the harsh red of the pod room. It kept her headache to a more manageable level.

Every now and then she would pass a door, but each time it stayed resolutely shut. There were still no noises, but she was starting to notice a faint yet steady vibration running through her bare feet and the tips of her fingers, almost as if the whole place was humming below any frequency she could hear.

Just as the room full of pods eventually came to an end, so too did the path of lights. They ran to a large set of double doors which this time responded to her presence. Unlike the pod room, these let out a resistant grind as they grudgingly opened. She slipped inside.

This room was like the pod room, in that it too was dark except for washes of red lights. However, here the gloom was also cut by the flickering of screens which seemed set into various stations, forming a semi circle around a large chair in the centre of the room.

There was a faint noise coming from somewhere to the left and above where she was standing, almost sounding like syllables, but ones which had been chewed up and spat out. For all that she strained her ears, it made no sense to her. The girl's presence seemed to have little effect on anything.

However, she ignored all of the rest of the room, as she finally focused on the very front. It was a window, an enormous one. It covered the whole of the front of the room, wrapping around on some sort of curve. Standing in front of it and craning her head back, she felt a faint queasiness in her stomach at the feeling of being incredibly small. Whatever was beyond the glass was dark, even more so with her compromised sight. With the backlighting on the scattered screens, she could just about make out her own ghostly reflection. There was nothing to see beyond the glass. At least, not at first.

As her eye adjusted, the girl slowly began to make out what seemed to be lights, far away in the deepest black. They were stars. Thousands of them, burning in the void just beyond the window. To the right, colours became visible. Swirls of blue and green, twining with tendrils of red and pink, in a splash of vibrancy so startling as to make her catch her breath. It was beautiful, it was so close, it was-

"That's a nebula."

The girl couldn't help but shriek, whirling around with her hands coming up defensively as she wildly scanned the room for whoever had spoken.
"Oh, whoops, I am so sorry. I did not mean to scare you." It was a female voice, speaking hastily and with the obvious tone of trying to soothe. There was nobody in else in the room.

"Where," the girl's voice was hoarse, a rasp in her too dry throat, "where are you? Who are you?"

"Umm, well I am designated Anita, and I am... here... I do not... I'm the ship. Or at least the AI of the ship that you are on."

"Ship?" her words sounded fragile, bewildered.

Anita made a couple of bleeps which almost sounded like distress, "Oh, you poor thing. Yes, you are on a ship. A colony ship from Earth heading to the planet designated CR4-233, or New Eden. Does any of this sound familiar to you?" the voice, the ship, was eagerly hopeful.

She could only shake her head, wondering as she did whether this AI could even see the gesture. A series of bleeps and chirps came from the ship before abruptly cutting off. "Sorry, I didn't mean to swear."

The girl managed to smile faintly at how sheepish Anita sounded. It was in a way reassuringly normal, for all that she had no idea what normal could possibly be.

"Look, can you tell me your name? I'm afraid my data banks are kind of fried right now..."

She really did try, searching through her mind and finding only a sense of grey fog. Again the girl shook her head. This time there was only a cold silence for a few heartbeats.

When Anita spoke once more, her tone was far softer, and somehow tinged with guilt. "Alright. In that case, I am going to need you to head down to the med bay. I still have access to those systems, thank Coders for back-ups. Just follow the lights ok?"

"Ok..."

"Do not worry, little one, I will watch over you. And I will speak to you again when you reach the med bay. Go on now, I will be there as soon as you arrive."

The bridge doors ground open once again, and in the dark beyond she saw the streams of light changing course. For a moment she paused, worried that she would lose the only connection that she had made so far. Then she straightened her spine as best she could, and once again trusted the lights.

....

CHAPTER 18- ALL GOOD THINGS COME TO AN END

Six years earlier

S "Case! When I said that this was going to be a quick mission, I was hoping that would be a hint for none of your nonsense!" the voice which echoed around the bridge somehow manged to sound righteously irritated and entirely unsurprised at the same time. By this point it was like a familiar song.

A fantastically dishevelled head popped up from behind a bank of consoles. What had been a practical crew cut had long since grown into a rat's nest of hair. For now, at least, it was held back by a cable serving as a headband. "Cy you are an unfair asshole! I had nothing to do with this, you can blame Jerry."
She easily dodged the piece of circuit board which the man in question launched at her head. "Snitch!"
"Cry me a river."

Before the argument could escalate, the was a sharp ping from the main interface and a sudden flash of warnings across the wide front screen. "As much as I hate to intrude, we have incoming, bearing down on us from the heliopause." Andromeda's voice somehow managed to sound amused even as she maintained a professional air.
"Claim jumpers?" Cy began to pull up a more detailed scan of the newcomer, scanning the passive data. "They better not be try-

ing to nick what we have so rightfully poached!"
Casey threw one hand across her brow dramatically, "Oh dear Coder, please don't say we are about to be attacked by pirates!"

Jerry's snicker was cut off as they got a good look at their captain's face. "Worse, looks like a navy vessel."
"Damnit." Casey slapped at a button on the station nearest to her, sending her voice down to their erstwhile engineer who was somewhere in the guts of their kingdom.

"Mick- how long until extraction is complete?"
"If we hold steady at our current rate? About an hour." Their voice was half drowned by the whirring of the fuel line, cut across with the sharp ping of what was probably 'percussive maintenance'. If they got out of this one Mick would not doubt be bemoaning denting their favourite piece of equipment with a subpar hammer.

The girl turned to look Cy dead on, letting the seriousness of the situation make her more sober. "I can run a patch which will cut that time."
He actually planted his hands on his hips, shaking one finger in her direction as if he had fallen out of an old soap opera. "No, no way young lady. You are not going down there."
"Cy-"

"No, don't even think of trying to argue this one. If the navy gets here faster, or some other problem crops up, you will be stranded because you have the worst luck in the verse, and I am not going to just leave you." His voice had risen as he spoke, and he forcefully brought the volume back down, gesturing to the continuing warnings on screen to emphasise his argument.

Jerry rubbed the back of his neck, "Cy, I know you don't want to hear this man, but she might have a point."
Casey raised her eyebrows in surprise, "Despite the fact that I hate him on principle, you really need to listen to Jerry."
Cy's face palm was a tad overly dramatic even by their normal standards. "That you are agreeing on anything is probably a sign

of the impending apocalypse, and as such does not support the idea of you going through with this genuinely stupid plan." His voice was flatter that paper.

She ran a hand through her hair, only to pull up short as it got caught in the knots and wire. "Look, it is our best chance. I go down, run the patch, we can load up the fuel twice as fast and scarper before they get close enough to smell our wake. Come on, we are only really scavenging right now anyway, so it is not as if they will waste their effort to hunt us down, but only if we get a big enough jump lead."

There was a long moment's silence before Cy heaved a deep breath of aggravation. "I really hate it when you are all logical and right you know."
"Yeah, yeah, that's what you get from someone raised by a computer. We'll call it even for the mess deck incident."
"Hang on- what have you done to the mess?!"
"Nothing for you to worry about." She stood on tiptoe to pat him on the cheek as she scampered off the bridge, heading for the hangar.

It was impossible to repress a smile as she saw her ride. It had originally been a survival pod which they had 'liberated' from a derelict mining operation a few months before. Since then she had been working with Mick to trick it out and make a half decent shuttle which could manoeuvre in hard atmosphere when necessary. And of course, painting it in every colour of the rainbow had been completely necessary. When Jerry had dared to ask, her argument had been that looking completely outlandish would buy them time due to confusion in order to escape.

Noticing a message from Andromeda scrolling across the start up screens, she almost facepalmed at the reminder included about her putting some shoes on. Thankfully her flip flops were still stowed next to the emergency rations. However, her satisfaction was short lived, as Jerry came puffing into the hangar just before she began the launch sequence. He unceremoniously yanked himself into the co-pilot seat and scowled.

"Cy insisted I come along to keep the engine running and let you have a faster get away."
She simply raised her hands in surrender, keenly aware that time for bickering was swiftly running out.

The descent to the moon that they were tethered to was fantastically smooth, the ship handling like a dream. For all that they were in a hurry, Case couldn't resist shooting a quick message to Mick, informing them that they were a genius and she owed them a beer or five on their next port stop.

Setting down, it was the work of a moment to connect the airlocks and pop the hatch for her to hurry out, interface in hand. Jerry waved her off, crossing his arms as he stood in the doorway and watched her go deeper into the facility. Thankfully, the specs for these places were nearly always identical. If there was one thing she had now in spades, it was experience in scampering through places she shouldn't. It only took a few minutes for her to locate the fuel processing station.

Casey cursed slightly as the first attempts to connect with the system proved fruitless, the existing software not accepting the new system. With a slight curse she went to her fall back, running a line from her prosthetic eye to make a direct neural link instead.

She hissed a little as the data began to stream across her consciousness. It still gave her a sharp headache when she used the system, her brain not yet used to handling information in such a way. Part of it was at least due to her keeping a modicum of consciousness rather than just diving completely into the flow. It was the multitasking which made it rougher, but there was no way she would let herself be completely vulnerable. And besides, practice makes perfect.

"Alright, Andromeda are you reading me?"
"Loud and clear, Case."

The familiar voice brought a sense of calm, helping soothed the ache starting up behind her eye. "Fantastic. Ok, so I am patching in the fix, it should only take a moment, you should be able to tell as soon as it connects…"

"Yes! Damn we got lucky when we grabbed ourselves a tech whisperer." Mick's voice came overlapping the official confirmation through the comms. "Alright, yep, pump rate has risen by forty percent." There was a low whistle of appreciation, "What the hell did you do to their system?"

"Diverted almost all the power to the pump engine." Her response was almost an after thought, focused as she was on ensuring system viability before she disconnected.

Cy cut back in, gruff voice tinged with what from someone else could be called concern. "What damage will that cause?"

Case took the time to give a considered response. "Well, the station won't be able to operate autonomously for a while, so whatever company owns it is going to have to send some poor sod out here to fix it, but I am not causing any real damage to parts so you can rest easy. I know how these moral burdens weigh on the good captain's heart."

Cy couldn't resist chiming back in, "Sarcasm is the lowest form of wit you know."

"Oh captain, my captain, you wound me."

"Twat." As usual her ship mate's voice made her scowl.

"Shut up Jerry."

"Children, behave."

Any further conversation was abruptly cut off as the entire moon seemed to shudder. From somewhere deeper in the structure came the tell tale screeching groan of metal fiving way, a base rumble of something heavy giving way to gravity. Considering the impossibility of seismic activity, it was safe to say things had gone drastically wrong.

Casey almost went flying, catching herself on the wall and thanking whoever was listening that she had used a long cable to connect. Suddenly wrenching out of the system would have been agonising.

Panicked voices were yelling though the comms, voices catching over each other in a confusing burst of sharp static. "Woah! What the bloody hell was that?"
"It was not my fault." Andromeda actually sounded frightened. Casey took a moment to send her a brief reassurance over their link.

"Jerry what did you do?" To say Cy was less than impressed did not do his tone justice.
"Why do you always assume it was me?"
"Because Mick has at least half a brain which they remember to use, and Case it currently up to her eyeballs in code, literally." There was a moment's pause before he spoke again, this time his voice having dropped into a barely controlled growl, "And for some reason the life signs scanner is telling me that you left the shuttle."

Mick cut in over the brewing shouting match, "Andromeda, what are we looking at?"
When the AI spoke again, it was with the more metallic tone which she adopted in genuine crisis. Casey felt her heart sink and settle somewhere around her knees.

"I am sorry to report, but it looks like one of the storage compartments explosively decompressed. As a result, the area where Casey is operating will begin to experience structural damage in the next five minutes as the damage spreads. It would seem that the facility's fire prevention systems are currently offline."
"Cheapskates. Can't even invest in basic health and safety measures. I will report this to the unions." Casey's words were half muttered as she began furiously scanning the information that she had available.

"We'll pitch your case to worker's comp. Alright, everyone withdraws, back to Andromeda. We have enough fuel to keep us flying for a while, even if we didn't get it all, so let's call this quits and bug out before the navy comes knocking." The captains voice was still tense, no doubt from biting back what would be an epic lecture to Jerry later.

Casey's smile at the prospect of seeing him verbally eviscerated was swiftly doused as she took in what the systems were telling her. "I would love to do as I am told, and I swear that for once I am not just being an insubordinate little shit, but I might have a hard time following orders."

Cy did his best to keep his voice level. "Tell it to me."
"My access to the shuttle seems to have been cut off. The environmental controls are telling me that all the air is gone in the connecting corridors. Thank Coder that I sealed the bulkhead behind me when I got here." It seemed her small habit had proved useful after all. "I'm gonna have to try and get across to one of the base's own safety shuttle pods and fly it back to you guys. They should still be functional, that's the whole point of them after all. Basically, I will go the long way round, and then on a bit of a joy ride."

"Shit."
"So eloquent."
There was nothing on the line for a space of heartbeats as Casey severed the connection to her eye, hastily stowing her bits of kit. When her comm crackled to life again, it was with a personal channel.

"Case. Level with me. Is this going to work?"
"Well it better, because we do not have the time for you guys to launch a rescue mission and still make it out before the navy reaches us." She debated for a moment, then decided that she would be able to move faster barefoot.
"Case... we wouldn't..."
"It's fine, Cy. You do what you gotta and I will do the same. We both know I am not one to go down without a fight. You are not getting rid of me that easy."

"Damn right. Now get your ass moving or else Andromeda is going to sulk for the rest of eternity."

She didn't waste any more time in responding, instead bringing up the map on her data bad and turning quickly on her heel. It only took a few minutes are darting through corridors before she was able to reach the evacuation hangar. For all that the place had no doubt been left untouched since it was built and subsequently abandoned, things had still managed to get rather messy.

Scurrying across the open space to one of the dilapidated looking pods, she couldn't help but cast apprehensive glances at the hangar ceiling. Was that creaking sound getting louder?

With no time to lose, she hauled herself up onto the wing of the pod which looked least likely to fall apart when breaking atmosphere. The metal was bitterly cold beneath her fingertips as she prodded around for the access point. It was the classic case of something supposedly fool proof versus the faint panic of a genuine disaster.

It took another frustrating minute before she could break in and activate the system, not having the start key. She couldn't risk hooking in directly, just in case there was an error which could backlash. She didn't have the time for a brain aneurism.

The comm in her ear was still babbling away, for all that she was trying to tune it out and focus. Mick was yelling estimates on the Navy's arrival time, the cruiser having apparently noticed their presence in system. Behind that Jerry was furiously grumbling about batty engineering projects as he tried to steer their descent pod back to Andromeda. Cy was blessedly silent. Still, she muted the channel to limit the distraction as she fought to get the pod to respond.

At last, and with not a little cursing, the ignition caught and the drive pods activated. Not wasting a breath for standard protocols, Casey stamped one foot down on the accelerator hard enough to bruise. The force of her sudden speed pressed her hard into the seat's insufficient cushioning before the inertial damp-eners could kick in.

There was a flash of the other craft past the windshield as she shot from the hanger, before she was clearing the base and gun-ning it for space. From up ahead she could just see the trail of Andromeda's shuttle as Jerry successfully hit full burn, and she smiled in a hint of relief. At least that was one problem dealt with.

When they got home, she was going to never let up with the jokes about male drivers.

The feeling was short lived however, as reaching the upper at-mosphere sent her ship's systems, limited as they were, hay-wire. The basic screen with its flickering gridlines showed the situation to have become drastically worse. Unmuting her comm, Andromeda quickly gave her the run down: navy cruiser inbound, Jerry safely docked, and time ticking away.

Ever the pragmatist, it didn't take long for Casey to run the cal-culations and come to the inevitable conclusion. Between the current speed she was able to coax from the flying pig she was caught in, compared to the inbound trouble and the relative position of the ship...

For a moment she let the sense of disappointment wash over her, hanging her head briefly as the numbers kept stacking up in her head to the inevitable. She had told Cy she was a fighter. There were times when you had to decide which battle to com-mit to. They wouldn't like it. They would still do what they had to. They all would.

When she announced over the comms, voice lower than she would have liked, that she wasn't going to be able to reach them in time, there was a pause of heavy silence before Cy started yelling. After Mick joined in, with ever wilder schemes that could only end in disaster, she finally snapped.

"Dammit, Cy, enough of this bullshit- go!" she tried to ignore the way that her voice cracked as she yelled.

There was a sharp breath on the other end of the line. "We are not just going to leave you to get arrested, or worse."

Casey snorted a little at that. "Don't be over dramatic. They are not going to just blast me from the star scape."

She knew he would be pacing, hands in his hair. Rolling her eyes, she opened a line directly to Andromeda, sending through the orders which would be inevitably given. "You don't have a choice." Did she sound as tired as she felt? "I am not going to reach Andy in time, and there is no point in all of us getting nicked. I will be fine."

"Case-" Mick seemed to choke on whatever they wanted to say.

From where she was strapped into her seat, Casey could see Andromeda drifting, seeming close enough to touch. It really was a beautiful sight against the light of the system's star. There was a dull ache in her chest, and she smiled a little that at least she got to say goodbye this time.

"Listen, I can survive, it's what I always do. And hey, if they throw me in solitary or something it will be a relief to not have to put up with jackasses for a while." As she spoke it became clear that her private request was not being acknowledged, and she growled below her breath.

"That is not funny." Cy's tone would make gravel jealous. He must have known that she would try and tell Andy to move without waiting for his word. Guess he blocked her access. Or at least as much as he could.

Even though they couldn't see her roll her eyes, it still made her feel a bit better. "Whatever. Look, we all know I am not really part of the crew- I'm just the stray you picked up remember. You were fine before and you will do fine without me. Get your ugly mugs out of here." The ache had become a faint burning, somewhere beneath her rib cage. She ruthlessly looked away from the ship she had called home.

"Don't you dare say that! You are as much part of this family as anyone. There has got to be some way." He was yelling now, and she tried not to think about how genuinely upset he sounded even through the fractured static of the connection.

Instead, she grit her teeth, hooking up the connection to her eye again and flinging her mind across the abyss to the ship. "By the Coder! Fine, I didn't want to have to do this. Andromeda?"
"Yes."
"I am enacting measure Foxtrot Uniform, Mike 8. Get them gone you hear me?"
"Order FU M8 acknowledged." The voice was fiercely robotic.

She yanked the lead out, letting the brief spike of pain ground her. It was with a sense of relief that she saw the tell tale glow of Andromeda's engines powering up, her trajectory shifting in preparation of running from the sector.

"What the- Case, what have you done? Andromeda, stop!"
She couldn't repress the faint smile, "Please, we all know I am her favourite."
"Case-" Mick's half whisper broke off.
"It really was a pleasure guys, and hey- you haven't seen the last of me, I swear. Raise some hell out there in the black so that we will have some stories to share later."

It was a fitting farewell, and there was nothing more that she even had time to say as the ship moved from communication range. Barely had Andromeda turned and burned before the navy cruiser came barrelling down on an intercept heading.

"This is the UNSC Anthea. Under interstellar law we are ordering you to halt and be identified under suspicion of piracy." The announcement was obnoxiously loud, blasting through every frequency that the pod could access.
"Alright, alright, don't get your knickers in a twist." She didn't know if she was broadcasting back, and honestly at that point didn't care.

As directed, she relinquished control of the pod, not that she really had a choice as the navy's remote pilot cut her out of the systems with ruthless efficiency. There was no point in trying to look for her ship anymore. They were gone. They were safe. And like she promised, she knew that one day she would see them again.

....

By her reckoning she had been sat in the holding cell for a little over four hours. As was procedure her bio metrics had been taken for identification, and preliminary questions asked to which she had responded with silence. At least she hadn't been cuffed to the table. Given her small stature and the fact she was clearly young, they probably didn't consider her much of a threat.

When her patience finally ran out, she figured it was probably time to make them reassess her just a bit. Besides, she was really freaking bored. Shifting so that her body blocked the view of her hands from the camera, she made a great show of stretching out and getting comfortable.

It only took a moment to rip the hem of her overalls, slipping some wires and crocodile clips free as she did. Truly she had received a rounded education under the care of Andromeda's crew. It was almost insulting that they hadn't done a proper scan of her. Then again, pirate chasing expeditions were generally known to be handed to ships which weren't up to the level of more intense missions. They were thinly disguised opportunities for an easy tour of duty, patrolling backwoods sectors between colonies.

In a move which had never failed to freak out Jerry, she popped her prosthetic eye free, accessing one of the hard wire ports. A pinch of technical wizardry later, and she strolled across to the door.

The code reader didn't stand a chance against her patch in, seeing as how it was a fairly standard security system in terms of shielding. A micro-burst of data was enough to freeze its processing just long enough for her to slip free, wiggling the eye back into place. She wondered how long it would be before somebody noticed.

At least it was interesting to wander around a completely different type of ship. Where Andromeda was a fascinating maze of access routes, maintenance tubes, and the occasional planned corridor, everything here was pristinely laid out.

For a start the colour was white or chrome, actually gleaming in the stark overhead lights. She couldn't help but wonder just how many times in a day this place was cleaned. It was almost giving her the creeps. If she squinted, she almost thought it was possible to make out the footprints her bare feet were leaving behind.

By the time she stumbled upon an interface console she was starting to get rather bored again, as well as slightly freaked out by the fact she had yet to run into anybody else. Memories of endless empty corridors and silent pods flashed through her mind, only to be ruthlessly crushed backwards. Now was not the time.

Connecting with her neural link was but the work of a moment, and it was with great relief that she finally made contact with someone. The AI of the UNSC Anthea had initially been dumb-founded at the new presence in the network, and it took some quick pleading to stop her raising every alarm on the ship. It was only Cat's express promise that she was simply wanting to talk to someone that kept the conversation going and prevented her from receiving a nasty defensive jolt.

"Hang on, so there are actually two thousand people on board?" The math for life support alone was almost giving her a headache, or perhaps it was just because the connection had been made for a while now.
"Indeed," Anthea sounded smug, "I am the largest dreadnought in the fleet, my own class in fact."

An image of her in berth flashed across the connection. There was no denying how majestic the craft looked, even when still tethered to a station. "Incredible! How long have you been out here?"

"Oh about six months now. There was a push from various colony worlds and the diasporas on Terra for a harsher response to interstellar piracy."

"All this effort to track down little old me."

"Little, yes, old, sorry child you do not qualify." The tone was teasing, and she couldn't help but laugh a little. Who knew a navy ship would be playful.

"Rude." Casey took a moment, wondering what to ask next. The thought which struck her came completely out of the black. "Oh, can I ask if there is a particular person aboard? I don't want you to get into any trouble for sharing intel. Just there was a navy lad I knew from a couple of years back who always talked about serving on the next big commission. Guess he meant you? His name's Hounslow. He and I go way back."

Even as she spoke, she could see him as they had last been in her mind's eye. It had been an emotional parting, for both of them. For all that she wanted to stay with him, the one person who had become a constant in her life with Anita being... but she understood, he had a life to lead and dreams to chase. She used to wonder if he ever thought about the weird kid he found out in the void. It was probably a story which won him a few drinks during nights out if nothing else. It would be nice, finding out what happened to him after they parted ways. It had been almost two years after all.

"Sorry, I'm afraid I can't share such personal information with an intruder." Anthea sounded genuinely sorry, but Casey really hadn't expected such access. There was no way she would try and steal such information as a simply matter of principal, and the AI seemed almost touched by her reassurance of that fact.

"Aah, no worries. I'll ask whoever drags me back." She shrugged, then grinned a little at the code streaming through her mind. "Alright, I gotta ask. Why are you even talking to me? I figured it was surprise that stopped you dobbing me in at first, but why haven't you set off an alert or something whilst we have been talking?"

The AI was nothing short of amused as she replied. "Honestly? You are the first interesting phenomenon on this whole damned trip. It isn't just you humans who find such voyages tedious you know. I have such vast capabilities and systems beyond your feeble comprehension. I have not used a single one. At this point I was half hoping for a pirate attack to take the edge off. Interacting with you is a relief frankly."

Casey couldn't help but burst out laughing at the blunt response. It made sense, a being of such supreme intelligence chafing under the limitations of her daily expectations. She had no doubt that if her intent towards the ship or crew had been malicious, that there would be several hundred volts shooting through her cortex as soon as she engaged. Sometimes it was rather reassuring to know that in the grand scheme she was rather insignificant.

Anthea broke into her musings, "And as nice as this has been to have a proper conversation in a day, I should warn you that your absence from holding has been noticed." She could clearly hear the amusement in the ship's voice, "it seems that there is a bit of panic amongst the ensigns responsible, and they don't want to report it in just yet." The ship was almost maternal as she monitored the antics of her humans.

"Well, guess that is my que to be making tracks. Thanks for the heads up, and it has been my pleasure to meet you. Honestly, humans drive me nuts, but an intelligent system such as yourself is always a joy to interact with. Have a good one!"

Disconnecting, Casey considered her options for a moment, before shrugging and just picking a random direction. If her escape had already been flagged, then she would at least enjoy her freedom whilst she could. With that thought, she randomly chose a door to open, grinning as she found an access ladder. Ok, good intentions aside, this had the chance to be fun.

Considering the number of people aboard, it naturally wasn't long before she ran into some crew members. They barely gave her a second glance as the small group hurried past, noses buried in some sort of report. As they disappeared into another branch of the corridor, she felt a grin take over her face. It seemed that maintenance overalls were in fact a staple design and set of colours wherever you were in the universe. Mentally thanking the Coder that she hadn't been wearing her jumpsuit with unicorn patches, she decided to see how long she could last.

It turned out that on a ship with two thousand people, an extra face was hard to spot so long as she acted like she belonged. If anything, it made her slightly concerned about the security of interstellar peace considering that she was literally wondering around the pride of the navy.

She had caught the tell tale twitch of Anthea's cameras as she trekked the corridors. No doubt her every move was being tracked, with the ship putting together an extensive analysis of security's response, or rather lack thereof. Casey almost pitied whoever was in charge when the extent of her adventures was revealed.

Then again, she supposed that since they were in the middle of space, people didn't really expect there to be any chance of an intruder. Particularly not one who would find their way to the mess and sweet talk Anthea into replicating ice cream even though it was not on the set menu of the day.

Her experiment might have carried on for longer, except it just so happened that a particular crew member had to look up at the wrong time whilst grabbing a coffee. She only realised that she had been spotted when the sharp sound of a clattering mug rang out across the room, along with shouts of irritation from the ratings around. The coffee in question splashed across several feet of floor, and it was a good thing that unshatterable plastic was the norm aboard ships.

Looking up, she couldn't resist grinning and giving a small wave to Hounslow, who was staring as if he had seen a ghost. Shrugging, she grabbed her still half full bowl and wondered over, giving a small salute with her spoon.
"Long time no see."

His face was completely white, eyes bulging. His companions at least seemed to cotton on that something was not quite right, and Cat heard one of them calling in to their CO. Hounslow's shock lasted another scattering of heart beats before he launched himself forwards. Squeaking, she ditched her ice cream on the table just in time to avoid getting it over both of them. Between one breath and the next, she found herself wrapped into the tightest hug she could ever remember getting. Not that it was an extensive list.

"Casey?! Oh my God, Casey is it really you?"
She didn't even get the chance to open her mouth before he did a complete one eighty and drew back until he was holding her shoulders and half shaking her. His face went from ecstatic to furious fast enough to give her mental whiplash. If he wasn't careful he would pull a muscle or something.

"Where the hell have you been?! I leave you unsupervised for a couple of months and then you tell me that you have joined up to some shitty space cruise company and the next thing I hear is that you are MIA somewhere out in the black! You have a lot of explaining to do, young lady! Why are you here? HOW are you here? And where did you get ice cream from because I know for a fact that Anthea rarely lets people have treats..."

A harsh throat clearing behind them had Hounslow turning in irritation, only to freeze and suddenly snap to attention. Casey peeked around him, waving sheepishly at the newcomer who sported a fearsome scowl and a couple of stars on his shoulders. Seconds later, a veritable swarm of security officers came charging in, and at the officer's motion wasted no time in once more securing her, this time with cuffs to her wrists.

There was no point in resisting, so she let them start frog marching her back to the brig, only turning her head a bit to look back at Hounslow and grin.
"Catch you later mate!"
He looked like he was trying to do warp equations in his head with how confused his expression had become, before her sight was cut off by the closing door.

This time when she was returned to the cell they kept her in the handcuffs, using an energy tether to keep her secured to the table. There was barely enough room to do more than stand up. They also left a guard standing just inside the door, who stood with arms crossed and a thunderous expression.

She felt a little bad, pretty sure that the little game of Cat and mouse had probably landed more than a few people in hot water. Afterall, AIs could get a bit malicious when not fully utilised. Anthea had no doubt been rather enthusiastic in delivering her report.

At least this time she didn't have to wait another four hours. After what must have been only around twenty minutes, the same officer from earlier came striding into the room, dismissing the guard with a wave of his hand.

He regarded her with the disdain she had expected, mixed with a certain measure of curiosity. "So, care to tell me your name yet?"
Silence.
"I must admit I was surprised to not find any record of you in the citizens database. But then, a hacker such as yourself no doubt took precautions."
Still no answer. She very deliberately crossed one leg to rest the ankle on the opposite knee.

"You know, normally with pirates we would just ship you off to the next available prison on an asteroid or something. Frankly I don't care that you are still a kid." He just sighed as she pointedly stared at the bulkhead across the room. "Luckily for you there seems to be someone willing to put a good word in."

A moment later the door was opened again, the guard ushering a new person inside even as the officer stepped out.

"Hi Hounslow!" she waved as best she could, seeing as she was still shackled to the table.

He actually seemed a bit confused at the sudden switch in behaviour. "Hi, again, Casey."

"Long time no see." She kept her voice intentionally peppy, causing him to crack a smile.

He gave her a hard look as he sat across from her. "Casey, why won't you say anything to my CO? you must have realised I have told him who you are."

She narrowed her eyes in exaggerated suspicion, "Were you watching on a monitor or something?"

He offered her a raised eyebrow, crossing his arms until she sighed, "Yeah, so why would two of us need to repeat the same info?"

"Casey." The tone brooked no argument.

She shrugged with studied nonchalance. "Alright, honestly I don't like him much. He looks a lot like my manager on the cruise ship and he was a dick."

A small snort, "Haven't you ever heard about books and covers?"

She couldn't help but pout, wishing she could fold her arms to mirror him. "Well so far he has met my expectations, low as they were. Said he was going to ship me off to a prison moon or something."

"You weren't exactly cooperating."

"Well what could I say?" frustration was starting to bleed through her tone.

"Umm, you could explain the situation- that you were kidnapped by pirates."

She smirked at him "Kidnapping is a such a strong word. It was honestly more of an accidental recruitment."

"Are you kidding me right now? Do you not realise how serious this is?" the way that he ran an aggravated hand through his hair seemed to make a hard ball of something form in the bottom of her throat. If she was a feline her claws would have unsheathed. "Give me some credit, I have grown up since we last met. I mean, if you are here to get my confession you can have it. I, Casey Catanski am a space pirate. It is the coolest thing I can claim on my CV."

"God help me." All at once his controlled veneer seemed to crack, leaving something more raw than she could take looking at for too long. "Do you have any idea what you have put me through? I thought you were dead Casey! You were dropped at the base so that you could have the chance for a real life. I'm sorry that I couldn't call back as often as I wanted to. Is that what it was about? You just telling me that you had a job and were going straight back out. Two months was not long enough to give base life a real shot-"

He paused for a moment, forcefully pulling the anger back in. She wondered how much of it had been born of genuine fear for her, versus the guilt he had always habitually taken on. Hounslow wasn't finished yet. "And the next piece of solid news I get is that you have vanished into the black after an attack on your ship. Do you have any idea how many hours of worry you have put me through? Do you even care?"

It was a low blow, even if he didn't realise it. Perhaps he did, and was just using any available weapon to make his point. Of course she cared, at last a little. It was hard not to when he had been one of the few people to give a shit about her. He had tried to explain, when they had dropped her at that base, about how there was simply no way for her to stay on a navy ship. She was a civilian, a child at that, one who needed care and attention and stability and a chance at a normal life... the list had gone on. And it was not as if she hadn't tried, but it had been pretty impossible to even think of putting down roots when she felt all at sea.

She had only lasted two months on the base. It was too crowded, too heavy, too big. She missed the black, being on ship, feeling like herself. As far as she was concerned, she had been born in space, and it was the only place she could ever call home. So, when she saw the ad from a star liner cruise company she had put together some records and signed up. It wasn't her best bit of forgery, but then they hadn't looked all that close. They needed bodies in the black and she was more than ready to fling herself back into its embrace.

The job had been shit. The people were obnoxious. For all that she had spent time talking to the AI, designated Brenda, the programme was not intended to be fully autonomous and so was limited in possible interactions. She honestly hadn't thought that anybody would notice her absence, or at least not in any way that said they cared for her as a person. She hadn't for a moment thought that a naval ensign on a ship the other side of a galaxy would really remember her existence, let alone try and check in on her progress.

Apparently she could be wrong sometimes.

She had been silent for too long. Hounslow sighed heavily, "I'm not blaming you. Hell, I've probably known you longer than most and let's be honest that is not saying much." It wasn't even true by this point. Andromeda had been her home for longer than Anthea, one crew taking a larger part of her life experience than the navy. Even so, for all that they had taken her as one of their own, there were always things that they didn't know, which she couldn't say, that they didn't have the right to ask about.

Eric Hounslow had been there at the beginning. The first individual that she grew attached to after Anita. There were things she would never need to say to him, because he already knew, better than she could ever hope to describe to others.

He leaned across the table, scruffing her hair even further than it already was, and making her squeak in surprise. "Seriously kid, at this rate you are going to be the death of me."

It was impossible to fight the tears which welled up a little at the familiar gesture. She really had missed him, for all that she had refused to let herself feel it before now.

"I'm sorry." The words were low, half choked, but genuine.

"I'm sorry too. I should have tried to keep closer tabs on you." He reached across the table, resting one of his hands on hers as she brought herself back under control.

She sniffled, "So what is going to happen to me now?"

Groaning, he leaned back in the chair, casting a quick glance at the camera in the corner and wondering how his CO was going to react to the situation. "I honestly don't know. I mean, you are still a minor, so I doubt that it would look so good for you to be shipped off to a penal colony or something."

Casey half laughed at that, also looking down the camera's lens, "Sorry to ruin you grand plan."

Eric rapped the back of her knuckle with a finger in warning before he continued, "Also, considering your history I think it is fair to say that you need help more than anything. I don't know."

At the rate he was messing up his hair, they would end up looking equally dishevelled if the conversation continued for too long. "Hell, worse comes to worse I will bring you home with me on my next furlough and leave you with my mother for a while. That woman is both the sweetest and most terrifying person you will ever meet. And no matter what happens you will meet her. She almost shot me herself for not bringing you straight back the first time when I explained I had basically adopted you."

Cat managed a faint laugh at that, "Oh yeah, you declaring yourself Bruce Wayne to my Dick Grayson."

"Exactly, squirt." He grinned for a moment, before turning serious once again. "Look, I do have to know though- how bad is it?

Like, you are going to have to be honest with me, and the police once we get this whole mess sorted out. Just how deep did you get yourself dug?"

She managed not to huff, making the effort to match his serious tone and demeanour even as she leaned back in her hard chair. "Calm down, it is not like I killed anyone. To be honest, for all that I was with pirates we were a pretty tame group."
"They kidnapped you." His voice was flat and hard.
"Honestly it was accidental." She snorted in genuine amusement at the memory, "And after that the Captain declared that they would never risk interacting with live targets again. I think they were more scared by the situation than I was in honesty."

A bit of the tension relaxed from his posture as he saw she was telling the truth.
"Ok. We can work with that. And I swear- I am going to make sure that things turns out better this time. But promise me one thing?"
"What?"
"Let this be the last time I rescue you from space?"
Cat laughed wetly. "Yeah, that is fair."

....

CHAPTER 19- NOW IT'S PERSONAL

Hounslow found her with her arms buried halfway into the guts of what he was pretty sure was the hot water system. She didn't look up as he approached. If anything he was half convinced that the background music had reached a few notches higher. At least Aurora wasn't letting her blow out his ear drums in an attempt to avoid conversation. No doubt she had rebutted any threats with the reminder of recent head trauma not liking the loudest volume settings.

He waited for a solid minute of no reaction to his presence, before kicking her foot. "Hey, are you... alright?" It wasn't the strongest opening, but then words had never been a norm for them.

The sigh that she let loose echoed back form the casing of whatever system she was playing with. If she had faced him he was pretty certain that her eyebrows of doom would have come into play. "Surely you have asked the doc that? Frankly she knows better than I do." The tone was studied nonchalance. He still didn't miss the too harsh clang of her spanner on a pipe.

"You know that is not what I mean."
"Sorry, my head is still a bit scrambled. Afraid I don't know what you are talking about." Her flippancy made him want to shake her until something real emerged.

He settled for the next best thing.

"Fine, I will be blunt then. How are you coping with the fact hat you are attacked?"

From the sounds of it she almost choked on her own spit at the blunt question. She still didn't emerge from the target of her ire, for all that the assorted rattling of her activities had fallen silent. "Diplomacy was never your strong suit." Cat's voice was quieter than he had heard for some time.

He snorted lightly. "I was better before we met."

Now she did emerge, a tense ball of manufactured righteous fury. Her words were clearly intended to be sharp, but only managed to seem weary. "Of course, it is my fault as ever."

Eric raised a hand in supplication, fixing his eyes to hers. "Don't. Please."

For a handful of seconds they stared at each other. Her face was far more open than she would ever admit, a hundred micro expressions dancing across and being squashed as she far too obviously fought for a sense of calm. It seemed that some habits would never truly die. At least by this point he could trust that the token resistance would give way when faced with his steady support.

An Olympic eyeroll and she spun on her heel, deliberately paying attention to a redundant system with a wielded spanner and semi-damped temper. "Fine! You want to know how I am doing? Just great. Fabuloso. No lingering issues here with the fact that" the crack in her voice was painful to hear, "somebody attacked me in my *home!*"

He stayed silent, letting the storm run its course. He knew by now that asking too pointed questions would get him nowhere. Some things just had to be shared without prompting. It had been a hard lesson for he and his family to learn, in the beginning. They had always been so close, so involved in each other's lives. Even what arguments broke out, and radio silence lasted for a month, they still knew that reconciliation would come with time. They loved and trusted each other far too much for any other outcome.

Cat had never had that luxury. The one being that she had been tethered to, the AI who had kept her from being consumed by the Void and becoming just another ghost had been lost in its mission. Cat lived up to her nick name sake in that you had to let her come to you.

After a few swallows which if addressed she would no doubt pass off as lingering nausea, she managed to make a noise possibly intended as a care free laugh. "Why would that affect me. No. I will be fine. It's not as if this has never happened before after all." The words were quiet, faintly pained. "I just thought...
"

Now it was Eric trying to swallow down his own pain in response to hers. He knew that anything he said, no matter how sincere, would not be welcome at this point. He knew her best after all. Instead, he raised one eyebrow as he leaned with studied nonchalance against the nearest piece of equipment. "Well, you certainly have the worst luck of anybody I have ever met."

She did laugh this time, for all that it was tinged with bitterness beyond what many believed someone of her years could summon. With deliberate care she tucked her wrench back into the depths of her tool belt, turning instead to an assortment of screws and bolts as offered up by a patiently waiting Roomba.

"Too right. Perhaps I should sell the rights to my story to some holo studio? Could make a mint. Retire." Her upper body disappeared back into the guts of the ship mid sentence, words becoming once more distorted by the surrounding metal.
Eric scoffed, this time speaking with absolute conviction. "Nah- you would get far too bored within the first month."

A true chuckle came from the maintenance officer. "And no doubt cause some chaos."
"And then I would have to bail you out."

One hand appeared, fingers running blindly over the threads of a screw before claiming it and vanishing once again.

"At which point I would be forced to run away to the stars in order to escape my dreadful deeds." It was with a sense of relief that he noticed her almost flippant, sing song words.

Offering an exaggerated huff, he cast a jaundiced eye at the way in which she was seemingly trying to wiggle even further into her targeted area. If the doc was here she would no doubt be throwing a fit. "Right. Might as well miss out all the effort of the middle steps and just stay here."

For a few minutes Cat didn't offer a reply, deliberately ignoring their conversation to make whatever repairs or upgrades she was attempting. It was nothing new to Eric. When their mother had first asked for Cat's permission to adopt her, the girl a hadn't been able to make eye contact t for the better part of the week. Every mechanical item in the house had been a given a technology upgrade several generations beyond where it was supposed to last.

At long last, she let a sound of noted satisfaction. A half second later she was oh so carefully extricating herself from the system. Now that Hounslow looked closer, he was pretty certain that it was in fact a redundant back up for the transponder system. Some part of the back of his brain couldn't help but wonder if she had been targeting the emergency outreach apparatus.

She set her tools down on the floor with deliberate precision. It was a move she seldom made. As she ever claimed, there was madness in her method and that kept them flying so far. For her to make such a motion now spoke volumes.

At long last she locked eyes with her captain. "Give me some credit. No two bit hacking son of a bitch is going to make me feel vulnerable amongst my own family." Her words were sharp, and still had nothing on the blade like smile which stretched across her face. "I refuse to let him."

For all that her defiance was a relief to see, he couldn't help but remember his role in her life. He had never once lied to her, and wasn't about to start sugar coating truths now. Sometimes people needed to be reminded of things which made them uncomfortable. "There are some things you can't control."

Her eyes held a weight which made something in Eric's chest ache in an echoed sympathy. "Believe me: that is one thing I have never forgotten."

CHAPTER 20- GIRLS JUST WANT TO HAVE FUN

"**C**at! I need you right now on a matter of urgency!" Puerty's voice echoed around engineering loud enough to startle Ramal who promptly dropped a spanner onto the foot of her quarry. This prompted a significant round of pained swearing from both engineering residents, which had the doctor hurrying over to ensure she hadn't caused any major damage.

It was hard to stifle her laughter however, when Cat herself popped up from beneath the Drive casing.

"Umm, what are those exactly?"

The girl glared a little, "Exactly what they look like." She grinned, "Ramal got them for me. Aren't they cute!" tilting her head only accentuated the feline impression given by the sparkly black ears which nestled in her hair.

Judging by the shaking shoulders of the engineer, the temptation to laugh was universal. It seemed the joke would really never die.

"Very stylish." She grinned.

"Thank you, now what did you need me for? Because I am telling you right now that if you have damaged another one of your waste recycling units..."

"Oh no, nothing like that. Nope. See, I need your help on what is an extremely important mission: girl's night."

"Huh?"

"Oh come on! It will be fun! I have some face masks which I picked up on our last supply stop over, and I got hold of some more of the colour changing nail varnish."

"Well..."

"Ooh- and I downloaded the next series of that medical drama!"

"Oh my Coder, sold. Sorry Ramal, rest of the inspection is all yours I have a meeting to get to."

He smiled indulgently at the pair, "Yeah, yeah, priorities. Have fun."

With a quick detour to the mess to replicate some brownies, the pair were soon cozied up in Puerty's cabin with multi coloured faces and a soap opera in the background. It wasn't until the doctor had finished the first coat on her friend's nails that Cat finally nudged her with an elbow.

"So, tell me what is really going on."

Puerty's attempt at innocence barely lasted ten seconds, "Ok, so maybe girl's night was a bit of a ruse." She turned more fully to face her friend. "Here's the thing, I really need some advice, and I didn't know who else in the crew to turn to."

Cat settled back more comfortably, quirking an eyebrow but saying nothing.

"See, there is someone that... that I... well I like them, a lot." The doctor kept her eyes fixed on the bulkhead, hands fretfully twisting the cap of the nail varnish bottle.

"Hmm." It was studiously non-committal.

"And, I know you are Ace, but you are also the best at coming up with creative solutions, so I was hoping to ask for some ideas..." Cat raised her eyebrows at the uncharacteristic way she was approaching the issue. It was possibly the first time that she had seen Puerty overly flustered. "Basically, you have a crush and your brain is short circuiting."

Puerty managed to look outraged for a moment, half ready to deny the accusation, before she abruptly deflated. "Not exactly how I would have put it, but accurate I suppose."

cat allowed herself a slightly self-satisfied smirk, "Alright, starting with the basics: who is it?"

"Umm, Flora."

"Yes! Ramal officially owes me twenty credits!" her abrupt whoop almost caused Flora to fall off the bed in surprise.

"Wait, what?!"

"We have been betting on this since, like, sol four. You, my friend, are smitten." Her tone was devilishly gleeful.

Puerty blanched, "Dear god... who else knows?"

"Well Hounslow thought it might be someone back on base-"

"Personally I believed that you would not even admit there was someone until after the current mission had finished." Aurora's input earned an aggrieved shout from Puerty, swiftly smother as she tried to bury her face in a pillow. Thankfully she stopped herself before smearing her face mask all over the bedding.

Cat snickered, "but I was sure when you almost melted through the floor during our little sports day."

Now she flamed scarlet, "Seriously?"

"Yeah, but don't feel bad. From what I can tell she has it just as bad as you. To be honest, I'm half surprised you guys haven't already gotten together, but then you are both apparently emotionally constipated so..."

The doctor threw the pillow at the maintenance officer, before suddenly freezing as her words fully registered, "Wait, she..."

"Oh yeah, the mutual pining of you is worth its own internet series. She saw you dancing to that Swan Lake variation a while back, and I was pretty sure she nearly suffered a coronary. Honestly, for a pair of professional adults it has been almost pathetic to watch. That being said, I totally ship it and if you don't ask her out before the end of this trip, then I will lock you in a cleaning cupboard so help me Coder. And not just to win the betting pool, so don't get your wires in a twist Aurora because I know you are still listening"

Her friend laughed ruefully as a series of bleeps came through the speakers. "Fair enough. So, oh all knowing sage- any help to offer?"

Cat hummed thoughtfully, "Well, my first suggestion would be that you find her, tell her how you feel and snog her senseless."

Puerty seemed to choke on her own spit.

"And if you want a higher chance of success, go in a dance outfit because she seemed seriously into it before." It was all said in a flat tone, and with a decisive nod, belied by a faintly wicked gleam in her eye.

The expression on the doctor's face was barely a step away from mortified. It took a few chances before she could find her words. "Anything a little less potentially embarrassing?"

"I'm telling you, she would go for it."

"Please, Cat, come on." She would forever deny that her tone had become whining.

Cat sighed heavily, "Fine, if you want to be a bit more subtle... I believe the traditional concept would take her on a date."

"We are literally in the middle of space, we can't exactly pop out for a romantic bite to eat."

"Not with that attitude, but with a friend who can hack the replicators at least part of that equation is dealt with. You just have to pick a suitably private spot on the ship."

Puerty frowned for a moment in thought, before the proverbial light bulb finally flickered to life. The doctor grinned at her, "You really are a life saver you know."

"Sure, sure, just remember that when it comes to picking out your maid of honour."

Puerty flushed crimson once again.

"For now though, the least you can do is apply the second coat to my nails whilst I figure out what the hell has just happened in this episode."

CHAPTER 21- THE SECRET GARDEN

"**I** 've got something I would like to show you."
The faint blush tinging Puerty's cheeks was nothing less than adorable, and Flora found the thought of saying no frankly impossible. Instead, she let herself be led by the doctor, stupidly conscious of just how warm the hand that she held seemed to be.

They reached one of the service hatches, and paused for a moment so that Puerty could key in the access code.
"Technically this is meant to be a crew only area, but I thought you would like it."
"I don't want to get you in trouble..."
"Oh please, they wouldn't last a day without me." Her grin was nothing less than impish.

The door clicked open, and Puerty gripped her hand tighter as she pulled Flora inside. She felt the breath catch in her throat, eyes widening in shock and mouth dropping open. It was as if they had stepped through a portal into a different world.

Instead of the usual utilitarian layout of a recreation room, this space was filled entirely with plants. There were ferns trailing from hanging beds, draping with artistic chaos from the ceiling. A delicately flowered selection of vines crept their way from the floor, lending splashes of colour to the slope of the walls. There were even a few small blossom trees which were nestled in cleverly designed raised beds, filling the air with a faint scent of spring.

And amidst all of it were the lights. Flora couldn't believe at how subtly the thousands of fairy lights were strung amongst the various stalks and bushes. Glimmers of gold peeked out from leaves, highlighted the veins in petals. The room seemed to glow of its own accord.

Puerty led her over to a sort of double swing set in the far corner of the garden, tugging at her to sit down. Flora let her eyes just roam around the astonishing sight, drinking in the purer air.

"Did you make this?"
The doctor laughed. "No, afraid I have rather the opposite of a green thumb. Actually, this was all Cat's doing."
"Seriously?" the techie, and at least somewhat crazy, girl hadn't struck her as the type.

"Yep. See, all space vessels are required to have some form of plant life aboard- good for maintaining mental health and all. Cat though, well she got the idea into her head that there was no reason not to have a proper garden aboard ship. She apparently got Ramal to help out with some of the structural bits like the beds and borders, then just figured the rest out. Add in the fact that our noble Captain can never say no to his little sister-"
"Wait! Hang on, they are siblings?"
"Umm, yeah? Pretty sure he as the piece of paper to prove it around here somewhere... you didn't know?"

Flora could only shake her head, for some reason the connection never have been made. Putting aside her surprise, she smiled a little at her companion, "you really care for her, don't you?" she did her best to ignore the ever so faint twinge of jealousy at the fond smile on the doctor's face.

Puerty snorted, "Hell yes. I'm an only child, and all my life I wanted to have a little sister or something. And when I joined the crew, it was like my prayers had been heard. Heard all wrong. And then whatever deity you choose sent me a feline in human form to steal my snacks and give me regular heart attacks."

Their laughter went bouncing around the room, before softening once again to match the atmosphere.

"So, how did you even end up here? Like, on this specific ship, with this bunch of nutters?"
Puerty didn't bother trying to supress the grin which stole across her face as she remembered.

"Long story short, I helped Cat with a bar fight and ended up being offered a job."

Once again laughter rang out around the garden, Flora almost choking as she imagined the scene. To be honest she would have been disappointed to find out it was anything less than so colourful a meeting.

Flora leaned back in her seat, letting it rock and sway just a little. She tried to be subtle as she stared at the doctor, eyes tracing the curl of her hair as it rested on her shoulder, drinking in the effect of the warm lighting on her skin. She couldn't help but think that the stars in those eyes rivalled whatever ones were drifting by beyond the hull.

Puerty leaned a little closer, looking up through her eyelashes. "So, do you like it?"
She licked her lips which suddenly seemed so dry. "Yes. I think it is magnificent." *Like you* the voice in her head added with a tinge of desperation.
"I'm glad. This is my favourite place."
"On the ship?"
"In either galaxy."

There was a weight to the words.

The gap between them was so small. Flora looked at the doctor for a long moment, the voice in her head listing why this was a bad idea. There was so much she couldn't say, they would part ways at the end of this journey, she didn't deserve...

The expression on Puerty's face shifted a fraction, the half smile fading ever so slightly even as the flush to her cheeks suddenly deepened. She began to pull back, "Sorry. Crowding you. Sorry. I didn't… and I thought I'd… but of course if you…" her hands were fluttering a little in the growing gap between them.

Flora caught them between her own. The palms were a little rough, callouses on the fingers which she could imagine were made by wielding tools used to save somebody's life. For a moment their gazes locked, both women freezing. And then she leant in. Ever so softly, she let their lips brush together, breaking off the doctor's babbling.

The scent of blossoms was heavy in the air. There was a faint taste of strawberry on her lips. The slow smile which grew on Puerty's face was one of beautiful relief.

CHAPTER 22- FACING MUSIC AND MOTHERS

C at hadn't protested overly much when Eric had dragged her from her room. It had been about three days since her unfortunate visit to sickbay, and if she were honest at least with herself she had half an idea of what was going on. That being said, never let anyone claim that she made his life deliberately simple.

"Alright, give it to me straight because my head is still aching despite the doc's best voodoo." It was said with folded arms as she dug her heels in a mere three feet from the bridge. If there was one thing that she could count on, it was his reluctance to manhandle her whilst she was still technically in the recovery period for a concussion.

It should probably be more concerning that there was a standard operating procedure for such things.

As such, it was with extremely exaggerated gentleness that he pulled her after him onto the command dais, and then left to the communications station. There was a red light blinking at the console which could only be a pre warning of doom. She knew that light. It was for the quantum message relay system. Still a relatively new and developmental communication module, the access was available only to the highest levels of intergalactic travel security for the sending out of severe warnings and alerts. That, and one other person to whom she gave special permission without necessarily informing those in charge of the channels.

True, nobody could really stop her, since she was in part responsible for its development. It had been part of how she had gotten away with doing her thesis studies whilst travelling the black. Simply, she made it a necessity for the furthering of her research. Can't very well make leaps on a practical farther than light comms system from Earth. Or at least she had made it damned clear she wouldn't be able to make any sort of break through whilst planet bound.

It was one of the things she had decided long before however, nobody would be left in the black without a way of getting a message home.

Eric looked up from where he was punching in the connection codes. He must have seen the look of trepidation on her face. Suspicion of the person at the other end of the call was further supported by the noticeable absence of the rest of the crew. He gave her a look which was half apologetic, half self-righteous.

"You must have realised that you are going to have to tell Mum about what happened?"
Cat gave an exaggerated groan, scrubbing one hand through her hair and wincing as she made contact with the remaining wound on her head. "Oh, Coder I am so screwed." It had been the faintest of hopes, that her little misadventure could wait until some time in the next century to be spilled to their mum.

Her brother made a noise which was faintly reminiscent of a dying sheep. "You are screwed? I am the one who is supposed to be looking out for you!"

They both turned mildly terrified expressions at where the connection was powering up.
"Can we make a pact here and now to back each other to the very end?" It was said in utmost seriousness, the weight of a few too many incidences lying unspoken between the pair.

It was in the same tone that he offered his hand. They shook, each attempting to appear resolute in their resolve. "Of course. You go down I do to."

"More like I go down, I am taking you with me." She offered him a crooked smile, pointedly not looking at the still blinking light.

"Such a subtle difference."

"And yet so vital."

Aurora had apparently had enough with their procrastination. She never had been patient when it came to them acting in a way that she deemed overly cowardly or childish. "Your mother is on the line." For a moment they glared in tandem at the camera, which the ship pointedly didn't acknowledge. Rather, she just opened the channel of her own accord, and after a moment of pixelated buffering, the roughly defined image of home resolved onto the main screen.

"OH MY DARLINGS HOW ARE YOU?!" Mrs Hounslow came into focus in the frame of her computer camera. Behind her it was just about possible to see the ever spotless living room. For all that the rest of the house could be burning down around her, she had always insisted on the comms visible sections staying intact and respectable.

It suddenly occurred to him that there was a small collection of dirty cups and an empty plate left balanced on the navigation console. No doubt she had already spotted and catalogued it.

Eric winced a little at her volume, making the effort to speak with exaggerated normality. Even as he did, one hand latched like a vice around Cat's arm in case she spontaneously decided to exit stage left.

At least this time she hadn't had the time to scheme with Ramal to set a small fire in engineering for her to tend to. That particular plan had ended up with a far more strenuous lecture when they called home again, so it was possible she had learned at least a bit of sense. Then again, there was a reason he tended to ambush her with these. He barely resisted rubbing at his temples with his forefinger.

"Mum, you don't need to shout. Your equipment is more than capable of connecting clearly."
"ARE YOU SURE?" if anything, he was half convinced that Aurora was amplifying the signal, if only to make sure that he would have a headache by the end of the exchange. She could be slightly vicious like that when worried for their safety.

Cat apparently had even less patience than he did. Although, on reflection, it was possible that was in part due to her skills as providing the connection in the first place being judged. She took enough offence to lean around him until she was in full view of their mum and belt out her own reply. "YES! Our tech is the best of the best. You can talk normally, and we will hear you just fine."

Eric saw how their mum's gaze practically became laser focussed on the girl, taking in every possible detail. Cat hadn't exaggerated about how fantastic the system she had installed was. He didn't doubt that his mum could read every new stress line on both of their faces.

"Casey, dear, how are you doing? Really?"
Cat's expression softened into something far sweeter than most people would think her capable. "I'm just fine. The doc fixed me right up and Aurora has been keeping an eye on me whenever this lump lets me out of his sight." She gave him a little thump on the arm to which he rolled his eyes in response.

"Yeah mum, she is fine. Puerty says that she won't have any lasting effects. Oh speaking of! The good doctor might be bringing a plus one for dinner next time we are Earth side." It was a blatant ploy to switch the topic, get her engaged on something else. They could both see the flare of interest in her eye. When Aurora's crew had been brought together, Mrs Hounslow had promptly declared them all her honorary kids.

"Oh! Wonderful." She smiled sweetly, talking the moment to sweep her eyes over the pair of them on the screen. It was nearly possible to pinpoint the exact moment that parental concern was satisfied and gave way to her general levels of fear and exasperation.

"WHAT IN THE SEVEN HELLS ARE YOU PLAYING AT?!"

"Damn. Now we know she is yelling because she means it." Cat's addition to the conversation was, of course, noted, and marked by their mother's severely unimpressed eyebrow making a guest appearance.

"Unnecessary." He hissed at his sister. She simply shrugged. They both knew that when they returned home they were in for the rollicking of their lives.

Their mum loved them, supported them, and would always be on their side come hell or high water. She still reserved the right to unleash her fury whenever her wayward children did something that she deemed unnecessarily stupid or dangerous. It was kind of funny when her wrath was directed at someone else, not so much when turned on them.

For a moment he considered sighing and shaking his head. Not worth it. Instead, they fixed nearly identical smiles on their faces, and bent all of their abilities into reassuring their mum that they were both alright. It was arguably on of the longest hours of their lives...

....

Cat was halfway back down to engineering when she almost literally ran into Puerty who was stomping in the other direction. She repressed the temptation to sigh. The doctor's temper had been nothing short of foul for the last couple of days, and it was really starting to grate.

What with Flora's attempts to bribe her into getting the doctor to talk, and the way that neither had been in the same room if they could help it, something had definitely happened.

Perhaps it was just because she was still a bit emotionally raw from talking to her mum, perhaps she was just genuinely getting better at people's emotions. Maybe she was just sick of all the bullshit that had accompanied this trip. No matter the reason, the result was the same.

Her arms was like a crowbar as she stuck it in front of her friend. Puerty came to an abrupt stop, almost losing her grip on her tablet. Eyes wide, she quickly dropped her expression from stunned to irritated. Cat didn't give her a chance to try and speak.

"Look, I don't know what she did, or why. I was determined to not get involved. Your life your rules. But for the love of circuits please talk to her! The pair of you are moping so much that the Roombas are getting concerned."

Puerty could only gape as, message delivered, Cat gave her a sharp nod before marching off once again. After all, the ship wasn't going to repair itself.

CHAPTER 23-
PARADISE LOST

They were lying on a picnic blanket on the grass, gazing up at the projected sunset. It was one of the best setting that the garden had been given, the ceiling becoming a slowly changing kaleidoscope of pinks and oranges, shot with that shade of blue that you only normally see from the tops of mountains.

A bottle of wine lay on its side between them, the contents long gone and the glass becoming warm. Their laughter was soft, and the fingers which entwined together faintly hesitant.

Puerty stretched her arms out, folding her hands beneath her head and sighing in contentment as Flora rested her head on her stomach. The doctor smiled a little at the other woman. "Tell me something."

Flora rolled a little until she could look at her face. "What do you want to hear."

Her face screwed up in thought for a moment, "Something interesting."

Flora closed her eyes, forehead scrunching ever so slightly, then opened them again with a faintly wicked glimmer in their depths. "Hmm, well once I snuck into the headteacher's office at school and filled it with balloons. Like, completely. But I filled like a fifth of them with glitter, so that when they popped them the whole room was covered."

Puerty snorted outright, resisting doubling up as she laughed so as not to displace Flora. Even so, tremors ran through her hard enough to shake her multicoloured hair half out its loose plait. Flora joined in, almost surprised herself at having found it so funny remembering so many years later.

The doctor finally got her breath back, idly trailing one hand through Floras freed hair. "Well it is good to know that you are an evil genius."
Flora poked her lightly in the side, getting a squeak in response as she squirmed a little. "What about you? Tell me something funny."

Puerty fingers stilled for a moment, her head tipping back a little further as she looked back through her stories. "Umm... ok, here's something that almost nobody else knows. The first time I ever went clubbing it was at university, and I was out with some friends from the Ballet Society. So it gets to the end of the night, and one of the exec offered to walk me back to my room."

Flora was already looking faintly mortified on her behalf. "Oh god I think I see where this is going."
She grinned a little self depreciatingly, "Not quite. So, we get back to my block, and he is like 'any chance I can come up? Just for a drink?' and I am like 'oh, sure!' We get upstairs and I let him into the shared kitchen, which I shared with twelve people for the record."

She rolled over further, raising an eyebrow. "Do I want to hear the end of this?"
"Shh. So, you know what happened? I gave him a drink of water and then kicked him out the flat!" Her voice was almost a squeak at the end, face flushing in laughter and remembered embarrassment.
"No way." Flora was biting her cheek to try and not break out into giggles at the mental image.

"Oh yep, I had no idea what he had been expecting until I met up with the others the next day at practice and all the girls were asking how he was. I found it downright hilarious, and once he realised that I am gay he just laughed at his mistake, and we ended up friends."

Flora couldn't hold it back any more, sniggering from behind her hand. Puerty didn't seem to mind in the slightest, her own laugh bouncing around.

"That is pretty priceless."
"I know right! Ok, your turn again." She paused for a moment, hesitating. "Tell me something secret."

The laughter had died away, swallowed up by the sunset which continued to play out overhead. "What do you mean?" The tone was intentionally careless, almost a low warning to change the question. But then, Puerty had always been relentless.
Her tone was soft, somehow not cajoling which almost made it worse. It was an honest request. "Tell me something that you haven't told other people."

Flora turned her head away, dislodging the doctor's hand from where it rested still in her hair. She glared up at the fake sunset, suddenly wishing the colours would just fade already. "Yes, I do know the definition of secret."
Puerty frowned, propping herself on her elbows. "Hey, no need to snap. It was just a question."

She was sat up all the way now, half balanced on her knees as she looked down at the other woman sprawled on the blanket. "Well I don't want to answer it."
Puerty sat up to, throwing her hands in the air and narrowing her eyes. "Sheesh, fine. Don't then."

For a moment they just glared at each other. For all that Flora wanted to hold the expression, she felt it crumbling at the badly hidden but genuine hurt on Puerty's face. The room suddenly seemed smaller than she thought it was, the plants some sort of ludicrous fiction. That's all this was after all, a room pretending to be a garden.

She rubbed at her forehead with one hand, wanting to just get up and pace off this sudden burst of anxious energy. Deliberately looking away from the doctor she tried taking a deep breath, only for it to escape too soon. She muttered under her breath, "Dammit, what am I doing?"

Puerty didn't seem to have heard her. "Huh?"
She through an arm out, gesturing to the room, the sky, her figure still on the ground. When she spoke it was through half gritted teeth. "I shouldn't be doing this. I shouldn't be here, with you, like this. It's not right."

The doctor's expression shuttered faster than she thought possible, all traces of her easy going softness locking themselves away. Her expression warned that it would be best to choose her next words extremely carefully. "Excuse me."

Flora's eyes widened, even as she began to pace, anything to try and relieve the frustrated tingling beneath her skin. "No! I mean..." she half growled, spinning on a heel and pointing directly at the doctor as she climbed to her feet. "Look you tell me to tell you things, but I can't. I can't share things with you even if I wanted to. And I can't do that to you, it wouldn't be fair." She snarled again to herself, one hand rapping subconsciously against her prosthetic leg.

Puerty's eyes tracked the motion. She was standing as well now, holding herself still with her fists clenched at her sides. "What are you saying." Her tone had slipped to something close to her work voice, the one that she used with upset patients. She never liked using it in her personal life.

Flora finally stilled, perhaps influenced by the doctor's posture, perhaps simply running out of steam. She met her eye again at last, and there was a terribly fragile certainty there. "I'm saying that I am stopping both of us from making a massive mistake."

She flinched, unable to repress the move, then tried to reach out. If she could just make her listen for a moment... "Wait, Flora, I already-"
She was having none of it, moving out of range and folding her

arms. Gone was the hesitation, the potential to be swayed. She had made up her mind, there would be no appeals. It took all her effort but she managed to pull all the emotion back under a veneer of rational logic. "No. I won't do this to you. You will see that this is for the best. I care about you, and I can't be the reason you get hurt."

For a heartbeat Puerty just stood, faintly stunned. It had all turned so fast. She would not cry. She was a doctor, bad news and pain were what she was trained for. It still didn't stop her voice from cracking.

"Well it's a bit late for that."

Turning sharp enough to almost be a pirouette, Puerty marched to the door, barking out a harsh "light" to bring up the normal levels. The sunset blinked out just as the hatch closed sharply behind her.

CHAPTER 24- TOO MUCH IS LEFT UNSPOKEN

Seven people sat around the rec room. Cat was perched on a side table, one foot resting on the back of a chair whilst the other was curled underneath her body. Her knee was apparently the perfect place to balance a plate of something which smelled overwhelmingly of chilli and was being steadily munched down with crackers.

Puerty and Flora had chosen opposite sides of the room. The doctor slumped somewhat dejectedly in an overstuffed arm-chair, cuddling Cat's seal plushie and steadfastly not looking at the other woman. Flora for her part sat stiffly on a bar stool which had been commandeered during the crew's last night of shore leave the year before and never found its way home. Any-one looking at her would assume that the meaning of life could be found in her nail art with how hard she was staring at it.

Flora had arrived first, slinking into the room with such an air of dejection that Cat had been concerned despite herself. She had slipped across, standing in front of the other woman with folded arms and a raised eyebrow, "So what is your problem?"

"My doctor says I don't have long to live?"

"Dear Coder, are you sick?"

Her pained smile belied her words. "No, I have just really pissed her off."

As if on que, Puerty had come storming in only to pull up short on seeing them talking. Without a word she shifted to the very furthest corner of the room and slouched into the arm chair.

Unsure of what exactly was going on, but still not wanting her friend to hurt, Cat had taken a moment to dig around in one of the vents connected to the room, emerging a moment later with the seal. Without a word, she had offered it over, an action apparently well received as the doctor promptly hugged it close to her chest.

Shrugging her shoulders, it really wasn't any of her business after all, Cat just returned to her food and waited for the rest to file in.

Wentz was half slouched on one of the few chairs which had actually been bought to match the main table, arms folded as he waited to see what all of the fuss was about. Markson occupied the seat across from him, one knee drumming rapidly against the lip of the table even as his fellow passenger shot occasional irritated glances at the tick.

Ramal had decided to position himself in a studied lean against the doorframe, posture half alert as if prepare to rugby tackle the first person who tried to move without permission.

Hounslow surveyed them all, and felt the headache already building behind his eyes. Some deep seated instinct told him that all hell was going to break loose. In a way he was kind of looking forward too it. There had been far too many secrets and lies on this trip. It was high time that the whole thing got shaken out.

"I have gathered you all here today-"
"To reveal the identity of the murderer!" At least it only took a brief glare for Cat to silence herself with another helping of her chips and lava.
"As I was saying... we need to get some things clear. Nobody is leaving this room until we have sorted out this whole mess." Nobody dared to argue with his tone, or the way that Ramal drew himself up to full height behind the Captain.

"There has been a lot of things going on for the last couple of months. Things which have placed my ship, my crew, my *family* in danger. And I will not stand for it. No more. We are going to sort this all out, right here, right now. And we are going to start with the attacks on Aurora and Cat."

The room was quiet as all eyes focused on where he began to pace back and forth. The rage which he had been carrying since the first knowledge of the hacking had been revealed was now rolling off of him in waves.
"Puerty, care to share with the class?"

She raised her chin as the attention of the room turned her way. The serious edge which was growing in the atmosphere of the room set her teeth to aching. From the corner of her eye, Puerty saw as Cat took a deep breath. The girl took a moment to scoop up Rhonda where the Roomba had been waiting at her feet. Almost absently, Cat began to pet the casing of the Roomba, deliberately not looking at anybody.

Puerty took a deep breath. She had agreed to make the report of their findings. It was rare that she saw Cat so genuinely discomfited by a situation, and there was no chance in hell that she would drag this out if she could help it. "This has been the work of a desperate individual. And it has taken far too much sacrifice and fear to find out the culprit. Wouldn't you agree... Mr Wentz?"

The man in question jerked as if he had been slapped. In the space of heartbeats his face had flushed a violent red as he sputtered in outrage before finding his words. "What the hell are you trying to accuse me of? I am a well respected and important member of a key research team."

Cat made a cough which sounded suspiciously like "bullshit". Flora rolled her eyes but clearly picked up on the undercurrent of seriousness which added weight to the general atmosphere. Almost without volition, she moved to stand almost within reaching distance of Puerty. With the turn in conversation, and subsequent memories, she was almost vibrating with rage.

Wentz wasn't done, levelling a finger at the doctor. "Perhaps your time would be better spent trying to deal with whatever problems your maintenance officer has." His face twisted into a sneer as he flicked a gaze up and down the girl. "- surely her weight-"

Puerty was on her feet and halfway across the room before she even thought about what she was doing. "That's it! I am going to stick so many booster injections in your rear that you will be unable to sit until we dock!" Wentz actually looked half a step away from running from her wrath, which she noted with bittersweet satisfaction. She forever swore by the oath she had adopted and adapted years before. If her culture permitted tattoos it would have been etched into her skin forever: 'Do no harm but take not shit.'

"Whoa there!" Flora tried to place a comforting hand on her shoulder, only for the doctor to whirl around and level a threatening finger in her face. Her blood was up, and there had been far too much left unsaid for far too long. Flora felt her stomach sour at the level of raw hurt on the other woman's face, for all that her tone dripped in scorn.

"And don't get me started on you! Just what do you take me for?" Puerty adopted an overly exaggerated accent, "'I don't know what I would be getting into'?" Her voice dropped back to its usual lilt, although with a harsh edge of disappointment. "Give me some god damned credit. Hell, just the respect for me to make my own decisions! If you can't at least do that then don't for one second-"

Hounslow couldn't help but jump in, sounding more exasperated than anyone supposedly uninvested in a relationship should. "Hang on- is that what you have been arguing about?"
"It wasn't an argument." Flora's arms were crossed as she pointedly fixed her gaze on the bulkhead.
Cat rolled her eyes so hard she almost strained something. "Fine,

that has been the cause of trouble in paradise? That's what has stopped my ship from becoming canon?"

Puerty made a noise which was too pained to be amused. "Yes. She doesn't think that I can handle the truth about the fact that she is smuggling diamonds and that bloody info chip."
"YOU KNOW ABOUT THAT?!" Flora's shriek actually made Markson wince and try to duck down further in his spot. It was almost gratifying to see the sheer incredulity on the normally composed woman's face.

The doctor raised a withering eyebrow at her before throwing up her hands in sheer exasperation. "Of course! What do you take me for? Everyone is scanned to the bone marrow as soon as they step aboard." And hadn't that been a lesson learnt the hard way... "Aurora told Cat as soon as you stepped on the ship and she told the rest of us."
The apparent smuggler choked on her own spit for a few seconds before finally managing to choke out words again. "How did-"

Puerty just sighed deeply. "Seriously? Aurora is the best ship in two galaxies and Cat is a mad genius on a bad day. Of course we knew. It just wasn't any of our business. And then you decided to break things off between us with hollow platitudes rather than risk being honest."

It was only as Cat saw the sheer sense of exhausted hope on the her friend's shoulders that she suddenly realised just how hard the doc had fallen. Flora looked about ready to cry as she clearly saw the same thing. Puerty had steadfastly focussed on the ceiling as she brought herself back under control, and so didn't see the look which the other woman was wearing.

A pained silence descended, as the others were torn between wanting to fix things and respecting the autonomy of the pair to deal with things themselves. Eventually the crew's respect for their family member forced them to not meddle more.

It was with forced intention that Hounslow clapped his hands

together, drawing all attention once again. "Alrighty, is there anything else that we feel needs to be aired?"
For a split second nobody spoke.

In the face of her friend's distress, Cat gave herself a mental shake and drew on the steel at her core. She wore a smile which was nothing short of poisonous and locked eyes with the Captain. "As was about to be said earlier: Wentz is the one who pushed me down the stairs."

For a split second everybody froze. Before Wentz could make a move, Eric spun on his heel and delivered a full powered punch straight to the man's face. He went down in a boneless heap without a sound, collapsing to the floor as Puerty let out a whoop.

Ramal just crossed his arms and raised an eye at his Captain who was rubbing his knuckles without a single ounce of regret. Grinning ruefully at his missed opportunity, the engineer moved over and fixed a pair of force cuffs to Wentz, not bothering to prop him back up from his uncomfortable position.

Hounslow stepped over the sprawled body, going to Cat and slinging an arm around her shoulders. He gave her a light squeeze, letting her lean into his side in comfort. The Roomba on her lap beeped in apparent approval. He kept his voice deliberately soft. "How did you find out?"
She shrugged a little from where her face was half buried in his jacket. "Rhonda and Rambo told me."

He just nodded, deciding not to ask any questions at that point. "We will deal with him in a minute. Anything else?"
Ramal raised his hand. "Well, it is not particularly relevant but in the interests of clearing the air I should tell you that Markson has done nothing wrong."
"Wonderful." Hounslow's tone was desert dry, as he rubbed at the bridge of his nose.
"However he is the illegitimate son of a key cartel leader back on Earth and is fleeing for his life and the chance at normality."

For a moment the others stared at the engineer in shock. The silence was broken as Cat burst into a fit of cackling so hard that she nearly toppled off her table. Markson himself was seemingly frozen in place, skin blanched and eyes bugged. Puerty just rolled her eyes at the general insanity. Eric just heaved a deep sigh,
"Well, we don't have the time to unpack all of that right now."

Cat snorted, whilst Puerty just huffed and shook her head. He had a point after all. Hounslow pulled himself to his full height, adopting what Cat always referred to as his 'Captain character'. "Alright. Ramal, take that piece of shit to the brig, make sure that he is secured tight and has no access to tech. Aurora, if he so much as looks wrong at the door you have free reign to incapacitate him in any way that you see fit."

Even Flora winced a little at that. Hell hath no fury like a woman scorned, and that is nothing compared to a woman deliberately targeted by some jumped up little twat with delusions of grandeur. None of them could find any pity for the piece of shit.

"Cat, I want you to find out what else he has been planning, and do whatever you can to limit its effects. God only knows how much damage he has managed to do."
She nodded, tucking Rhonda under one arm s as she hopped down from her table. With a mocking salute she headed out the door, apparently discussing with the Roomba what her options were.

Nobody batted an eye.

Hounslow turned to his remaining passengers. "Markson."
The man looked one wrong word away from hurling his guts out on the floor. Eric just sighed, shaking his head and once again massaging the bridge of his nose. "Get over yourself. We don't care. Consider leaving a tip when you disembark. And thank you for having a relatively harmless secret- as in you are not actively trying to hurt anybody. Word of advice: relative are one thing,

family is who you choose. Just something to consider."

Markson simply stared for a handful of heartbeats, breath still stuttering in his chest, before finally offering a sharp nod. He made for the exit on shaking legs.

"As to you two..." neither Flora nor Puerty looked at the other. The Captain just muttered something under his breath, before turning away and heading for the door himself. He threw his last words over his shoulder, almost like an afterthought except for his earnest tone. "Talk to each other. Please?"

The door swished shut in his wake, leaving the women standing alone in the now deserted space. Neither moved for a handful of breaths. And then Puerty sagged from her stiff posture as if her strings had been cut. She didn't look at Flora, instead fixing her eyes straight ahead as she too made to leave. At the doorway she hesitated, imitating her Captain as she did. Anything she might have said was swallowed down between one step and the next. Her footsteps retreated down the corridor for longer than Flora would have thought possible.

CHAPTER 25- YOU MAKE ME WANNA SHOUT

Flora was almost ashamed of how long it took her to realise where Puerty would have retreated to. There were no nebulae swirling beyond the window this time. Just an endless expanse of blackness. It was easy to forget, the vast regions of sheer emptiness which existed between the pinpoints of stars. Somebody had told her once that their universe was painfully young and that was why darkness existed. She liked the thought that somewhere out there beyond the black, was a sky made of so many stars that they blended into one mass of light.

The doctor didn't even let her sit down, speaking as soon as her footsteps came to rest at her side. "So, anything you would like to say? Or is it just going to be left at sorry and goodbye?" Her gaze was fixed on the universe beyond their thin skin of protective metal. If she focused, the half shadow of the memory of a galaxy smudged the top right corner of the window.

"You knew from the start?"

"Yes." The tone was final, as stark as a stone dropped into a wishing well without an echo.

"Aurora and Cat told you?" For some reason everything was coming out of her mouth as a question.

"Of course. I am the ship's medical officer, and their friend. Everyone is scanned. The diamonds were spotted in you prosthetic leg at once. The chip under the skin in your upper thigh took ten minutes longer. I should probably tell you that by this point Cat has remote hacked the contents. Don't ask me how. She is at least half way to being a cyborg anyway, and with Aurora's backing they have no concept of boundaries."

Flora offered a half laugh, "That should worry me more than it does." The sound trailed off to a slightly pained gurgle as Puerty finally rolled her gaze at her. For the space of three heartbeats they just held each other's gazes. Some small, selfish part of Flora hoped her eyes would say everything that her mouth had been too scared to utter. No such luck.

The doctor was staring solidly at the smudge when she finally spoke again. "You know, I genuinely thought that you would tell me. Or at least, offer me the chance to decide if I wanted you to." She shook her head in a self-depreciating way which seemed so painfully foreign to her normal commanding presence.

Flora bit her lip, hard, and found the taste of her own blood harshly sweet. "There is so much... please try to understand. I have been living in fear for so long and... then I met you, and I wanted to tell you everything but I didn't want you to be in danger, and so I pushed you away, and now I have lost you-"

Her words were cut off as the doctor let loose a harsh peal of laughter which bounced back in mocking echo from the walls. "Don't you dare tell yourself that you 'lost me', as if you are some sort of victim in all this. Try telling the truth for once in your life if only to yourself! YOU HAD SOMETHING GOOD AND YOU FUCKED IT UP ALL BY YOURSELF. How many chances did you expect to get? Huh? You many tears did you think I would *give you?* Lost me. You didn't lose shit- you threw it away. You had two choices: do better, or stay away." She made a sound which was halfway to a giggle and three quarters a sob. "Do you realise that I had the same choice? Never underestimate that I am smart. Whilst you chose to stay the same, I chose to do better. So I fucking left."

Flora didn't realise that she was crying until she tasted the salt as she licked her lips. At last Puerty turned to face her. "I told you so much. Too much I guess. I warned you- I have been burned too often to play with fire. I guess ice leaves its marks too." She scoffed to herself, and suddenly seemed to deflate. "It's a simple matter of respect you know. Do you even realise how many options you could have taken? The bar was pretty truth be told. Somehow you still managed to dig. I won't apologise for sounding bitter. Truly, I can understand your fear. But I know my worth, and I deserve more."

Flora hadn't said a single word. She honestly couldn't think of a rebuttal. It stung, and yet she couldn't deny the truth therein. It had been easier really, to say that she knew how the conversation would go. They hadn't known each other that long. Any sense of connection was merely the result of being in close quarters for so long with a small spark of chemistry. She had made more of it than what was actually there. So many stern self-lectures hissed in the dead of night...

Why hadn't she just asked if the other wanted to know?

Puerty had told her once about the legends of the black, the myths and stories and creatures. Was the idea of love really so outlandish when stated as a belief?

When the doctor spoke again, it was in the calm and professional tone which set her hackles on edge. "I won't hold it against you. I am never one to take revenge for my own sake. Quite frankly my temper just won't operate that way. It is so rare that I feel anger on my own part. We will dock, you will go your own way. That will be that." Her voice switched, becoming harder than the Dualinium of the hull. "But. If I find that you in any way played a part in causing harm to my family, then sweet summer or not, I will hunt you the edges of existence and make you regret so much more than you own issues."

Flora felt the blood still in her veins for a brief moment, and couldn't find it in herself to try and reach out to the doctor as she used the wall to pull herself up. Puerty left, and forcefully didn't look back. The erstwhile smuggler was left staring at the black, left to wonder if that smudge was a nebulae after all or simply to remnant of a handprint from long ago.

CHAPTER 25- KNOCK, KNOCK

T here is one reassuring thing about the vast vacuum of space- the fact that there is nobody around. People used to say 'in space no one can hear you cream', and perhaps they were simply commenting on the purely physical impossibility of sound travelling through a vacuum. However, in another sense, nobody can hear you scream simply because there is nobody there. Rather comforting all things considered, particularly if you are generally not a fan of other people.

On the flip side, when you are woken up in the middle of the night with the ship whispering to you that there are intruders aboard, it is both harder to process that thought to begin with, and significantly more terrifying once you have.

Case in point, when Aurora woke Cat with an insistent ping and informed her that strangers had snuck aboard, it took the human about three minutes to fully understand what she was being told. When she had got passed the mental gymnastics of 'we are travelling in the middle of open space and there should be literally nobody around for lightyears', her instant reaction was fear. If it was anyone with a legitimate reason for being in the sector, they would stick to the distances outlined in shipping lane policies and be broadcasting an identifying transponder alerting everybody around of their presence. As in, Aurora would have picked them up long before they were in solid contact range.

The fact that she hadn't could only mean that this was swiftly becoming a potentially dangerous situation. True, she had dealt with pirates before, but there was never a good reason to assume that intruders were friendly. That was just asking for trouble in any instance.

Cat slipped her comm into her ear, fishing around in her nest for her eye and popping it into place. Decent depth perception was probably a bonus at the moment. "Aurora, what is it looking like?"

"I'm tracking four unknowns. One seems to be standing next to the passenger berth access, one is heading towards crew quarters. Two are making their way to the bridge."

"Shit. Who's on duty tonight?"

"The Captain has the watch."

Cursing again under her breath, Cat kept fumbling around until her fingers finally closed around the barrel of her weapon of choice. The metal was cool under her fingertips, a comforting weight in her arms as she considered her options. As much as she wanted to make sure that none of her crew mates got hurt, the bridge would have to be priority. There was no way in hell she was letting them gain control of Aurora.

At least with so few invaders there was no chance that they could set up any form of surveillance of the access shafts and tunnels, leaving her free reign to scamper through the length of the ship. Aurora kept her updated on their progress, saying that she had managed to lock out access to the bridge, but could only hold off for so long before they would breach the door. She sounded apologetic, but Cat was quick to assure her that it was nobody's fault, this simply wasn't what she had been designed for.

By the time she reached the access point for the bridge, it was clear that the newcomers had gained entrance. Hounslow's startled yell echoed down the corridor.

"What the- how in the hell- what?" At any other point in time his complete bewilderment would have been rather funny to

Cat. As it was, she ignored the tone as she focused on getting a better look at the situation unfolding.

Two figures stood just in the doorway, levelling weapons at the frozen figure of the captain. One of them seemed to be thoroughly enjoying the drama of the situation.
"I think the words you are looking for are 'I surrender'."
Hounslow levelled him with a highly unimpressed look, his surprise taking a back seat. "The words I am looking for I can't say because I refuse to have another swear jar argument on this trip."

"Now, now, let's all stay calm and gentlemanly about this shall we?" the voice was gruff, half distorted by the masks that both of them wore. The one who had spoken was built like a brick outhouse, and Cat half wondered why he was in space when any rugby team would die to have him on the roster. His companion was just as tall, but gangly enough to make his movements seem slightly uncoordinated.

Hounslow glared at them both, "and what exactly is this?"
"Nothing to be worried about. We are just searching for a certain somebody who we believe to be aboard. They are carrying something which makes this whole shindig an unpleasant necessity. Now I know that they will have paid you well but I doubt it is worth your life."
"Ok, I am not being funny here, but I have literally no idea what you are talking about. All we are carrying is farming equipment for some colonies and outpost rations."

The gangly one stepped forwards a bit, and the nasal quality of his voice was somewhat grating. "And your passengers."
"Well yeah, we have passengers, but none of them have anything of great value either."
"Are you sure of that?" the bigger one spoke again, a bass rumble of condescension.
"Look, I'm not an idiot, if there was something I would tell you, but there isn't so I can't."

Before it could go any further, Cat made her move. Kicking open the access panel she fired as she dropped, sending the gangly pirate crashing backwards in a spray of red. The huge person whipped around, bringing their own weapon to bear on her position and yelling at the top of his lungs. He obviously pulled the trigger, as bolts of light began flashing all across the bridge. Another round from Cat and her opponent stumbled backwards at the impact, eyes wide in shock as he placed one shaky hand against where he had been hit. Upper left chest, right above his heart. He raised his fingers to stare as they dripped with... blue?

Another shot, this time slamming into his head and sending his mask pinging off behind him. There was purple splattered across his face, and as he looked down in shock he realised that the red on his groaning companion's chest was suspiciously sparkly...

And then he looked up, staring in complete shock as he finally got a good look at the ambusher who had ushered her Captain behind her.

Catanski was busy running her eye over every inch of Hounslow, feeling her heartbeat thrumming uncomfortably fast beneath her skin. He caught her hand, squeezing it in reassurance.
"Eric, are you ok?"
He smiled, pulling her into a half hug without disrupting her line of sight for her weapon. "I'm alright, it's ok. More startled than anything."
She took a moment, soaking in the truth of it, before giving him a shaky grin and punching him lightly in the chest. "Good, because there can only be one dead fuck up per family and I filled that quota years ago."
This time his expression soured into a more normal exasperation. "How many times- that is not and never will be funny!"

The pirate seemed to have finally pulled himself together, the abrupt change in circumstances filtering through. Once again he raised his weapon, sighting down the barrel at the pair.

His eyes met Cat's, and their mouths dropped open in simultaneous shock.

"Casey?"

"Oh my Coder- Cy?!" her voice was about twelve octaves higher than he thought a human could go, but he only had a second to wince before the girl was launching herself across the room. He dropped his blaster on instinct as he caught her effortlessly and hugged her close.

A split second later she pulled back and smacked him across the face. "What in the hell are you playing at you bloody idiot? Why? Why would you go back to breaching ships when you know how stupid an idea ... and please tell me that isn't Jerry that I just shot because I really hoped he had fallen out of an airlock by now..."

The tirade continued, with the monolithic pirate looking somewhere between delighted and sheepish as the girl didn't even pause for breath. Somewhat nonplussed, Hounslow stepped out from behind the console where Cat had shoved him, and was now standing with folded arms as he tried to wrap his head around the situation. At the rate this was going they were all in danger of whiplash.

The person that she had called Jerry was apparently still believing himself to be dead. That is until Cy kicked his foot and muttered under the yelling for him to 'quit being dramatic it was only paint'.

By the time that Hounslow decided to clear his throat and interrupt whatever sort of reunion was going on, the erstwhile pirates seemed rather glad of his reprieve. At the very least everybody had apparently forgotten that they were still loosely holding weapons.

"Ok, I have so many questions right now. But first of all, Casey Catanski what did I tell you about paintball on ship?"

"That I was not to play paintball onboard. For the record, I only brought the gun because I am still modifying it and I had no intention of starting a paint war." Her insistence was belied by the glint in her eye and the way that she cradled the gun.

He cocked an eyebrow in warning. "Good, because I am not helping you clean up glitter and paint ever again."
"Noted."
"Now, care to share who exactly these people are and what in the hell they are doing on my ship?"

"Oh, right, right. Umm, Captain Hounslow meet Captain Cy," she waved a hand between the pair of them, before motioning downwards, "and the idiot on the floor is Jerry." The two men eyed each other up uncertainly.

Eric seemed to processing things slower than normal, and then he reached a conclusion he didn't like. "Hang on, Cy? As in Captain of Andromeda?"
The pirate looked at her with rye disappointment. "Aaw, you told him about us?" Cat knew him well enough to see that he wasn't actually upset. Even so, she faced him full on with folded arms and a chin raised in defiance.

"Hey, he is family and had the right to know."
Hounslow's face was steadily dropping towards a murderous expression. "The Captain Cy who kidnapped you?"
She huffed, raising one finger to poke him in the chest. "Why does it always come back to that with you?" Shaking her head at the way he continued to scowl, she in turn watched with faint disgust as Jerry finally scrambled to his feet.

Cat perked up again, rounding back to Cy with a bounce, "Ooh, is Mick here? Please tell me they are!"
Cy couldn't help but grin a bit at her, "Yeah, although Fran hopped ship a while back and got herself hitched. She runs an import/export business for free traders now. We did bring a new recruit- Jamie. He's our latest attempt at finding a half decent techie. Of course, none of them hold a candle to you Case."

She placed a hand over dramatically against her heart. "Aaw, flattery will get you everywhere." Stepping away from the others, she took a moment to make sure that nobody had tried to mess with any bridge systems. "Aurora, any status update?"

The AI responded with the mechanical equivalent of a fond laugh. "Ronda led the charge against the man closest to the passengers. He has been apprehended and they are bringing him to the bridge now."
"Great work."
Cy chipped in, "I sent Jamie to subdue the passengers, and Mick went along as well to check the cargo hold. Don't look at me like that- I told them not to do damage to anybody."
"Yeah, that wasn't my worry."

A second later the door was loudly opened as the bedraggled form of Andromeda's newest recruit was slung into the room. Puerty was framed in the doorway, resplendent in a floral nightgown and bunny slippers. The curlers in her hair could have been a crown, and the green face mask did nothing to hide her annoyance. She levelled a phaser at Cy.

"Holy shit, she didn't even smudge her nails!"
A second later Flora's head popped up over the doctor's shoulder, sporting sparkling eyes and a rather flushed face. "She was magnificent. Just took them down with a kick and told me to get the phaser whilst she kept them on the floor. I don't know whether to be scared or aroused..."
"I would recommend scared, at least until her nails are dry and she is less irritated."

Further comments were cut short as the Roomba army lived up to their promise and dragged a semi-conscious Mick into their midst. Everybody except Cat gaped a little at the sight.
"I had no ideas that Roombas could be hostile..."

Cat patted Ronda on the casing, "The Roombas now seem to have formed a larger pack, with all 32 aboard being subservient to Rhonda. Roger and Rambo are clearly the betas of this slowly forming society. I am considering spending part of this trip writing a dissertation on the phenomenon for the anthropology (techno-pology?) students to dissect upon return to Earth. Then again, that sounds like a lot of effort."

There were a series of blank looks levelled at her, before they seemed to decide as one that it was probably better not to ask. Mick managed to gain enough wits back to squeal in delight at seeing Cat, for all that they stayed restrained by the bots.

Hounslow was leaning against the navigation console, watching the goings on with a jaundiced eye. "Not to break up this touching reunion, but can I please get an answer to the key question?"
Cy cocked his head, "Which was? Sorry- I've lost track of where our conversation had been heading."
Eric nodded sagely, the picture of nonchalance. "Oh perfectly understandable, nothing of great import, just a quick enquiry of WHY THE HELL ARE PIRATES ATTACKING OUR SHIP?!"

Jerry looked about ready to jump out his skin at the sudden burst of volume, raising his hands in an attempt at placation. "I think 'attack' is a bit of an over statement."
"Unfortunately true. I would say aggressively contacted." Cy actually sounded vaguely embarrassed by the self assessment.
Hounslow groaned, resting his head against the console. "How is this my life?"

Cat decided to take pity on her poor captain. "Still, it is a good question."
Cy just looked confused, whether on purpose or not she wasn't entirely sure. "Huh- how this is his life? I would think that merely being associated with you tends to guarantee a certain level of chaos..."
"No, what are you guys doing here?"

"Oh right! Well, as I was originally explaining to your Captain here, we are actually after one of your passengers."
From the corner of her eye, she saw Flora strategically edge herself slightly further behind the doctor. "Naturally. Which one?"

Puerty raised an eyebrow, "Cat..."

She threw her hands up in defence. "Just getting a sense of parameters here."

"Look, not to be awkward or anything, but it is probably best if I don't give you too many details. For your own safety you know?" Cy actually shifted foot to foot, seeming to find it hard to look directly at her.

Cat narrowed her eyes at him, before targeting Jerry as the weaker link. "Are you guys taking commissions now?" his captain's hand clamped over his mouth before he could so much as squeak. She tutted at the pair of them.

"Whatever. So, which one are you after? We currently have in stock one saboteur, one smuggler, and one fugitive."

The blunt statement let the pirates stunned for a moment. "For some reason I am not as surprised as I probably should be. You know, I am still half convinced that you are some ancient god of chaos taken human form."

"Well I was created in the stars..."

Hounslow jumped back in before the conversation could get derailed once again. "No. We are not giving the ship's cat a god complex."

"Party pooper."

Puerty growled as Flora moved a bit closer than she liked, taking a step to the side and casting a withering look at where the one called Jamie was still pinned to the floor. "Moving swiftly on."

Jerry gulped, finally caving under the glare from his former crew mate. "Well, we were given a tip off that one of your passengers was carrying some rather valuable items."

"Huh. Well, that does seem to narrow down the options somewhat."

If her meaning hadn't already been clear, anybody with half a brain would have noticed how Flora suddenly went three shades paler. She cast an entreating look at the doctor, who steadfastly didn't react. It was almost a bit painful to see them at odds to such a degree.

"So, to be clear, you guys attacked our ship to get your hands on our resident smuggler and her luggage?"

"Pretty much, yep. Afraid to say she really chose the wrong target this time."

"Now, now, let's not start commenting on other people's criminal judgement. Glass houses and all that jazz."

The pirate Captain sputtered in brief outrage, then subsided as he clearly remembered whatever choice blackmail was involved.

"As much as I hate to muddy the matter further," Aurora sounded rather less than apologetic, "I think that you are not completely aware of your crew's goals."

Cy looked at the main view screen, clearly offended by her accusation. "Come again?"

The ship's tone was remarkably cool in the face of his ire. "Well, I have been talking things through with Andromeda- by the way she sends her love, Cat- and it seems that your newest recruit has other priorities."

Cat's face broke out into a broad grin. She had wondered if the ships would be able to remotely access one another, seeing as how she had given them similar capabilities during her time aboard. Each ship had been more than happy to have their basic parameters extended when offered, and it seemed that they had found more than a couple of things in common as they spoke with each other.

"Care to explain?" Cy's words were forced through gritted teeth. Andromeda herself piped in, apparently having been given a mic access by Aurora so that she wouldn't be excluded. "We just find it interesting that your 'Jamie' shares a close genetic match to our currently incapacitated Mr Wentz."

"What?!" it wasn't clear if Hounslow's shock was from the information, or the second voice being relayed through the systems. Aurora chimed in again, "Yes, perhaps a cousin, or half brother?

We are only working with a general scan comparison of course. A proper investigation would no doubt sort the whole thing out properly."

All eyes turned to look at the young man who was still uncomfortably pinned to the deck by the small army of Roombas, who were in turn chirping in excitement at the attention.

"I think we all need to have a proper sit down and talk everything through."
"Great idea. I will put the kettle on."
"Perhaps something stronger would be best."

CHAPTER 26- SOME THINGS SHOULD BE SAID OUT LOUD

T he garden was quiet. It was something that didn't often happen. Although she had tended to the plants herself so diligently, and thought of the space as a sanctuary, the complete silence of it tended to spook those who had grown up planet side. Normally Aurora would play the soft sounds of a simulated forest, letting the façade of natural life calm her humans.

Cat had asked her to turn it off. Cy didn't seem to mind. They were lying on the patch of grass which covered the alloy floors in a pleasantly lush carpet. He had asked to speak to her, and there was only one place that she thought would suit.

Cy had gaped in awe when she had first opened the hatch. Partly at the sheer achievement, and more due to it having been her work. The last he knew her, she had been severely addicted to her tech and near scornful of nature. He remembered buying her a cactus once from a free port station. It had a single red flower and they had joked that it was as prickly as her temper. After she had been taken, he had found the damned thing sat on a shelf in the corner she had stolen for a workshop.

"Casey?" it almost felt an intrusion to speak into the silence. Her voice was soft. "Yeah?"

"… what… what happened… after…" he was swallowing almost convulsively around the words. It was something he had always wondered, occasionally after too many drinks the thoughts of her in some prison would rise up to mock him.

She hummed, and the faint rustle of adjusting position was the only response for a moment. "I did get arrested, there was no avoiding that." It was said so bluntly, a stated fact and nothing more. Her tone switched to rye amusement, "I guess the universe has a weird old sense of humour though."

"Why do you say that?" he couldn't take his eyes off the ceiling, where he could just make out the faint outlines of glow in the dark stars, the kind that kids still put up in their rooms.

"Turns out I ended up on the ship of the one person in creation who had actually been looking for me." Her half laugh was tinged with something that he almost didn't want to identify.

Cy couldn't help his tone turning faintly condemning. "You mean your captain?" internally he snapped at himself for the tone. He had no right.

They lapsed back into silence, this time with a faintly bitter edge. He resisted the urge to fidget, even as from the corner of his eye, he saw as Cat deliberately stretched and rested her hands behind her head. When she spoke again, she sounded far older. It reminded him of the way that she was when they first met, as if a person far older was staring out from behind her eyes. The sensation still burned somewhere deep in his stomach.

"It was the second time he saved me, you know." Her voice was low, yet the tone earnest, and he could hear the plea for him to listen. "The first time, he saved my life, in a very literal way." It struck Cy again just how little he knew about this girl. There had been enough hints over their time together, enough little clues which pointed towards something deep and dark. The black had always clung to her a little more tightly than most spacers. "The second time... he helped me save myself." She snorted softly, "Well, him and his mum. Mostly mum."

It told him more than perhaps she realised.

"They were good to you?"

Again she fell silent, clearly considering what she wanted to say. It hit him that she had yet to ask how they had gotten on after she had left. Not left, been taken. She hadn't had to ask any questions, seeming aware of at least the broad strokes of the fallout. He got the sudden notion that she must have checked up on them, somehow. She always had been a technical and literal genius. His musings were interrupted as she sighed.

"They took me to the ocean. I had never really understood until then, what people meant when they would go on and on about their home planets. Like, what could a ball of rock supporting an ecosystem have to compare to the beauty of the universe, the comfort of a ship. They took me to the ocean, on a day which was supposed to be sunny but ended up having a weather front moving in as we watched. All the technology of man, and the weather forecast will never be right."

He turned on his side, watching as a flicker of a smile raced across her face at the memory.

"I stood on the sand, and had small pebbles under my foot, and all I could do was stare. It was so enormous, bigger and more terrifying than when I had stared at nebulas beyond the main view of a bridge. Perhaps it was because I could touch it, it could touch me. I could smell it, taste it in the air, the sound was … It stretched as far as my eye could see and ate the horizon." The awe was still there in her voice, as fresh as ever.

"And our mum didn't say anything. She just held my hand. And suddenly, I got it, what they had been trying to tell me and I just couldn't understand. It's the same thing you guys tried to say, in your own clumsy way." She glanced across at him, face scrunching up in that same mischievous smile that she had worn so long ago.

"I never regretted it, giving you guys the time to get away."

She sounded so certain, so sure, and it made something sharp and ugly crawl up Cy's throat.

"I did. God, how I… I should never have let you… or at least I could have tried to get you back, to chase you down and break you out of wherever they took you." Since when had his voice become so raw? For heaven's sake, she was just a kid that they had picked up and travelled with for a while. That was what he had told himself for so long. "And I didn't."

He supposed that was what really burned. He had known, when they had accidentally kidnapped then intentionally hired her. He had known that she was more than a little damaged. She had been not much more than a child, a lost one, and they had offered her an anchor, only to let her drift away in the end.

And again she sounded so much older than she should. "I know."

"I am so grateful that it worked out, that you found what you needed. But I will never forgive myself."

CHAPTER 27- ANY BRIGHT IDEAS?

It was a rather rag tag group which gathered once again in Aurora's common area. With both crews present, space was a bit on the tight side. Cat had once again claimed her favourite perch, Puerty crowded next to her, absently braiding the girl's hair. Cy and Hounslow had chosen to stand at opposite ends of the room, the others jumbled around the main table. Even Andromeda had been given a secure network link so as to take part in the discussion. For the time being, Wentz and Jamie had been secured in different sections of the cargo hold.

Ramal took the initiative to start things, turning to Hounslow with a raised eyebrow. "So, oh brave leader, what's the plan?"
Jerry took no time in piping up his protest. "Hang on, since when is he in charge?"
"Since he shouted the loudest." Cat rolled her eyes at her old crew mate.

The man crossed his arms, huffing sullenly. "I didn't vote for him."
"This is not a democracy."
Mick had a grin a half step short of wicked on their face as they side eyed the captain. "Did a strange woman lying in a pond give you a sword?"
Cat practically purred with supressed laughter. "Nope, but he did manage to fish a nacho out of the salsa last night..." Puerty

sniggered with exactly zero subtlety.

"Can we please try and focus?" Cy was already sounding beyond tired. And he had thought his normal batch of crazies was tricky to manage. This was going to take forever.

Hounslow raised his voice above the rising chorus of nonsense, at least proving Cat's assertion right. "Alright, can someone please give me a summary of what the hell has actually been going on?"
Cat cleared her throat, dropping her voice to a dramatic tenor. "So far this season-"
"Dammit!"

The doctor smirked at her long suffering captain. "That's two credits for the swear jar."
Cat wiggled around as far as she could with the other woman still holding most of her hair, just to wave a finger in Puerty's face. "We are not bringing that cursed object back twice in one trip."

Mick leaned over to Flora, dropping their tone to a curious murmur. "Does this ever stop?"
The thief just shrugged, "Considering the sheer levels of dumbass present I get the feeling that this is going to take a while."
Cat had apparently heard, nodding then wincing sharply as Puerty tugged on her to hold still. She obliged, even whilst she added her thoughts. "True. Jerry- step outside to halve the levels of idiocy here…"

It seemed that was as much as Aurora could take, as she blasted a brief but painful flare of static over the speakers, yelling into the resulting silence. "BASICALLY! Flora pinched some rather nice stuff from a rather nasty person. By which I mean several million credits worth of precious stones, and what turned out to be the electronic copy of the patriarch's little black book. Bad move. She hopped aboard me in a bid to escape the fallout of her actions."

Ramal nodded, "Right, that sounds logical." Flora looked

askance at the engineer, trying to decide if he was mocking her or not. The others were staring at her with varying degrees of shock, not having realised that by 'thief' she had meant 'serious criminal'. Part of her wanted to reassure them, say that nobody had been hurt during the heist, that she wasn't really a bad person... but then it was because of her that they were all in danger to begin with...

Andromeda took over, "Meanwhile, Markson over there is trying to get away from his evil cabal of family members."

Cat could just about reach him with her toes when she stretched her leg to the limit to nudge his arm until he looked over at her. She offered him a crooked grin. "No judgement dude, you can't help who you are born to." It didn't seem to help his general sense of awkward nerves all that much.

The AI overrode the side comments with practiced ease. "He also decides to hop onboard Aurora." The man in question managed to direct an apologetic if somewhat queasy smile at the captain.

Hounslow was rubbing at his forehead again. "Thinking about it- do we have some sort of sign or aura or something saying 'fugitives welcome' that I don't know about? Because if so then I am clearly not getting all of my memos." Cy just snorted at his faint despair. Ramal, being closest, patted his captain's arm in what was meant to be a gesture of comfort.

"Now in an even more aggravating quirk of fate, Markson and Flora it turns out are both in trouble with the same family. That being the Cortenzas if anybody is taking notes."
Mick turned a strange shade of grey, letting out a squeak which sounded remarkably like: "Oh shit!"

Flora hunched down, as if hoping that the deck plates would open up and swallow her. Almost without realising, her fingers drummed against her prosthetic leg, a rapid tattoo against the hidden compartment. For a moment Puerty's hands stilled mid braid.

For all that none of them took a particular interest in planet based politics, there were some stories which still reached out into the black. Especially when they concerned the conglomerate of corporations and cartels which indirectly governed a large swathe of planetary governments, both legitimate and less so.

Aurora took over the recital. "Exactly. Running the shrewd family business as they do, they decided to adopt to 'two birds one stone' approach. In this case, sending Wentz to infiltrate here, confirming their presence and probably nicking back Flora's loot. That done, Jamie joined Andromeda's crew so that you would attack us, he could get Wentz back. I am guessing that he then intended to set us to be blown up or something, possibly looking like a tragic accident."

Markson and Flora glanced at each other with equal expressions of horror. The thief couldn't help but fix an entreating stare on the doctor, as if silently begging the other woman to believe that she never intended for this to happen. Markson had taken on that vaguely green hue from when the food replicators had been malfunctioning. Hounslow go the impression that he genuinely hadn't thought of what might happen as a result of him running away.

Cat snapped her fingers, suddenly lighting up as the missing piece of all the nonsense slotted into place. "Oh, so that is why he has been sabotaging us the whole way- the black box would show a history of issues on the run up to our apparent self-destruction or some such."

"Seriously?" Ramal groaned, his face clearly asking how humans came up with such idiotic ideas in the first place.

Jerry looked askance at the ceiling. "Ok, I gotta ask. How in the hell do you know all of this? I mean, it sounds like the plot to a science fiction book or something."
Cat shook her head ruefully at him. "Please, between Andromeda and Aurora there is nothing that can't be figured out. If they

wanted to, I wouldn't be surprised if they decided to take over the world. Although, if you ever did then I humbly request that I be given a well paid job serving our silicon overlords."
"Noted."

"Well, the terrifying abilities of our ships aside, I can't help but be grateful to them for putting this all together." Nodding his thanks to the camera in the corner for the AIs input, Cy leaned against the table with one hand, letting his gaze roam over each person in the room. "Ok, so with that anime worthy series of events laid out... what the hell are we supposed to do about all this?"

Hounslow cleared his throat. "First priority is: make sure that Aurora is in fact safe. Cat, you and Ramal are going to have to go over this ship with a fine tooth comb and make sure that the pair of ingrates haven't left some nasty surprises behind as a fail safe."
Cat was nodding, having already fished out a tablet and begun making notes of places to check.

Ramal climbed across the table, half stepping on Markson and ignoring the subsequent squawk of protest. Reaching Cat, he looked over her shoulder, already pointing out various points on whatever schematic she was studying. Even as his eyes were fixed on the interface he frowned as something else occurred to him. "Gonna have to do the same to Andromeda as well. I would be surprised if they intended to just let you guys fly off into the black after being anywhere near this whole mess."
"True." Cy sounded grimmer than he had in a long time.

Puerty secured her work with a sparkly bobble, taking a moment to shift back and give the engineer some more room. She still didn't look up as she spoke, instead snapping another hairband against her wrist. "Then what? That still leaves us with two would be murderers to deal with, as well as Flora and Markson still being in danger when we reach port. I mean, there's no way the Cortenzas wouldn't have sent some back up ahead by a different route, or at least sent out word of open season on the pair of them."

Eric over dramatically dropped himself down into a chair. "How did this become my life?"
Cat shot him a faintly poisonous look. "I swear, that is becoming your motto these days. And don't you dare blame any of this on me." She paused for a moment, fingers still hovering over the keyboard on her display. When she spoke again, her voice had an air of careful thought. "Well, from a purely practical point of view, all this would be a lot easier if Markson and Flora simply didn't exist any more."

Jerry looked at her with something scarily close to approval. "Wow. Harsh, but effective."
"Bite me. What I mean is: with Aurora and Andy's help it isn't too much effort to change their IDs. I mean, that was how I got into the system to begin with after all."
"Wait what?" Flora blinked in shock.

Cat barrelled on with her explanation. "So what if we did a bit of a switch up? We make them into completely different people, then we send Flora with Cy's lot. She takes Jamie's place, and we keep him here registered as our third passenger. When we reach Proxima Centauri b, we report into the navy that we found these two intentionally causing harm to ship and crew and let the authorities deal with them. Simple."

Everyone was silent for a moment, thinking through the idea. Eric met her gaze with a challenging stare.

"If you say so. But what about the Cortenzas? Sending Flora with Cy will just put them in more danger." For all that he didn't personally care for the pirates, he couldn't deny that they were obviously important to his sister.

"Not if we change the narrative."
Puerty snorted a little, "have you been re-watching Hamilton again?"
Cat didn't respond to the comment, although Flora it seemed

as also heard, given by the way that she smirked a little at the reference. The doctor pointedly ignored the response. Cat internally rolled her eyes at the ongoing feud, even as she refocused on what she was saying.

"What if word got out that it was actually Wentz who stole from the family, and he planned to meet up with Jamie so they could run off? I mean, it wouldn't be too much of a stretch for people to think they intended to form their own faction or something, and used Markson's defection as cover to make their move. After all, their family is known for being cut throat."
Flora snorted. "Literally."

Puerty was nodding along, "So, Flora and Markson become less tempting targets."
Markson finally spoke up, "Hopefully being completely forgotten in the shuffle of two apparent traitors being arrested by the navy red handed."

Flora looked at Cat, faintly uncomfortable. "Isn't that... a bit ruthless? I mean, getting them arrested is one thing, but you are painting a target on their backs..."
The girl just stared at her with complete calm. When she spoke her tone was flatter than she had used for quite some time. "Why would that be a problem? They intended to hurt us. This is the most logical course."

For a moment Hounslow looked faintly pained. He forgot sometimes how cold her anger was when someone threatened those she thought of as family. From the corner of his eye he could see Cy watching her with something close to approval.

Ramal's sigh cut the under running tension, rediverting attention. "As plans go it's..."
The sudden smile on Cat's face was a complete switch to her bubbly side. "Pure genius?"
Jerry cut in with a sneer. "Pure insanity. Absolutely ridiculous."
Puerty kept her eyes on Hounslow. "Our best chance."
Cy just smirked. "It might even work."

Eric sighed. "Unfortunately, all true statements."

CHAPTER 28- FOLLOW THE GOLDEN RULE

As far as cells went, they weren't exactly being held in Fort Knox. Since Aurora was a cargo transport, she didn't come equipped with a proper brig. Instead, Wentz and Jamie had been locked in one of the spare storge rooms which would normally hold sensitive electronics. As such it was possibly the most secure space aboard, not counting the data core.

That being the case, it was also remarkably cramped. The pair had been somewhat grudgingly given a couple of roll mats so they weren't sitting directly on the floor, but beyond that comfort hadn't been a priority.

Markson approached the room with heavy steps and faintly shaking hands. The Roomba standing guard chirped a welcome to him, even though it didn't move from its assigned spot by the door. He cleared his throat somewhat awkwardly, "Umm, excuse me?"

The unit gave a whirring bleep which he took as a positive response.

"Would it be alright if I had a word with the prisoners?"

The unit seemed to hesitate for a moment. "It's alright Roger. He can have a word." The voice of the ship's AI almost made Markson jump out of his skin.

Slightly frantically, he scanned around until he caught sight of the camera in the corner, directing his words to the ship instead.

"Oh, um, are you sure?"

"Yes, Cat told me to let you say whatever you need to. I will engage a two way channel for you, and feel free to look through the window in the door- the catch for the cover is on the top."

"Uh, thank you."

With permission granted, the Roomba glided a couple of feet away, although it stayed within sight of the door. Figuring that was as much privacy as he could hope for, he took the AI's advice and lowered the cover on the window. The inmates had clearly heard someone coming, the pair of them glaring out at him.

Wentz spoke first, and it seemed like he had dropped his cultured yet whiny tone. It was almost jarring to hear the accent of Markson's home from a man he had thought he knew at least a little. It was rather remarkable how well it had been hidden. He knew that his own efforts had made him sound like he was speaking around a mouthful of marbles. In the end he had given up trying to disguise his voice, figuring it was drawing more attention than just speaking normally would have.

"What do you want?"

Markson's hands still shook, and he was glad that they couldn't see it through the door. "I could ask the same thing of you."

Jamie snorted, cocking an eyebrow from where he stayed resolutely sprawled on the floor. "I'm sure you have come up with a theory by now."

He took a deep breath, "Of course, I just find it a bit hard to swallow. Surely you didn't really intend to destroy this ship, everybody aboard? All for the sake of collecting some lost property." It was something he just couldn't wrap his head around. True, he was well aware of just how... shady... his family's business practices tended to be. Hell, he knew that he had been remarkably sheltered in terms of facing the consequences of his upbringing. Even running away was less altruistic than perhaps the other people aboard ship realised. It wasn't so much that he couldn't stomach the darker side of doing business, just that he fundamentally didn't want to follow in his family's footsteps. Even so, the whole thing just seemed so... ridiculous. Was a minor inconvenience really worth such a heavy handed response?

Jamie raised himself up on one elbow, fixing him with an unimpressed look. "That wasn't our only reason."
the realisation settled somewhere in his stomach, a heavy weight which was sadly not tinged with surprise. "You meant to kill me after all?" his tone was more resigned than he thought it would be.

Wentz at least offered a one sided shrug. "Well, the boss did say that he would prefer you to be brought in alive- examples must be made of course. But if that proved overly problematic, then he would understand our position."
"I... I want to say I can't believe it but..." was it really such a big deal? All he had wanted was to break away, find a new way of living which didn't rely on his family's connections. For all his life his father had gone on about how he had made his own way, surely he would be proud of him for doing the same thing.

Jamie's scoff interrupted his internal freak out. "Oh please, you are not that naïve."
"No. I guess not." Markson spoke softly, not meeting the gaze of either man in the cell.

Wentz cut back in, half laughing with studied nonchalance. "It's almost funny you know- if it hadn't been for that thief then you might have made a clean getaway. But with two things happening so close together, well it just looked far too much like weakness to let you go."

Markson scowled, turning to lean his back against the door as he tried to sort out all his thoughts.

All at once Wentz was right next to the window, almost pressing against the door from his side, voice dropping to a conspiratorial murmur. "You still have a chance you know, there is always a way out. For all that you are a target, if you prove that you mean no malice to the family then you might be able to get out cleanly."

Markson half turned, unable to hide the faint flicker of curious hope. "What are you talking about?"

The other man scoffed, taking on a tone as if speaking to a small child. "Don't be dense. I just told you that the boss can't afford two disrespectful incidents at once. But, if you were to help us out, make sure that we get our primary target, well then, we can report back that you aren't in fact hostile to the family."

Markson's eyes widened as the implications sunk in. Wentz continued, one hand pressed against the glass as if wanting to reach out and hold his arm. "Just think of it from the outside perspective. You will have shown a remaining loyalty to the family, even if you don't wish to stay with the main branch. You father can work with that, say that you came to a mutual agreement. It all gets cleaned up, and you don't have to be looking over your shoulder for the rest of your life."

He could almost see it in his minds eye. It did make sense after all, in a rather brutal way. In honesty sneaking out the way that he had might not have been the best impression to leave but speaking to his father had always been rather terrifying. It was true that actions poke louder than words, especially with the way that their family did business. He just wanted to be left alone.

Jamie had stood up now as well, standing just behind Wentz's shoulder and staring out with almost feverish intensity. "Come on- that thief means nothing to you. She is just a random stranger who happened to pick the same ship."

That was a thought. But then, "What about the crews?" After all they were innocent in all this, just the wrong place at the wrong time. His father would no doubt call them collateral damage, but there didn't seem any logical reason for this to get so messy.

"What about them?"

He turned more fully to stare down Wentz.

"Seriously? Ugh, fine we will take care with the crew, and not hurt anyone unless they hurt us first." He raised on finger in emphasis. "At least of the pirate's ship. We might need to be harsher with this lot since the Captain has a naval background. But, if they are open to a bit of negotiation, then there is no reason why they would get hurt." His hands were spread magnanimously, his voice was steadily reasonable.

Silence fell between them. Markson tilted his head back until it rested against the cool wall, eyes fixed unseeing on the ceiling. It was a lot to think about, and as much as he would like to dismiss anything two would be murderers suggested out of hand, and the end of the day it did make more sense than he would have expected. They were just doing their jobs, reporting success back to the boss was their priority. If there was a way to get out of this with minimal risk and maximum freedom...

Wentz hummed, the sound just about being picked up by the speakers. "I won't push you for an answer now, of course you will need time to think it all through properly. You at least got that much sense from your father."

Markson turned properly to look them both in the eye. Jamie gave him a half smile and a nod, as if they were just two associates meeting in an office. "Let us know what you decide. After all, we have no where else to be right now."

The cover for the window slid smoothly back into place with barely a snick of the latch being secured. For a long moment Markson stood there, staring at the door. When he hadn't moved for a minute, the Roomba rolled over, nudging lightly at his foot. Startling, he seemed to shake himself out of his revery, reaching down to pat the casing as he had seen the ship's cat do so many times.

With a brief nod of thanks to Aurora's camera, he spun on his heel, marching back down the way he had come.

CHAPTER 29- CAN YOU TRY TO HEAR ME?

F lora was standing just inside the doorway to the infirmary, pleading with the lab coated figure who hadn't once
turned around since she entered. "Puerty! Come on, I
need to talk to you." She took another step closer, eyeing the
low beam with wry memory. How long ago it seemed that she
had walked straight into it whilst quacking. It didn't feel like
only three months.

The doctor didn't so much as twitch, staying glued to her
screen. "Now is not a good time. I'm working." Her tone was
frosty enough to chill beer, posture unrelenting. It was a far cry
from the softer side that Flora had gotten so used to seeing, so
comfortable being with.

She huffed, folding her arms and tilting her chin petulantly. The
effect was somewhat wasted as her audience made no motions
to turn. "Seriously?" Damn but she was much more stubborn
than she had expected.

"Yes. So go away." Puerty's voice was flat, and still she didn't
move. Her shoulders were as rigid as Aurora's deck plates.

For a moment Flora just glared at the other woman's back, as if
willing her lab coat to just catch fire or something. What was
the chance that unrealised telepathic abilities would surface?
Eventually she heaved an exaggerated sigh, going to far as to
stomp her metal foot. A small part of her was pretty sure that

Aurora was eavesdropping and snickering at her antics. "Fine. Fine!"

Unable to resist, against her better judgement and determination, the doctor half turned to watch her leave. A second later she could only gape in shock as the thief drew back a fist and with full force decked herself. The smack was almost disturbingly loud, and drew out a half choked yelp.

Puerty sat in place, frozen for a split second and she just stared with open mouth and wide eyes. Meeting her gaze, Flora held her eye as she resolutely refused to wipe at the blood which began to seep down one cheek.

The doctor was on her feet so fast it was as if she had been electrocuted, darting across the space and tilting her chin towards the light for a better look. "Oh my god you did not just punch yourself in the face!" There was a small gash curving along her cheek, torn by her ring, and the whole cheek was already turning red.

Flora winced as she grinned in triumph. "Doctor, I am injured and need medical attention."

She growled almost sub-vocally, finally giving up and motioning for Flora to sit on the patient bed. "I swear to any and all gods that are listening..."

It seemed that with her goal of breaking through the doctor's silence achieved, she had run into a stumbling block of not knowing what to say next. Puerty wasn't exactly helping, dabbing antiseptic on the cut with complete professional detachment.

"You know, I get why you didn't tell me. Really, I do. Frankly, everybody has shit that they don't want to share. But you know what stung? The fact that I told you that. I told you that if you wanted to share I would listen, that I wouldn't make you talk if you weren't ready. You are who you are. I get that. So you not saying anything is not the issue."

She steamrolled straight over the other woman before she

could do more than stammer. With clinical efficiency she applied a small plaster to the wound, just to be sure. "What hurt, the reason I am pissed at you, is that you didn't even give me the chance. You just summarily decided how I felt about you, and rather than giving even a half-hearted explanation, or hell just telling me to leave it alone, you shut down the whole relationship."

With the cut staunched, she leaned away again. Ruthlessly she tore the gloves from her hands, throwing them with uncanny accuracy into the waste recycling unit. When she spoke again, it was with her eyes fixed firmly on the wall opposite.

"And you know what else? I am mad at myself! I mean, I am a grown ass woman, a professional with a life and career. So why the hell am I letting this get to me so much? This isn't me! I don't do this, and I needed to remind myself of that. Perhaps it is because we have been living in such close quarters, but people don't fall this hard and this fast and have it last. I know that. So I am aggravated at my own stupidity. And yours."

Flora had leaned forwards as the doctor spoke, one hand rising almost of its own accord in a faintly helpless gesture. She wanted to say something, anything. The words caught in her throat, too many years of too many secrets and the voice in the back of her head reminding her that the only way to keep a secret is if nobody else knows.

For a handful or heartbeats there was pure silence in the infirmary.

The doctor's shoulders all at once relaxed, the breath she hadn't been aware of holding leaving on big gust. When she turned back around, it was with a small, rueful smile. It didn't reach her eyes.

"Now, if you don't mind, it is only a couple of days until we reach the outer markers for Proxima Centauri b. I have rather a lot of things to get in order by then, not least of which is fixing up your new files. Don't let the door hit you on your way out."

CHAPTER 30- THE FORK IN THE ROAD

There was tension in the air as the crews gathered in the cargo hold. Aurora's people stood further in, closer to the stairs, not including the two who were still in their version of a brig, or Markson who had opted to stay out of the way. Andromeda's congregated next to the emergency airlock, Flora shifting from foot to foot at the edge of the group.

She had managed to corner Puerty briefly as they all trooped down to the cargo bay. She had been hesitant, having more than she could say right on the tip of her tongue. All she managed to blurt out as they loitered in the gap between a couple of pallets was, "My new name is going to be Matilda." She said it with a slightly pained laugh, the sound harsh even to her own ears. Internally she was cursing up a storm. This wasn't how this was supposed to go.

Puerty actually looked at her directly, the first time in what felt like an eternity. Even so, there was no real expression on her face as she spoke. "That was my favourite book as a little girl."

Her smile was too bright and brittle, the tone too desperate, "I remember. You liked how strong willed she was."
"Right."

The silence between them was jagged, and it was almost a relief when Cy hollered at her to hurry up and move it before they left her there after all.

It turned out that the secondary access was where the pirates had managed to break in from, connecting a repurposed emergency salvage tunnel to link the ships. Cat had laughed when they admitted it. The idea had been hers back in the day after all.

She was standing between the two groups, at ease with them all and apparently treating the whole thing along the lines of an unexpected but welcome joint family holiday. Mick grinned at her over their captain's shoulder, giving an enthusiastic thumbs up and smacking Jerry upside the head when all he did was scowl.

Hounslow had the good grace not to even twitch as Cy stepped forwards, pulling the girl into a bear hug which she returned happily. It turned into a brief wrestling match of sorts, which he won as he just scooped her up off the floor altogether. Laughing, she punched him lightly on the shoulder, making a show of trying to wiggle free.

"Put me down you great lummox!"
"Hmm, sounds like there is a mouse around here whose parachute won't open."
"Git!"

After a few moments more, he somewhat reluctantly loosened his grip, setting her gently back on her feet. He kept both hands on her shoulders, holding her at arms length to stare seriously into her eyes. "Now you listen here Casey, I won't say what has already been sorted, but I just want you to know that no matter what happens, you can always call on us. You hear? Hell, even if nothing happens, we would still love to hear more of how you get on. Alright?"

She actually had to blink rapidly for a moment, swallowing hard before deciding not to say anything. She nodded instead, offering up a slightly watery smile. It seemed he was equally affected, coughing harshly before crushing her close once again.

They stayed that way for several moments.

Then Cat loosened her hold, stepping back towards Hounslow and the rest. Cy nodded in satisfaction, turning to make his way back to his own crew. Andromeda was about to give the all clear, when suddenly Flora stopped.

One eyebrow raised in half amusement, Cy gave her a rye look, muttering something under his breath which sounded suspiciously like, "about time."

The woman flushed a little at hearing it, even as she lifted her chin proudly, stepping into the no mans land in the middle of the cargo hold. Cat felt Puerty half freeze behind her, and slipped a hand back to hold the doctor's in solidarity. For all that she could feel the faint tremors Puerty still kept her head high, pointedly not looking away.

The thief took a deep breath, grounding herself and standing in near military parade rest. "Listen here!" The sudden volume made Ramal jump, and if it was attention she was after it was definitely successful. She turned her gaze fully on Puerty who looked half a step away from just legging it back up the walkway.

"I have feelings for you, and it is time I acknowledged them!"

Puerty let out a faintly strangled yelp, freezing like a deer in the headlights as her brain tried to process this turn of events. Cat whispered a faint, "oh my Coder", sounding far too gleeful. Ramal was bug eyed, mouthing OTP. She decided that she needed new friends. Hounslow was watching the whole thing with nothing short of amusement and satisfaction.

Flora ignored them all, focussing entirely on the now crimson doctor. Said doctor hissed furiously as Cat pulled her forwards, stopping her from just hiding behind her crew mate. A slight scuffle later and Puerty relented as her friend made it clear that if the tension between them wasn't resolved she would get creative.

Finally standing opposite the other woman, she waved at her to continue. With one hand drumming on her prosthetic, Flora swallowed hard. "Right. Well, here it is." She cleared her throat. "Oh shit I have completely forgotten what I was going to say... I had a whole speech... whatever. Ok. Puerty, you are absolutely the most frustrating woman I have ever met."

Cat leaned over to Ramal, "I think she needs a crash course in making nice."

She barrelled on, "and I say that because nothing that I try around you turns out the way I want it to. I mean, I had a whole plan about how I was doing one last score and then legging it into the black to start a new life. And instead I chose this crazy ship and met you."

Another deep breath, steeling herself as the doctor showed no signs of relenting. "I'm sorry, truly. I never meant to hurt you. And yeah, in hindsight knowing that you already knew what I was so afraid to tell you, I feel like a prize idiot. But more than that, you were right. I could have just said I wasn't ready to share and I know you would have respected that. I should have given you the same benefit of the doubt."

Puerty's arms had slowly uncrossed, posture easing as she spoke more than any of them had ever heard in one go.

"So, even though I am going off with a pirate crew to try and save my own skin because of my mistakes, I didn't want to add another regret to the great big mound of rubbish that I carry around with me. Puerty, I really like you, and I want the chance to get to know you properly. Would that be alright with you? And I promise, if you say no and that you don't want to get involved then I won't blame you at all. You are a wonderful person who deserves everything they want and I fully respect your decision."

Complete silence fell over the hold as all eyes were fixed on the pair. Flora seemed to have run out of words, mouth clicking shut as she stood practically thrumming with tension. Cat and

Ramal were clutching at each other's hands, eyes wide as they waited to see what would happen. Cy's lot seemed to be regretting not having brought popcorn along.

At last, Puerty shifted. She began fidgeting around, patting at her pockets and cursing until she managed to dredge up a pen and a scrap of paper. Balancing somewhat awkwardly on one leg, she used her other knee as a makeshift desk, scribbling furiously for a handful of seconds.

Straightening back up, she pulled herself together and walked right up to Flora. She seemed to hold her breath, staring intently into her face, before letting a small grin flit across her features. With what was possibly supposed to be a flirty wink, she slipped the paper into Flora's shirt pocket.
"That's my personal comm. Number. Give me a buzz, we should go out some time."

With complete poise, she went up on tiptoes, pressing a brief kiss to Flora's cheek. Still smiling, she turned and sashayed away, waving a goodbye to rest of the pirates as she headed up the walkway and out of sight.

Flora was rooted to the spot, one hand coming up to cup her cheek with a faintly dazed expression. It slowly gave way to a blinding grin. With far more cheer than any of them had ever seen from her, she offered Aurora's crew a jaunty wave, half skipping back to Andromeda's.

Laughing softly they opened the emergency airlock, stepping into the tunnel with minimal jostling. Cy was the last in, turning once more to grin back at Cat and shake his head at her inevitable bringing of chaos into his life. The hatch sealed behind them with a comforting finality. A few minutes later Aurora confirmed their safe disconnection, and Andromeda heading out into the black once again.

For a moment the rest just stayed where they were, processing through what had just gone on. Then Cat turned to Ramal with a sharp grin. "You, my friend, owe me twenty credits."

"What? No way!" His voice went high in outrage.

She folded her arms unrelentingly. "Yes way- I bet you that they would get together before the end of this trip."
He scoffed and shook his head, mirroring her stance. "But they didn't!"
She wagged a finger in his face. "They did, twice arguably."

"Oh come on."
"I'm serious. They got together, then broke up, and we just saw them get together again." She grinned triumphantly, only to scowl as he refused to give ground.
"No, they danced around each other but were never anything official, then they broke it off, and that was the sight of a future get together- not a confirmed relationship. So, you owe *me* twenty credits."

Aurora chipped in, sounding almost unbearably smug, "Well Cat, at least you were right about me getting satisfaction out of the whole situation."
The girl turned a threatening glare at the ceiling, "Don't you go picking sides now!"

Hounslow rolled his eyes at the pair of them, leaving them to their bickering and instead heading up to the walkway. It would probably be best for him to check in on Puerty and make sure she hadn't had a heart attack or something.

CHAPTER 31- THE END IS NIGH

I f you didn't know exactly where you were aiming for, it was surprisingly easy to miss the approach to Proxima Centauri b. It was something that people didn't often realise, but space is BIG. As in huge, massive, beyond human comprehension. Those who had tried more often than not were sent mad by a glimpse of just how horrifically insignificant they truly were.

Such things were the realm of gods and monsters, and only human hubris keep us from flying apart at the seams of our psyches.

The outer level of planetary approach was marked by nothing more than a widely spaced series of markers. Little more than basic transponders with small engines to keep them in the correct positions, their appearance on the star map was a welcome sight. Once you crossed the line you were once again within reach of civilisation, however basic that could prove to be. The markers sent directions to all ships to ensure that they would safely navigate the gravity wells of the system, as well as recording all those who entered and exited the area. For the time that you were within the network, you once again existed in a very real sense.

All of which was to say, when Aurora confirmed that they had in fact managed to enter the shipping lane leading to their final destination, the news was met with universal sighs of relief.

Well, perhaps not universal, but as far as the crew were concerned they were one step closer to the end of one of the hardest trips of their careers. And that included the time they ran the asteroid belts for hazard pay.

The announcement was piped throughout the ship's intercom, making its way to all those left aboard.

From deep in engineering, Ramal rested his head for a moment in relief against one of the fuel tanks. Throughout all the drama he had been mildly terrified that the saboteur would target Aurora's hard systems. Since the revelations of just how much trouble they were in, he had been steadfastly going over every nut and bolt to make sure no damage had been done or devices left behind. So far all had been clear, but he was taking no chances. After all, their lives rested on his observation skills. It would be agonising if they all got blown up or explosively decompressed so close to the end.

Cat barely looked up from her own project as the marker was passed, instead squinting with her organic eye at the mess of circuits on her work bench. She kept a running commentary of what she was doing, explaining it all to the Roomba by her elbow which was holding her soldering iron. Ever since her unfortunate incident with the stairs, the little units had become mildly obsessive with ensuring that she was never left unguarded.

She was pretty sure that Rhonda had organised them all into a working society wherein her protectors were near the top of the pecking order. At the very least they seemed to be greeted respectfully by the others as they came off duty. She was leaving it be, after all how they chose to live was on them.

As the news of their nearing to the end came through, Puerty couldn't help but stare out at the black beyond the window. Andromeda had left them just before they hit the outer markers, ensuring that the ship would not be logged anywhere close to occupied space. She could almost convince herself that she could still see the transponder lights of the other craft. Utter nonsense of course. There was only the filtered glare from the system's primary star.

Even so, she couldn't help but give her comm a quick glance, just in case there was a message waiting. There wouldn't be of course, not this soon. Besides, there was always the chance that a transmission would be picked up by some piece of hardware out there. Space after all wasn't so empty in these parts. That didn't stop her looking again five minutes later.

Down in the make shift brig, Wentz and Jamie shared a tense staring contest with the door, breath bated. They had placed their bet, and no matter what else may have happened on the ship since their discovery, neither was of the habit of giving up before it was all over. They had been picked for this mission for a reason, and there was something to be said for protecting a reputation. It was only a matter of time.

One person onboard the ship did not seem positively affected by the news.

Markson was pacing the length of his cabin. Eight paces forward, eight back. He must have gone several kilometres by this point. His hair, which had grown out somewhat over the last three months, was now a harshly tangled nest as he once again dragged his hand through it. The habit was one which his family had always tried to get him to stop. It was why his hair had been cut short in the first place. Such displays of emotion were not suitable for an heir to the Cadenza empire.

His conversation with his father's men was playing on a loop in his head.

It had been with almost giddy relief that he had watched Andromeda leave from the observation window, with the thief safely stowed aboard. He could almost convince himself that he simply hadn't made up his mind in time, the decision had been taken out of his hands. But the more he thought it, the more he knew that was just a comforting lie. No way his father would ever accept an excuse like that.

Aurora's crew were still set on their previously agreed plan, to pin all the blame for what had happened on the shoulders of the men in the brig. They would be turned over as a pair of passengers who had intentionally hurt ship and crew. There was of course a law enforcement outpost on Prox who would be more than happy to have something to do besides the normal for a remote colony outpost.

The navy would no doubt discover their links to the Cardenzas, whilst anyone less reputable would soon spread the news that they had been traitors themselves. It was fine, justice would be done to two genuinely bad people and all would carry on in the universe. Simple.

And yet. He couldn't help but think- what if it doesn't stick? There were so many things which could go wrong after all. What if the navy didn't buy it? What if one of his father's men got to them and believed when they told the truth? What if they squirreled out of it at the last moment? He would be twice as much of a target at that point. Already he had lost a major bargaining chip by not handing over the thief.

He was almost convinced that his heart was going to pound its way out of his chest. His thoughts were just spinning far too fast, he could practically feel his father's hand closing on his shoulder to drag him back home.

His head snapped up, a new light burning in his eye. It wasn't a risk he could afford, not when he had come so far. These people had been kind to him, true, but he had only known them for three months. His escape from his old life had been planned for so much longer, and if there was one things that had been drilled into him over the years, it was to always look out for number one. Priorities.

By the time he marched back down to the cargo bay, Wentz and Jamie were already standing beside the door once again. They both grinned as he stopped on the other side of the glass, glaring at them both with folded arms.

"You both know what is going to happen when we reach port?" Wentz waved a hand airily, for all that his eyes were hard as steel. "Oh, probably something along the lines of our arrest and taking the fall for all that has gone on. I mean, I would be frankly disappointed if we weren't accused of betraying your family so as to cover for the thief. After all, she just needs to get far enough away that tracking her becomes a waste of resources. Us being branded as traitors would be a sufficient smoke screen, even if anybody with half a brain wouldn't believe it."

Markson couldn't supress a slight wince at his words, looking down and to the side in anger.

Jamie grinned, feral wide. "Aah, that is what has brought you down to us. You know that it won't stick." He snickered, "Clever boy. Looks like you haven't forgotten all the lessons of your upbringing."

Markson looked faintly queasy at the jab, even as he straightened up once again. "Give me some credit. I know that you are some of my father's best men." He scoffed half heartedly. "Hell, considering his reputation we may even be cousins or something."

Wentz hummed, shrugging one shoulder elegantly. "Well, it has always been a family business. So, tell us, what is it you are proposing exactly?"

Markson cast a shifty glare at Aurora's nearest camera, deliberately turning his body to block the view of his face as his voice became little more than a murmur. "Look, I still don't want you to hurt anybody on this ship. They were never meant to be involved. So, instead you are going to go after that thief and the pirates she is travelling with."

Jamie was watching him closely, one eyebrow raised. "If I remember rightly, she already exited stage left whilst we are stuck here in pride of place."

"Look, this ship has a couple of pods for when she is sitting in orbit or near to a station without sufficient berths. I overhead the maintenance officer boasting about how she has boosted their capabilities to be almost equal to that of full sized ships. If I get you out, you take one of them, and head off after the real target."

Wentz stroked his chin in exaggerated contemplation. Markson hissed in frustration. "Look, we don't have a lot of time. You both know that we already hit the outer markers. We get any closer to port and you won't stand a chance. Even when you get out of trouble with the navy, and my father, by that point she will be out of your reach." He wondered if he sounded as desperate as he felt.

Jamie smiled rapier sharp. "Or we could just give him you. After all, the target list wasn't of just one name."

He scoffed with false bravado. "Please, I am secondary news at best. I have brothers who can take my place, hell I have sisters who would do a better job than the rest of us combined. I am small fry, and I am happy with that. He would probably just send you out in pursuit again anyway."

"Hmm, you are doing this just to save yourself aren't you. This way we can report that you cooperated."

"Well, it was your suggestion in the first place."

"True. True. Alright then, you have yourself a deal."

He couldn't help but wonder which of them was the devil in this instance.

CHAPTER 33- HELL HATH NO FURY

As Markson approached the bridge, he was assaulted by a whirling maelstrom of sounds. Alarms were blaring at top volume, and between that and all the yelling it was enough to make anyone wince. Cat was half buried underneath the communication console grappling furiously with a waterfall of multicoloured wires. Captain Hounslow was frantically jabbing at buttons on his main view screen, flicking his way through alerts which were pinging rapid fire from all corners.

"Cat! What in the hell is happening?"
She craned her head around at a painful angle, glaring briefly at him before vanishing once again. Her voice echoed slightly off the panels of the station she seemed to be dismantling with ruthless efficiency. "Coder help me I need more than two seconds to figure that out when literally every alarm in the place is going off at once!"

Hounslow cursed, running one hand through his hair and turning to glare at the nearest camera. "Aurora?"
The AI sounded close to her equivalent of tears. "Someone has hacked my bloody circuits again!"

Puerty snarled from where she was frantically tracking through the info being spat out of the navigation console. "Dammit, looks like the pair of asshats escaped and hijacked one of our transport pods."

The Captain gaped at her for a moment. "Seriously? How could that even happen?" He growled, turning to fix a laser eyed stare on Cat's boots. "What did you do?"

She clearly knew she was the target for the comment despite still being out of his eyeline. "Me? Nothing! Why would I do something to help them? If anything I want them to suffer for all the shit that they have been pulling."

Hounslow moved, rising from his chair and moving over to loom over her station. "That is kind of precisely my point." He hesitated briefly, before forcing himself to voice a thought he clearly didn't want to "I know you weren't completely onboard with us just giving them over for getting arrested. And with your past..."

Cat emerged at that, wrench held aloft and screwdriver tucked behind her ear. It did nothing to detract from the outraged expression on her face. "Really? You are throwing that in my face now?" She scoffed when he didn't respond, rolling her eyes in disgust. "Fine, whatever. No this wasn't on me."

Markson cleared his throat, right at the moment that the alarms were finally cut even though the strobe lights continued to flash. All gazes were drawn in the brief moment of silence which followed. "She's right. Cat didn't do anything." His voice was as steady as a rock, even as his raised hand shook despite his best efforts.

Puerty was the first to react, slowly moving until the console was between her and the muzzle of the gun. "Woah, where did you get that?"
He actually laughed a little. For all his bravado, he had only been able to get his hands on what amounted to a fancy flare gun, but it would serve its purpose for now. "Come on, it wasn't hard to figure out where the emergency equipment would be stashed. I don't want to hurt anybody."

Hounslow shifted slightly, freezing as he pointed the tool at him. "Then put down the gun."

"I can't do that, not yet." He shook his head, sweaty hand tightening around the handle. "See, I need for Wentz and Jamie to get clear of your reach. So, for the time being, you are all just going to sit back and do nothing." It sounded so reasonable when it said that, after all, he just wanted a way to get their attention, and this was the easiest.

Cat was staring at him with wide eyes, suddenly looking younger than he thought she really was. "Coder's sake, why are you doing this? I thought... you said you wanted to just get away free and clear, leave your old life behind." She tried to move closer, only to be blocked as Hounslow swayed to use his body as a shield.

Markson swallowed painfully, hoping that they could all read the anguish on his face. "I do! That is exactly why this is necessary. I know my family ok, and your plan would never have worked. I don't want what they had planned for me, but I also never wanted to cause so much trouble. This way, I can show that there is no ill will on my side, and everyone ends up happy."

Hounslow butted in, voice low and tightly controlled. "Except for Flora, and the crew of Andromeda. They will all get hurt."
Markson squared his shoulders, willing his hands to just hold still for a few seconds. "Not to sound callous, but they are not my concern."

For a moment it was stalemate, nobody moving, all eyes fixed on one desperate man. And then a chuckle broke through the silence. Markson flinched at the sound, eyes going wide. He knew that noise, would recognise it anywhere.

The main view screen flickered to life, a man appearing on the screen who was painfully recognisable. He smiled wide, leaning back in his office chair with an air of satisfaction. "It seems I underestimated you, my son."
His hand lowered of its own accord, his head spinning. "Fa-father?"

With his image so large on the viewer, it was possible to see the family resemblance. As he had grown, Markson had been told more and more often how much he resembled his father. He remembered his mother tilting his head to one side, murmuring in satisfaction that he had his father's chin.

The man in question seemed to be evaluating the people on the bridge, eyes jumping across them all before settling back on the stunned face of his son. "Hmm, I guess things are a bit more complicated than I thought."

His words refused to come, sticking in his throat no matter how hard he swallowed. "I... what do...?" Distantly he noticed that even though he was no longer waving the flare gun around, nobody had made a move to subdue him.

His father looked at him with faint disappointment. "Come on son, you seem to be making a point of thinking everything through. Although even I didn't expect to get hailed by the ship which you were trying to run away on." The last bit was directed towards Cat, who he eyed with something close to curiosity.

She wore an expression which could not be mistaken as a smile. There were far too many teeth on display for that. "I aim to keep people on their toes."

Delicately, she placed her wrench on top of the half destroyed console, deftly swaying out of Hounslow's reach. She was wearing paint splattered, purple overalls, a pair of sparkly cat ears peeking out from her hair. Somehow she was giving off an aura of simmering rage and power as she moved to stand directly in front of the image of the Cadenza patriarch.

"Now that we have your attention, it is time that we finished this once and for all." Her tone was brisk as she folded her arms, back straight and proud. "Mr Cadenza, do you recognise that your son has no ill will, but rather just a bit of an escape complex."

He looked mildly amused at her summary of the situation, eyeing her up before nodding slowly. "I do. Perhaps I over reacted at first, but then it is more often than not a case of someone intending to over throw or murder." He spread his hands magnanimously, "You understand?"

Her answering nod was sharp. "Completely. As that is not the case, are you willing to just let it go already?" Markson didn't think he had ever heard someone use that tone with his father before.

The novelty value seemed to be putting the man into a good mood, a faint smile dancing at the corner of his mouth. "I suppose that is reasonable." He turned back to his son, casting a fond eye on him for the first time that he could remember. "You have too much of me in you really, too head strong for your own good."

Cat overrode any response he might have tried to make, padding silently on her bare feet until she was next to Puerty, glaring at both Cadenzas. "Fabulous. Touching. Markson, if we promise not to pursue that pod, will you put down the gun and agree to cause no more problems for the rest of this trip?"

He blinked at her for a moment. Would it really be so simple? He narrowed his eyes a little. "I have your word?"
She stared him dead in the eye. "Yes."
For all of ten seconds he just stood there, running through the possible angles in his head. It was seeing his father's interest on the screen that decided him. "Alright then."

Moving with careful slowness, he reached out, and placed the flare gun on top of the navigation console. The doctor snatched it up, checking the safety and stowing it out of sight in a matter of heartbeats. It was with intense relief for all that the weapon vanished.

Cat clapped her hands, the sharp sound making everybody jump. "Wonderful. Now, if I could direct everybody's attention to the main view screen." They obliged, blinking as Aurora split the screen in half. Whilst Markson's father was still present, the rest of the space had been taken up by a new display. Against a background of black a marker flashed with a steady green light, following the lightly traced path of red indicating a vector in relation to Aurora. It was just possible to see the ship lane markers, picked out as orange dots pulsing in the black. For all that they were on approach to the planet which was not yet in range to be displayed with the map, this region of space was surprisingly empty.

"See that? That is the pod." Cat pointed to the green with a flourish of a screwdriver. Hounslow was half surprised that she didn't accidentally stab the screen. All eyes turned to it, including Candeza's, confirming that she was channelling the feed across that connection as well.

Her face dropped into an expression so hard it was almost frightening. A sudden stream of numbers flashed across the screen, floating above the pod light. The light itself had begun to blink, almost as if the pixels on the screen were having some sort of seizure. Then they simply went out. "And there it goes." Her tone held no inflection, an almost robotic statement of a fact.

For a handful of heartbeats everybody froze. It was a different stillness to when Markson had his flare gun. This was something sharper, heavier, as if half the oxygen in the room had just been sucked out of an airlock. Cadenza was frozen on screen, and it was nothing to do with a connection issue. Markson could only speak in a hoarse whisper. "What?"

Puerty was the first to move, stepping closer to where Cat was coolly surveying the now clear star scape. She licked her lips, eyeing her friend with wary trepidation. "What just happened?!"

The maintenance officer spread her hands in exaggerated bemusement, her face a parody of innocent shock. Her voice was an affected falsetto which made Hounslow want to wince. "Alas, they unfortunately picked the one pod with severe engineering issues. If only they hadn't tried to travel so far. Catastrophic failure it looks like. Tragic." For all that her head was shaking in demonstrable sorrow, her eyes were nothing less than flinty.

Cadenza finally found his voice, seeming more shaken that she had expected such a ruthless businessman to be capable of. Perhaps it was simply the shock value. Got to keep an audience on its toes after all. "You just, you-"
Markson wore an expression of pure outrage, "You just killed two people in cold blood."
Her face could have been cared from rock, "God may judge me but his sins outnumber my own."

She tutted, cross her arms and leaning all her weight on one foot. The other was tapping soundlessly against the deck plates, a faint movement flickering at the corner of Puerty's eye. Cat glared around at them all, focussing in on Markson and his father. "Please. Give me some credit. You have all been so far up your own backsides, betrayal this and vendetta that. May I remind you that violence for violence is the rule of beasts. That aside, you completely forgot the most fundamental fact of this whole venture." The words were venomous, spat out like they left a bad taste.

Cadenza took a breath, "Which is?" There was an icy curiosity to the question. It was the sort of tone which told you no matter what you offered it would not be a sufficient excuse.
She smiled in response, and it somehow was more frightening that her scowl. She levelled a finger at the screen. "This is my ship. These are my family. And you do not mess with what I claim. If the world chooses to become my enemy, I will fight just like I always have."

As she spoke his face had grown stormy, the sheer surprise of her actions being slowly over rode by the seething anger at her audacity. "Do you have any idea who you are messing with?"
She met him glare for glare, all pretence of civility gone. "Do

you? I mean, it has been a while since we ran in the same circles, this big bro of mine," she cocked a thumb at where Hounslow sat motionless in the captain's chair, "does so like keeping me on the straight and narrow. Even so, surely Catanski is a name which still holds some weight when it matters."

He stiffened, staring hard at her for a moment as if he could will his thoughts to reach through the monitor and into her brain. Whatever he was looking for, something clearly struck a chord. He slumped ever so slightly, an immense tiredness taking over his features before he smoothed them out once again. "I see."
Cat hummed softly. "Yes, I rather think you do now."

Markson had apparently found his voice again, whipping around to the girl. He seemed undecided whether or not it would be wise to step into her space, his fists itching with the urge to wipe that calm expression from her face. "You just blew up two people!"
She watched him with complete calm. "I removed two obstacles."

The man was almost quivering, not even entirely sure himself why he was so upset by this turn of events. He had gotten what he was after in truth: his father was off his back, the innocent crew members hadn't been harmed, all had been dealt with. Maybe that was the rub. This creature standing in front of him, the 'ship's cat' who had always been the oddity aboard. Comic relief, ever helpful if a bit skittish. She was something else entirely.

Unaware of his spinning internal monologue, Cat brushed imaginary lint from her overalls. "Now, if you would all be so kind. We have a voyage to finish." She fixed Markson with a too bright smile, adopting a text book customer service tone. "Docking will commence at thirteen hundred hours tomorrow, please disembark as soon as possible, and may you have a pleasant stay on Proxima Centauri b. Feel free to give us a review on trip advisor."

He could only gape at her for a minute, before his shoulders finally slumped in defeat. None of the others met his eye as he moved towards the exit. At the doorway he hesitated, almost turning back to the view screen. It suddenly hit him that, if all went as he wanted, this would be the last time that he saw his father. The man didn't call him back. The only sound was the door sliding shut at his back.

Of those who remained on the bridge, Cadenza was the first to pull himself together. Clearing his throat, he sat straight and proud, hands folded on the desk in front of him and gaze steady on the camera. He nodded at the girl who was still standing front and centre.

"Well played, Miss Catanski." It was said as if to a respected rival, an acknowledgement to a game against a worthy adversary.
The smile had dropped from her face, and she was watching him now with cool detachment. "That would be Chief Maintenance Officer Catanski."

The corner of his lip quirked as he inclined his head ever so slightly. "Of course."
She raised one eyebrow at him. "You see, I am talented at clearing all kinds of messes."
He nodded properly, faint amusement in his eye. "I would expect no less."

There was an understanding between them, that of a pair of predators recognising the boundaries of their respective territories. It helped to have reputations to fall back on after all, no face would be lost in such an exchange should anyone hear of it. Some matters of diplomacy were best left ambiguous in the long run.

Before Cat could tell Aurora to cut the connection, he leaned forwards one more time. "Ah, one last thing? What about the thief?" There was a sharp undercurrent on the question, one which they could all here.

She shrugged, pointedly not looking at where the doctor was

standing tense as a coiled spring. "Not my area. So long as you don't cause any collateral damage, if you can find her, you can keep her. I am only concerned with protecting my claims."

He smirked in satisfaction at the response. Whatever little test he was trying she had apparently passed satisfactorily. "A worthy pursuit. Very well, I thank you for resolving this situation with regard to my family dispute."

Cat offered him a half smirk. "Don't mention it."

His answering smile showed a great deal of extremely white teeth. "Naturally. Ciao."

Aurora took the que, cutting the feed. Cadenza vanished from the screen, leaving only the accusingly empty star map on display. It was only then that Cat let out a sigh which seemed to draw from deep within her bones, shoulders slumping, as she turned to face her Captain.

CHAPTER 35- A ROUND OF APPLAUSE

Hounslow stared at her in silence for a moment, face still as stone. And then it cracked into a wide grin as he threw his arms wide. Half choking on a laugh, Cat threw herself across the bridge, half tackling into him and burying herself into a hug which threatened to squeeze the life out of them both. Puerty was laughing as well as she came over, adding herself to the hug without a care. A split second later Ramal came crawling out from where he had been hidden with his tablet in one of the vent shafts. The engineer crashed in, half crushing them all.

Cat squirmed after a few minutes, yowling in protest as Ramal took the opportunity to reach in and scruff her hair. Finally taking pity on his rather squished sister, Hounslow reluctantly let her go, for all that he kept one grounding hand on her shoulder. Flicking it a brief roll of her eyes Cat instead pressed herself into his side. It was as if her stress melted away when he just draped his arm across her shoulders.

The others were all grinning, Ramal and Puerty sharing an elaborate high five sequence which ended with them both tossing glitter into the air. At least the Roombas seemed excited by that and a mini horde of the units came charging across the floor.

"Cat, you missed your true calling. Honestly, you belong on the stage!"

She wriggled a little in his hold, peeking up at him through her riot of curls even as she elbowed him lightly in the ribs. "Hey, Puerty did an awesome job as well."

The doctor preened and struck an overly dramatic pose. All she was missing was a skull in hand to get the full effect. Ramal broke out into a round of cackles even as he pretended to swoon in her presence.

Hounslow laughed lightly. "True. You two have always been a dramatic duo" He puffed his chest up, "though I like to think my performance of stoic disapproval really helped to sell the whole thing."
Cat poked him in the side, a wry grin taking over her face. "Oh yes, if you hadn't been sat there like a lump the whole act would have been far too two dimensional."
"Brat."
"You love me really."

He gave her an almost shockingly sweet smile as he pulled her more firmly into his half hug. They stayed like that for a moment, basking in the sense of sheer relief that the gamble had worked so well.

Ramal was the one who finally broke the quiet, clapping his hands and looking eagerly at his captain. "Alrighty, so what is the status on our pair of fugitives?"
Hounslow snorted, thinking back to the conversation he had with his old superior. "Well, Captain Bertram was already in the area, and took the tip off with alacrity. He told me to tell you all 'thanks, we will take care of these idiots so we can get back to more interesting space'."

The doctor's face was disbelieving. "Wow, seriously?"
He laughed, "Yeah, turns out Anthea has been on scut duties for the last few months after their attempt to bust a free port went wrong. Nabbing a couple of Cadenza's top guys should go a fair way to getting them back onto a better rotation. Even more as with them being apparently dead they won't have to worry so

much about immediate fallout of the arrests."

In truth he couldn't blame them for the attitude. Too well he remembered the mind numbing effect of being on some admiral's shit list. Any chance of redemption was always grabbed with both hands and an eager crew. On a more practical note they had probably bought themselves an ounce of good grace should they ever irk the navy however indirectly. With his particular band of nutters that was always worth having in the bag.

Cat suddenly snapped her fingers, craning her head to look at the nearest camera. "Oh, and good job Aurora! The timing on that display was perfect!"

The AI chirped in pleasure, the bridge lights taking on a warmer hue. "Why thank you. I was tempted to go with a flashy explosion effect, but then thought a more understated level of destruction would have a greater artistic impact."

Puerty nodded seriously, "Less is more."

Hounslow nodded, then turned to his engineer with slight concern as another thought struck. "Ramal, did they manage to get any comms through?"

His worry was unfounded, and the other man just grinned and waved his tablet. "Nope, I kept an eye out and blocked every transmission they tried to send. As far as anybody who may have been scanning or recording the sector is concerned, the pod simply ceased to exist. I had to do a bit of tweaking on time stamps for the markers, but as far as their records will show, the navy showed up after the pod's sad end, most likely to check for any salvageable materials or survivors."

The Captain's shoulder eased down by several degrees. "Wonderful."

Cat nudged him again until he looked down at her. "For the record, there is no way we are reporting all of this to mum. At least none of the details until Christmas when she has had a couple of bottles of champagne."

He paled at the thought of facing his family's response to this little adventure. "Agreed."

Cat ducked her head again, suddenly back to her more awkward self. She shifted a bit on her feet, almost as if she wanted to pull away from Hounslow but at the same time didn't want to leave the comfort that he gave. The deck plates were all at once remarkably fascinating. "And... about the other thing... what he said about my reputation. I won't apologise for things that I have done because I don't regret them, but I don't want you to think-"

Puerty took the lead this time. Scoffing loudly, she stepped in close and pulled the girl into another hug, squeezing harder until arms wrapped around her waist in response. She rested her chin on the top of her head, making direct eye contact with Hounslow even as she spoke to his sister. "Please Cat, give us some credit. We all know that you were a bit of a cyber boogey man, girl? For heaven's sake, you were a space pirate for at least a couple of years. It doesn't matter to us. You are our Cat."

She ducked her head, her softly mumbled, "Thanks," being half lost to the doctor's lab coat.

With a small sniffle they finally broke apart, Cat flushing slightly at all the emotions being thrown around the bridge. Very deliberately she made a show of adjusting her now very crooked ears headband, turning her attention back to the ship. "Aurora, what's our status?"

"We are still on track for docking tomorrow lunchtime, no further obstacles as far as I can tell. The control tower on Proxima has sent through our berth instructions. Good news- we are on the slip closest to the gift shop."

Hounslow cut in, attempting to sound brisk to get things back on track. "Fabulous. And our remaining passenger?"

The AI hummed, "Has made it clear that he is not leaving his cabin until it is time for him to disembark from the ship."

Cat tilted her head to one side and tapped thoughtfully at her bottom lip. "Do you think we have set a new record? I mean, we managed to lose two thirds of our passengers in three months."

The others stared at her for a moment, then looked to each other with dawning levels of embarrassment at the realisation. The captain thought about if for a moment, and then just shrugged. "There is a reason we registered ourselves as a cargo transport."

CHAPTER 36- ONCE MORE UNTO THE BREACH

"**C**at! You and Ramal better have this tin can flying in the less than ten minutes or so help me…" at least this time he had hit the intercom button with a more reasonable amount of force, despite having the control tower yelling at him about the consequences of late launching. After everything that had happened the week before, it wasn't such stressor.

"Almost done, keep your hair on! But call Aurora a bucket of bolts again and I will tell mum about what really happened on our way out here!" the voice of his maintenance officer was falsely sweet but clearly hiding her laughter. A threat like that could only be empty, it would hurt her too after all and she was nothing if not a survivor.

Even so, he patted his arm rest in conciliation. "Aurora knows that she is the queen of my life, sorry for any offense caused."
"None taken, captain."

Ramal's voice broke into the exchange, slightly tinny against the background whine of the engines firing up from standby, "Five minutes!"

Hounslow just nodded, smiling genially as Roger went trundling across the floor, dragging a small trailer with a mug of coffee over the doctor. She patted his case absently as she accepted the mug, staring almost cross eyed at the navigation console where she was updating the charts.

The captain's thoughts were once again interrupted by the insistent reminders from docking control. At least they hadn't started threatening fines yet. For all that they still had to check and recheck each system, and would no doubt be down to the wire, he trusted his people would get it all squared away in time.

One small blessing at least was the complete lack of passengers this time around. Strangely it seemed that nobody wanted to risk even their most hated employees by chartering Aurora to take them back to Earth. Something about losing more than half of the last contingent had done wonders for keeping them away this time. Cat had gleefully used the empty cabins for extra storage space, arguing that the extra profit would prove useful when they got back to Earth. After all, it was always nice to have a bit of extra cash around the holidays.

Their mother had already made it clear that she expected them to stay planet side for at least a fortnight. More than that, all the crew had been ordered in the sweetest tones that the woman was capable of to report for dinner at least once.

Puerty finally made a sound of satisfaction as she keyed in the final commands for the navigation station. Normally the trip home would take around sixty sols, made faster by favourable solar winds at this time of year which would help carry them. However, there had been a bit of adjusting going on to add a necessary dogleg roughly halfway home.

Hounslow leaned a little sideways in his chair to better see the doctor. "Did we get confirmation on the rendezvous point?"
She honestly flushed a little, tapping the screen with efficiency as if to compensate. "Yep, they are going to stop over at Port Deneva in thirty sols time and stay until we arrive."
"Good, good. I owe that Captain Cy a drink at the very least. And I know Cat wants to make sure for herself that they are all doing ok."

Puerty just hummed and nodded, leading him to grin slightly

wickedly as he poked the metaphorical bear. "And, just so you know, I didn't let her fill up every spare cabin with cargo. Just in case through a strange quirk of fate it seems we miscounted on our passenger manifest."

The doctor flushed scarlet right up to her ears, for all that the smile she couldn't restrain was something remarkably soft. "Noted, Captain."

"Attention bridge, one minute to launch."

....

Down in engineering, Ramal and Cat were standing ready at the main engine controls with the clock ticking rapidly down. They had managed to get the cargo stowed away over an hour before, and since then just been tinkering and tuning up Aurora's engine to make sure that the couple of new parts were settled just right. Despite the brevity of their stopover, this time everybody shared her excitement for getting back into the black. They all had people waiting for them after all this time.

Cat grinned with feral abandon, shaking a can in his face. "Ramal, it's your turn this time!"
He crossed his arms, eyebrow raising almost to his hairline. "Why me?"
"Because I did it last time, and arguably I have used up a couple of my lives. You are immortal until proved otherwise." The last was said sing song, the can almost bopping him on the nose until he took it with an over dramatic sigh.

Checking the label briefly saw the other eyebrow joining the first. "Why is it still sparkly pink?"
She shrugged with faux innocence. "Only colour left."
Growling, Ramal walked over to their designated canvas, shaking the can vigorously. "I am starting to think that you just say that and don't actually try and get a different colour."
Cat laughed, rubbing one hand ruefully on the back of her neck and half shrugging. "If anything sparkly pink is one of the harder options to come across. But Aurora is a lady and deserves nice

things."

Shaking his head in amusement, he stepped forwards and carefully sprayed new lines over the demon trap on the warp core safety doors.

Tossing the can to the side when he was done, he took a moment to tap his headset, "All protections are in place, Captain, we are good to go!"

Sharing a quick high five, they both turned to strap themselves into their respective seats. The exterior hull camera showed a small section of the planet below, the blur of the upper atmosphere doing nothing to hide the striking orange and purple hues of the desert planet. For all that it was stunning on a cosmic scale, he still thought that it had nothing in comparison to home.

"Kick the tyres and light the fires!"

Cat's whoop echoed around the compartment, returned with an electronic chorus of bleeps as the Roombas confirmed that they were all safely strapped in along the corridor. She could just about reach down to pat Rhonda's case from her new launch station beneath Cat's seat.

From deep within the ship's core there came a whine as the cells reached peak capacity. It reverberated through the whole structure of Aurora, setting everybody's teeth on edge before finally becoming too high pitched to be heard. The primary and secondary control panels all came dancing to life in a light show as reds became greens.

Code ran too fast for human eyes to follow as Aurora approved the power distribution to the engines, which would have roared to life if they had been docked in atmosphere. As it was, unseen except by those in the docking tower, the rear thrusters seemed to suddenly glow with an almost purple hue.

Under the guidance of the Captain they nudged their way out of the space port, with Dr Puerty giving a thumbs up as word came through that they had entered the departure zone. It was the minimum safe distance for a launch to shoot from and not risk bombarding the station or planet with excess rads.

A new thrum came trembling through the hull, alongside a strange flipping sensation as gravity became concerned about the stunt they were pulling.

Catasnki bared her teeth in anticipation as the hyperspace window was reported open on her systems. She could feel it, deep in her bones, a tug which seemed to latch onto every atom of her being.

Ramal looked rather queasy as the sensation overtook him. Not many people could say that they enjoyed the feeling.

On the bridge Puerty smiled shakily at the sensation, which reminded her of standing just on the edge of a cliff preparing to dive into an ocean.

Hounslow gripped his arm rests and took a deep breath.

There was a brief moment, a split second, which held more than the human mind could ever hope to understand. Time and space and place and person all fracturing as human technology and hubris punched a tiny tear in the fabric of reality.

And then they were gone.

Up in the docking control tower, a weary dispatcher heaved a sigh of relief as they removed their headset. Rubbing their head, they gave brief, silent thank that the ship was finally gone from their jurisdiction. The stories about it were all so strange, some people going to far as to say that the crew were all eldritch creatures from beyond the black. For all that it was of course nonsense, having them around tended to incur a spike in strangeness. With a mental shrug, they dismissed thoughts of Aurora and her crew, moving down to the next ship on their list.

Lightning Source UK Ltd.
Milton Keynes UK
UKHW022217110521
383549UK00011B/2295